IT DOESN'T HAVE TO BE THIS HARD

Mile High Heat
Book 1

CHRISTINA HOVLAND

For rights information, please contact:
Prospect Agency
551 Valley Road, PMB 377
Upper Montclair, NJ 07043
(718) 788-3217

Development Editor: Kristi Yanta
Line & Copy Edits: Erica Russikoff
Final Proofreader: Shasta Schafer
Editorial Goddess: Beth Carbutt
Typo Terminator: Suzie Waggoner

Cover Design: Christina Hovland

This book was originally put on pre-order as
Everything's Fine, Emmaline.

Author's Note

*There are so many people who have believed
in all the drafts of this book.
Thank you to every one of you.
Emmaline is a character that I was destined to write.
Her story is my privilege to share.*

*As with the creation of this story, I'd encourage you to always
remember that history is just how we got here.*

**This* is the moment that matters.
So I'll use this space to encourage you,
my friend, to fight for what you believe.
Ask for what you deserve.
And always believe in yourself.*

*xoxo
Christina*

Chapter One
EMMALINE

THIS FIRE? Not her fault.

Well, mostly not her fault.

Fine, a little bit not her fault.

Sonofabitch, it was *totally* her fault.

Her fault for always saying yes. Her fault for marrying the wrong man. Her fault for divorcing him. Her fault for thinking she deserved an orgasm to celebrate closing the loan on her new home in her new life. A life where she did not plan to blend in with the curtains anymore. A life where she planned to stand up and shout, "I'm Emmaline!"

But now, flames licked up the inside of the dumpster as though they were starving and the metal came coated in chocolate syrup.

She sighed. Mostly, the fire was her fault for purchasing a knock-off-brand battery-operated-boyfriend that began smoking before things even got good.

Here's the thing: she was the daughter of a firefighter. He had lectured her about how fires start. Never once—*not once!*—had Dad mentioned the peril of knock-off vibrators.

She should've gone brand name.

Emmaline Eaton learned this lesson in the hardest of hard ways.

Light the neighborhood dumpster on fire the first night in her new home in Denver? Check that box right off the list. She was officially the worst at all things decision-making related.

This was not the way she'd planned to make herself stand out.

The neighborhood stayed quiet this close to midnight, and no one was around. Small blessings and all that. The thin mountain air of Denver's summer was sure feeling thick right about then—and not because of the burning garbage fumes, either.

When the "thing" started smoking, she'd panicked. Tossed that pretend lump of a man right in the trash and took that bag to the neighborhood dumpster.

Em had considered putting out the flames quickly, but she couldn't risk anyone digging through the trash to figure out what had started this mess. She'd briefly hoped that maybe no one would connect the dots on this one. They'd find the who-dittily-do and have no idea where it came from.

But then she'd remembered the mail with her name that she'd tossed out in the same bag. So it made lots of sense to just let it burn for a minute. Not too long. Just long enough to destroy the evidence.

Burn, baby, burn.

The neighborhood HOA had the foresight to place the dumpster way off at the end of the cul-de-sac with nothing in the direct vicinity but some soaked grass from the sprinklers. Nothing flammable close by—other than the contents. Contents that needed to burn, burn, burn.

Not to worry, she had a plan to eventually put out the

fire where Bob was burning. Bob being the name she'd given her battery-operated boyfriend when she still had hope for his usefulness. Being a responsible adult, she had a fire extinguisher and a hose with her—she'd even turned on the water at the spigot nearby before she came to battle the flames, something Bob couldn't do. Turn her on, that is. She could just get a Roomba and name *him* Bob. Then she'd at least get clean floors.

Next time she bought herself a vibrator, it'd be top of the line, and she'd name it Banks or something even more unique. Something *creative*.

She used to be creative, but that was before the divorce. Before the marriage, really.

Definitely before the current dumpster fire.

Grr.

"Mom?" Fiona, her ten-year-old daughter, called from the porch of their new home. Oh geez, she had apparently woken up.

"I'm here, babycakes," Em replied, not as loud as her daughter, but with enough volume to be heard through the distance that stretched between them.

"Why are you outside?" Fiona asked, sleep still present in her voice.

"Taking out the trash."

"Why's it on fire?" Fiona asked, like this was totally normal and not that big of a deal.

Which was good because it wasn't *that* big of a deal.

"Everything's fine, baby," Em whisper-yelled down the street. She didn't want to wake the neighbors. You know? "Go back inside. I'll be right there."

She would be once she dealt with this whole situation successfully.

Now was the time to stand tall and deal with things. She was going to deal-the-shit out of this situation. Yes, she stood taller. She was not the Em of yesterday who let the world roll right over her. No, she was doing this life thing right and not hiding anymore.

This was her fault. Look at her owning it. Owning all her mistakes.

"Should I call 9-1-1?" Fiona yelled back. "Grandpa always says to dial 9-1-1 if there's a fire."

"No, babycakes, this is like a campfire. We can sing songs and roast marshmallows next time I take out the trash." Lying to her kid? She shouldn't do that.

"Are you going to use the hose soon?" Fiona yelled again, but at least she stayed at the front door. "Or should I find marshmallows?"

"I'll be right back inside soon," Em assured her. "See if you can find the marshmallows I bought at the store."

Please, dear goodness, go inside.

Blessedly, with the promise of midnight marshmallows, her daughter went inside.

Deep breaths, Em. Deep. Breaths.

She hopped from foot to foot like she was a boxer getting ready for the ring instead of a new homeowner ready to put out a fire at precisely the correct moment.

"The fire brigade is on the way," a man yelled from up the street.

Well, damn.

Hopefully, that fire crew would not include her dad.

Dear God, let it not be my dad. It couldn't be her dad. The universe wouldn't figuratively screw her that hard.

Would 'fessing up to the situation be an admission of guilt? She should probably talk to an attorney before she made another mistake. Did divorce attorneys handle accidental arson via vibrator?

She should google the melting point of silicone. That's what she should do. She had a few minutes of time. The average response to this neighborhood was three minutes and twenty-seconds. See? She knew her Denver fire trivia.

"Grab a hose, mate," the guy hollered from down the road.

Was that an accent he had? Sounded sort of British. But not British.

A bit like those Hemsworth boys—the Chris and Liam guys.

Australian!

"I have a hose," she yelled back.

The hose she was prepared to use once the garbage was good and destroyed. Not one moment before.

"Then use it," the man yelled, coming closer.

Nuh uh. Not yet.

"Why aren't you using it?" the man asked, breathless from sprinting up the street and getting closer by the second.

Oh hey, he was a cutie pie.

"Use it," he hollered again.

Ugh. Fine.

She pointed the fire extinguisher at the flames like the good little firefighter's daughter she wished she was, and let it rip.

Well, hey now, this was actually pretty damn fun. Fire extinguishers were powerful.

She got it. Got why her dad and her brothers all enjoyed this. Heck, maybe she should set vibrator fires more often.

The flames died down thanks to the water and white powder burst. She double fisted it, the hose in one hand, extinguisher in the other. Even she wasn't sure how she managed, but it involved her shoulder, some creative movement with her hand, and a bunch of badassery.

She let the hose work on the residual licks of heat as the wailing siren of a fire truck came closer.

"Y'okay?" the Australian accent guy asked, a touch breathy.

She looked at him and really wished she wasn't wearing her Peppa Pig pajamas. The ones that matched her daughter's jammies, which they both thought were super cute.

Because, *ooooh*, this guy was a good-looking one.

He was handsome, and she was single. She glanced at his left hand. No ring.

Bad. Bad Em. Focus on the issue at hand, not on the cutie pie.

Still, she couldn't deny that this guy was a looker. Messy blond hair, dear-God-blue-eyes, and that freaking accent women all over the country wanted to tuck into a Sprite bottle and savor. He wore a white tank top that stretched tight across some nice muscles, with steamy swirls of tattoo ink all the way down his arms—though he wasn't a gym rat. Pajama pants slung low on his hips, but she didn't glance down past his waist because, about the time the flames started, she'd given up on sex in all forms.

"I'll have a go." He grabbed the hose. "Let me take it a sec."

She let him. Mostly because he said it so cute with that accent of his and she was reconsidering her no sex manifesto.

"What a freaking disaster." She rubbed between her eyebrows with her fingertips while he finished up with the flames. "I'll never live this down."

Even if it wasn't her dad who came on the fire truck, he'd hear about it and then the holidays would never be the same. Thankfully, her brothers didn't work at the fire station for her neighborhood. Yep, that'd been the requirement she gave the real estate agent when she'd begun her search.

This wasn't her dad's usual station, either.

Also, a requirement. But he floated between stations as one of the Division Chiefs so one could never really know.

"Ya did this?" Hot Blond Guy asked, still spraying the water into the dumpster even though the flames were gone.

She nodded. Willed her pulse to calm down a little. "Not on purpose."

"I've started a load of fires," he said, still spraying away. "Never intentional, either."

This was sweet—the whole hey-I-also-start-fires schtick. And the way he said *never* like *nev-ah*. Freaking adorbs.

Wait a second. Was he flirting with her?

She slipped her glance to him and, oh yeah. He was checking her out.

Her cheeks heated at the blatant perusal.

"I'm sorry to interrupt your night," she said it, she meant it. Now what were the odds she could convince him never to say anything, ever, about what happened at the dumpster tonight?

"You should probably go back to your girlfriend." Was she fishing for personal details? Yes, yes, she was.

"No girlfriend, I'm afraid." His grin could've melted those piggy jammies right off her body. "Not at the moment."

The way he said that? Implied…oh, she'd been out of the dating game for a helluva long time, but even she remembered how it felt to do this dance with a new potential someone special.

This guy probably stole the show wherever he went.

Why did he have to be cute? Why couldn't he be mediocre? Then she could totally flirt right on back.

Sirens up the street wailed, and her face heated. They were coming for her.

"Oh my God, this is going to be so bad." She took in a deep breath of air.

"Nah, don't let it get to you. It'll all be okay. Fire's out."

She shook her head. "No, I…just… I'm something of fire department royalty in Denver."

He looked at her like she'd lit the entire street on fire. Not just the dumpster. "You're what? Like a flames princess?"

"My family. They're all firefighters. This has the potential to be very…familial."

"And you keep them in business, eh?" he asked with a tilted grin fit for the handsomest of handsome cartoon heroes.

She sighed internally but kept her expression neutral. At least she hoped it stayed neutral.

"Not usually. Just moved back." She slid her gaze to her petite house that was perfect for her little family. "But I'm still never going to live this down."

"Gotcha," he said. "Family trouble is special trouble."

While that nugget settled between them, things got busy super quick as the fire crew arrived to do their thing, even though the fire was already out. Seriously. Why did they need to hoist around those gigantic axe things? She didn't know.

Thankfully, her dad was not among the crew.

Unfortunately, her oldest brother—James—stepped from the truck with a big ol' axe.

Damn. Damn. Dammit. Damn.

The other firefighters sallied forth, but James paused when he glimpsed Emmaline. Then he frowned.

"Uncle James!" Fiona shouted, marshmallows in hand, running toward them in her matching Peppa Pig pajamas.

"Fiona?" he asked, his face screwing up with many

questions and a heaping dash of happy-to-see-her. "What are you doing up so late?"

"Bringing the marshmallows for the fire," Fiona responded, eyes bright, holding up the big ol' bag of marshmallows. Then she took in the lack of flames and her expression fell.

"Fire's out," Em said, refusing to look at anyone but her daughter. "Head on home and we'll have marshmallows when I get back." They could roast them over a candle or something.

Though, that might not be the best idea. One fire a night already seemed like too much.

James evidenced this by clearing his throat. "I'd like a post-fire marshmallow, Fi. If you're handing them out."

"Yay." Fiona grinned, pulling open the bag and handing one to her uncle. He went over the top taking it from her fingers and making ridiculous *nom-nom* noises.

Then, without even checking with Em, he handed Fiona one and she also made *nom-nom* noises while she ate it. Hers were, however, way cuter than his.

"Go on home now?" he asked Fiona with a wink.

Fiona nodded, and Em scowled while ensuring Fiona made it back to the house, the marshmallow bag swinging in her little hand.

"You can have two more before I get there," Em said before Fiona went inside, loud enough for her daughter to hear. And not only because she was trying to one-up James, but also because Fiona was a good kid and a couple of marshmallows would be fine.

Unless she lit the house on fire roasting them…

"Em?" James asked in that big brother's voice that was not awesome.

She glowered at him. "What are you doing here, anyway?"

He glanced at the smoldering dumpster, eyebrows raised. "This is my literal job."

"I mean *here*." She pointed to the asphalt. "This isn't your station," she clarified.

He shook his head like he always did when he didn't want to answer her. An outright, not-worth-the-time dismissal.

That. Sucked.

She may as well have disappeared into the dark of night. Unnecessary, and all—

"Em, tell me you did not start this," James said, with substantially more criticism in his tone than was entirely necessary.

Oh, *now* he looked at her like she existed.

"Knock it off, James." His assumption got her hackles raised right up. "It's not like I'm a serial arsonist."

He guffawed.

"It's only happened a few times," she assured.

Yes, she accidentally lit fires, and all of those times she'd been much younger. Not one of them involved sex toys.

James made wide eyes at her. "A few times? That's not giving you full credit. Should I go through them all?"

"Only if you want to get kicked in the nuts by your sister," Em countered.

"Not her fault, mate," Hot Blond Guy said with that really yummy accent. He pointed to himself. "My bad."

Was Hot Blond Guy seriously taking responsibility?

"Your bad?" James raised his eyebrows toward the guy.

"Yeah, the fire's my bad." Hot Blond Guy lifted his hand. "Name's Ethan."

Yes, yes, he did take responsibility. Em's mouth fell open the slightest bit.

Okay, so, whoa. Coming to her rescue made him even

sexier. Too bad he was so handsome, and probably super good at upstaging everyone in his vicinity.

"Ethan," James confirmed, shaking the wonderful man's hand.

She was going to make Ethan Rice Krispies Treats— her personal specialty. James, however, had practically called her a serial arsonist, so he was getting MiraLAX in his treats. *Don't eat the ones with the pink wrappers! Ha.*

James did that thing again. The one where he seemed to forget she existed because his entire focus turned to Ethan. Yeah, this was the problem with charisma-soaked hotties.

"James," one of the other firefighter guys called. "Check this out."

As her brother walked away, she seriously hoped they found a crapload of drugs that would distract everyone from the real culprit.

Chapter Two
ETHAN

"EM," Ethan said her name, taking his cue from James's use of her nickname and savoring that syllable on his tongue like his favorite taste of watermelon and mint.

"Emmaline," she said. "Officially, I'm Emmaline, but most people call me Em."

"These would be those delicate family politics?" Ethan asked, low and only for her.

"You have no idea." She took a massive breath and then firmed her spine, seeming to prepare herself for whatever James was going to toss her way next.

Ethan liked that. Liked that she stood up for herself with James.

"You all right?" Ethan asked, hoping his concern was clear.

She blew out between her lips. "It's my fault. I threw it away when I should've dunked it in water. I didn't mean for this to—"

"No worries. It's all good," he assured. "No more fire."

"There are still a lot of worries." She pursed her lips as

the fireys went to work digging through the mess in the rubbish bin.

"I like to think that when dodgy things happen, it opens the door for better things." He did. Although, the dodgy things in his life lately were just bloody pissing him off.

"That is remarkably positive," Em said. "I'm not feeling it right now."

"Not with that attitude," he said with his best cheeky grin.

She chuckled. So it worked.

"I'm still a little punchy from the whole lit-a-fire part of the night. I'll get to the better things someday."

"Don't be *too* hard on yourself until then," Ethan said.

"Just a little hard?" She made an adorable little bit motion with her thumb and index finger.

"Just enough so you don't light up the dumpster again."

"The fire's your fault?" James called from near the dumpster, disbelieving, his words clearly meant for Ethan.

"Yeah, mate, sorry," Ethan said, going for bashful. "Won't happen again."

"This is yours, sir?" another firefighter guy asked, holding up a green, glow-in-the-dark, phallic slab of…silicone…with charring all down the shaft that left nearly nothing of the tip.

Ethan squinted a little and had an intense desire to protect his own prick by covering it with his hands. He looked from the object that was not a corn cob to Em.

"I did not see this coming," James said under his breath, but loud enough for all to hear.

"Me bloody, either," Ethan said. Of all the things Em could've used to start the fire, this was not on his list of suspects. "It's…uh… I think that there was a… yeah, uh, it happens sometimes when… oh, bloody hell."

He glanced to Em, hoping she might have some kind of story for him to share that wasn't as embarrassing as all this.

She shrugged and obviously there was no story.

So, then, he was on his own. He heaved in a breath. Then let it out. Then heaved it in again. "Alright, I'm going to just be honest here…"

But what was that honesty he was about to make up?

"Believe it or not you can use one of those to…uh… stir the custards." Dear God, that sounded awful. "Or, uh, it helps when I'm making dessert and need a little extra help to bring things—in..ingredients—together…" Oh, bloody hell this was sounding worse and worse. "I mean you can't cut a steak with the damn thing, can ya?"

Was it getting hotter out there? He felt warmer, for sure.

James and Em both stared at him like he had tried to fix them a custard.

"It's not his. It's mine." Emmaline held her hand out for the…thing…making a gimme motion to James. "Unless the department needs it as evidence?"

Did that happen?

"Actually, yeah, you should probably keep that." She pulled her hand away, sliding it in her pocket. "That's fine, you just keep it. You might need to fix a custard or something later."

Ethan usually enjoyed using his words. It was part of his job. But he couldn't find any of them at the moment.

The pause in the thin nighttime air was only punctuated by a feline meowing somewhere up the street.

"He was just being nice," she clarified. "Ethan, I mean." She pushed her toe at the asphalt before glancing back to Ethan. "He was being nice to me, and covering for me, and he didn't know. Nobody actually cooks with these things. I'm pretty sure."

Honest to all bloody hell, Ethan thought his life was complicated, but he had nothing on Emmaline.

This was the bit where he should be the knight in shining pajama trousers. He understood this, embraced it —but he couldn't seem to spit the bloody words out. Not with the green slab o' silicone still fresh in his mind.

Also, because Emmaline was absolutely adorable, with her brown hair ruffled up into a mess of a wreck on top of her head, her pink pig pajamas, and massive rubber clogs.

And again, because under all that adorable she was a real looker with an underlying strength, and the thought of her and the green wand o' wonders conjured all sorts of illicit images to his brain cells that had no business being there.

That was a non-starter that could get sticky quick. Ethan didn't do sticky. Not when he had a daughter to raise, a television empire to rebuild, and a whole life to untangle.

Also, he'd learned early in his life that a woman with a penchant for flames was best left to her own devices. Wisdom best not forgotten.

"Righto." Well. Ethan went for the charm he'd been known for once upon a time in Nosh-Land. "The culprit's nabbed. No harm done. Onward."

They all stared at him like he was a mortadella sandwich short of a picnic.

That look on all their mugs? The precise expression his business manager had when Ethan pitched his plan for opening his chain of restaurants in Denver, Colorado Springs, and Fort Collins while he waited for an opportunity to get back in good graces with the Nosh Network.

"The dumpster is scorched," James said, his voice pitching higher. "There's harm done."

"Well, could've been worse. Amiright?" Ethan asked, even though he knew he was bang on the money.

"Is this going to happen often?" Ethan asked Em, all cheeky like to lighten the mood. "I should stay in the know so I can notify the HOA board if we'll need to redo the budget."

"The HOA board?" Emmaline's eyes got big. "The HOA board does not need to be involved in this."

"I was pulling your leg. We'll definitely keep it on the down low." He winked. "Our secret. Right, James?"

He could fully understand her desire not to involve others. She would probably prefer they keep this little nugget of intel among themselves.

Emmaline's bloke of a brother harrumphed and glanced away from them, back to the residual burnt out rubbish bin, the wheels spinning in his head.

"Right, James? Our secret?" Ethan asked.

James frowned, thinking way too hard. "Secret, huh?"

"Because it's nothin' to be embarrassed about." Ethan nodded along with his train of thought. "Could happen to anyone."

Emmaline quirked an adorable eyebrow. "You're saying *this* could happen to you?"

"Never." He was confident in that answer, and perhaps he said it a touch too quickly. But he'd never lit a fire via unmentionables and didn't plan on starting.

"How do you normally light your fires?" James asked, unimpressed. Hands on his hips.

That was a tricky one.

"Some things are best left to the imagination," Ethan dodged.

"You said you also don't generally light them on

purpose." Emmaline turned to him and assaulted him with the gorgeousness of her brown eyes.

"I'm also curious about this," James said, readjusting his stance like he was ready to dig in and hang out at the end of the cul-de-sac all night.

Well, Ethan's fires were a tad more contained and a touch more straightforward.

"Grease fires, mostly." He shoved his hands into his pockets instead of commenting on how her eyes had a hint of the same shade as her bedside wand— "Or the occasional flambé gone wonky every now and again."

"Holy crap. You're a chef. I know you." James's eyes went wider. "Yeah. I know you."

Best not to make him think too hard on it, wasn't it? This type of thing definitely wouldn't go over well with the executives at Nosh if it got out.

"Ethan Greene." Ethan nodded, since it was who he was. "Formerly, of the Nosh Network. Currently, of Bradbury Drive." He gestured toward the direction of his house.

"Who?" Em asked.

"The man who created the meatsicle," James said with an awe that made Ethan uneasy.

"The what?" Em asked.

"You know," James said. "Nosh Network? Barbecue show?"

Em shook her head. "I… I guess I missed that one. I don't watch a lot of television."

"This is the man who started the Barbecue World Championship," James said, again with more awe.

"And the man who would be grateful if we could make tonight go away for my new neighbor here," Ethan said with a pointed glance he hoped would do the trick. "Perhaps I could drop off a gratitude cake at the firehouse sometime? For your trouble?"

James pursed his lips. "You are *the* Ethan Greene." He shot Em an unreadable look. "I'll see what I can do."

He strode back to his mates.

"I'm not enjoying tonight." Emmaline frowned.

Ethan didn't care for that frown.

Of note, she didn't mention a thing about his celebrity. He appreciated that. He was more than a bloke on the telly, but women rarely saw that in him.

"Your secret *is* safe with me." He held his pinky out to her.

She stared at his pinky like he'd sprouted an extra off the side.

"You know." He linked his pinkies together to illustrate the way his daughter had him make promises.

"Oh." Emmaline linked her pinky briefly with his. "Right."

"Em," James said, her name curt and abrupt.

Oh wonderful, brother bear is back.

"You're off the hook," James said, drawing the last word out a tad too long. "The guys all agreed this didn't happen. All that jazz. Somebody tossed matches. Happens all the time."

"That's great news." Ethan smacked his palms together.

Emmaline, however, was letting off an odd energy. The way she crossed her arms? She did not seem to be so friendly about the way this was working out.

Yeah, not with the way she stared at her brother like a feral animal ready to pounce.

"I know you," Emmaline said, staring daggers at James. "This isn't over."

"You're right." James nodded, his villain grin the stuff of sibling rivalries. "I'm going to hang on to this one."

He winked. The wanker winked.

"That's an odd thing to hang on to," Ethan murmured, because it was.

James gave him the empty picnic basket look again. "I meant the knowledge that this happened. Hanging on to that."

"Righto. For the next time you want something from her? So you can…what's the word?" Ethan paused for a moment. "Blackmail your sister."

He may not have had siblings of his own, but he'd seen how these things played out.

"I take it you don't care for the cake, then?" Ethan asked.

"It wouldn't be right to take your cake." Well, look at that, James could smile. "And blackmail's not the word I'd use. Just sticking some knowledge away for another day."

"It's fine." Emmaline held up her hands in faux defeat. "I'll *owe* you, James."

"Right." Yes, that was another genuine wanker smile from the brother.

Ethan couldn't have that.

"I'm afraid that's a negative, mate." Ethan took a slight step forward. Why? He wasn't entirely sure.

"What do you mean that's a negative?" James asked, clearly having breathed in too many of the toxic silicone fumes to understand English.

"I can't let you blackmail my new neighbor when she's had a helluva rough night."

"It's fine," Emmaline assured. "He can have this one. I still have video documentation that he's the one who dinged our dad's car three Christmases ago. I think the whole family would be more interested in that than *this*."

This was a right mess, wasn't it? "Is this what brothers and sisters do? Blackmail each other with Wands o' Wonder and videos of wrongdoing?"

"Yes," Emmaline and James both said at the same time.

Ethan rocked back on his heels. Time to skedaddle on home where things still made little sense, but they gave it a fair shake. "Another reason to be glad I'm an only child then."

"You don't even know," James said under his breath.

Emmaline took a right hook to his shoulder for that comment.

James draped his arm around her shoulder. "No more fires, Em."

"I'll do my best." She saluted him. "Captain."

They did the required handshakes and good nights. Then the firefighters packed up.

"Can I walk you home?" Ethan asked. Wasn't that the decent thing to do?

"You don't have to, I'm good," Emmaline said, again with the low chuckle in the back of her throat. "Thanks, though. And thanks for standing up to James. He's not used to that from anyone but me."

Families could be a real pain in the bum. "Happy to help."

"Right," she said, heading toward her house.

"Righto," he said, heading toward his house.

This was, in fact, heading in the same direction.

"I live up here, too," he said to clarify.

He also gestured toward the house he rented while staying in Denver.

"I got that," she said with a grin.

"I'm over here." She gestured toward the house nearest them, the one up for sale until that very day.

"If you find yourself in need of a cup of sugar or anything." He waved toward his house. "Third from the stop sign. That's me."

"I totally owe you one for this," Em said. "I'll make you Rice Krispies Treats, and you have one entire free favor from me. Whenever you need it. I'm serious, you just ask."

"That's very kind," he assured. "But don't even think twice about it. No worries."

"Just like that, no worries?"

"You've got enough worries with that brother, I think."

"Are you always this nice to everyone?" Em asked.

"Are you always surprised when people are kind?" he countered.

She flinched. Just a tad, not a lot. "It's not the world I come from."

"The world with James?" he confirmed.

He'd believe that.

"Oh, gosh, no. That's family. That's different." She waved in the direction of the fire truck. "My family is invasive, but they're good people. I meant my divorce. That's what I meant. Before my divorce, the circles I ran with. They were more shark infested than kind. Anyway…" She tucked a stray hair behind her ear. Thank you for being nice to me."

"Anytime, Em."

He said it, and he meant it.

And damned if he didn't look forward to what came next.

Chapter Three
ETHAN

"ANNIE," Ethan hollered from the kitchen. He finished wiping down the stovetop from brekkie. The rest of his house may have been a disaster worthy of the Defense Force Reserves, but he drew the line at the kitchen. This was the one place he didn't allow clutter.

"Thirty minutes," he shouted, snatching up a towel to dry where he'd cleaned.

He was still in his sleep shirt and today he finally landed a meeting with one of the Nosh producers to discuss his return to the network, so he'd best get upstairs and put on his business shirt. He always wore jeans—it was part of his Ethan Greene character and that wouldn't change. But occasionally, like today, he'd dress it up a bit.

Annie didn't respond, so he tossed the towel over his shoulder and moved to the banister before shouting up the stairs, "Thirty minutes."

Still no reply. Drat.

He headed up, grabbing a stray water bottle and her schoolbag from the floor on the way to her bedroom.

Annie was a new feature in his life because it was only

in the recent past he discovered she existed. Her mum hadn't mentioned their affair had resulted in a souvenir. Not until Annie was six years old and her dear mum needed a paycheck and a permanent break. Four years later, and now Annie lived with Ethan, but they were still figuring each other out.

She had become used to doing things herself when she lived with her mum.

And he'd never known what it was like to be a dad.

So their introduction hadn't been a cakewalk, that's for bloody certain. Caused a whole commotion at the Nosh Network and he had to walk away from his television career to care for his kid. In return, though, he got a daughter, and he loved her more than his own life. He'd loved the bachelor life before Annie. Not realizing there'd been an Annie-sized hole in his heart ready to be filled.

He knocked three times before pushing her bedroom door open. She sat with her back to him, headphones on her ears, typing something into her laptop. She was blonde, like him, but she'd inherited her mum's green eyes instead of his blue ones. Only ten, but he could already see the woman she would be someday. Which meant he was in trouble because she was going to be a looker like her mum.

A quick glance at the screen and he froze.

Another dating website? With his photo up on the screen? Bloody hell.

Even if he wanted a relationship—and he didn't—he didn't have time to give his partner. That wasn't fair to either of them. It just wasn't. He'd already covered this with Annie on multiple occasions.

"Annie?" he said, hurrying toward her before she could post anything.

She jumped about three feet off the chair. "Dad."

"What on God's green earth are you doing?" he asked,

gesturing to the screen. Though he already understood what she was up to.

"Nothing." She hastily pushed the laptop closed.

He reached around her and lifted the screen. "You're still off to find me a date? Is that it?"

"Dad. Yes. You need this." She was ten years old. Only ten. And yet, she was slick as bloody hell with the computers and such. And as manipulative as her great-grandmother on his father's side, with no care for consequences.

"Annie." He closed his eyes so he didn't have to stare at his face on her screen. "Delete it," he said. "Now."

She frowned at him. "Uh, this is how you get a girl-friend when you never go anywhere."

He didn't want a girlfriend. He'd had loads of them over the years and it never quite stuck.

"We've been over this," he said, frustrated that his daughter navigated the bloody Internet better than he did.

"You are not to find me any dates?" he asked.

She didn't react.

"You heard me?" he asked again.

She tossed her hands up in the air. "It's for your own good."

Fantastic, now she was throwing his own words back at him.

Annie hadn't had a proper mum figure, since her mum had sent her off with babysitters and such. Now that they'd settled into something of a routine, and she got comfort-able, well, she got on Ethan's case to meet someone. She wanted him to find a missus so she could have a mum.

When he refused to take the bait, she started searching for him. He'd taken away her laptop and mobile, and she'd only recently earned them back through chores and grades and all the things he figured she needed to do.

"Delete it." He pointed to the laptop, and they were down to twenty minutes to get out the door, get her to school, and get him to his meeting at the restaurant.

He watched carefully while she removed the posting, to be certain it was well and truly gone. "Are there any others?"

"Websites like this?" she asked, innocent as the day she was born.

He nodded, hands on his hips, still holding the damn kitchen towel between his fingers. "These matching-people-together sites, yeah."

"No." She blinked up at him. "But, c'mon, Dad. You know this is what we need."

"You've lost the Internet again, love." He lifted her laptop and tucked it under his arm.

"Daaaaad," she whined. "How long?"

He didn't answer because he had no bloody idea. "The mobile, too."

"Dad. No." She crossed her arms, the phone tucked under her armpit as though that would keep it safe from dear old dad. "For real?"

He made a gimme gesture. "You go to school and come straight home. No dallying at the bus stop."

"I'm grounded?" She scowled at him and if looks could kill, he'd be a puddle of goo stuck in the carpet.

"I prefer to call it helping around the house." He dug in. "Now get your socks on so we can go."

"Why?" she demanded.

"Because if you don't wear socks, you'll get a blister."

"No, why do you want us to be miserable forever?" She tossed her hands up with a hefty dose of drama.

Drama that didn't work on him. He was immune to her drama. That was his superpower.

Still, the miserable part? That stung quite a bit. But that was being a parent, he'd learned, wasn't it?

"I'm that bad?" he asked.

"Dad." She frowned.

"Annie, love, my hands are full. Two restaurants, one house, one daughter, and a try again for a show on the telly? *You* get my attention. There's no time for funny business with a girlfriend."

"You're not even trying." Annie slid from her chair, stood, and marched to her dresser.

She pulled open the top drawer with the wrath of a ten-year-old who lost her mobile. She nearly slammed it closed, but glanced up at him at the last moment and pushed it quietly shut with one finger.

For whatever reason, that seemed to make her point more than if she'd slammed the bloody thing.

"Annie?" he asked.

She turned, but it was clearly not because she wanted to, but because she understood she had to.

"There's a new girl from up the street. If you see her at school, be kind to her, all right?" he asked.

She nodded before she pulled a pink sweatshirt with little hearts over her head.

His daughter may look for a mum in all the wrong ways, but she had a heart the size of the whole outback. That was *her* superpower. It's what made being her dad worth every second.

"Fine." Annie slunk out the door to the hallway. "Fine. Fine. Fine."

Maybe not this particular second. She may have said *fine* four bloody times, but it still didn't sound fine. Not at all.

Chapter Four
EMMALINE

EMMALINE STIFLED HER BUILDING YAWN, stopped sketching—she'd been playing with a cartoon drawing of a chef that looked a little like Ethan Greene—and refocused on the computer monitor.

She now used her art degree to design insurance billboards. Uh-huh, say hello to the newest head of graphic design for National Country Insurance based in Denver. This post-divorce gig sort of used her skill set.

Unfortunately, this job would kill every creative neuron in her brain, numb as they were from the drag-and-drop process she'd gone through so far for insurance agents all over the country. After a while, all of their faces started to look the same as she plugged in their photos and updated their names, addresses, and phone numbers.

Of course, that meant the branding was cohesive. But it also meant the branding was dull as all hell.

She heaved a sigh and stared at the computer screen.

Persistence itself was attached to the sudden knocking on her door, jolting her from the drag-and-drop hellscape.

"Yoo hoo, hello," a female voice called. "I know you're in there, Em!"

Emmaline grinned harder than she had in months.

Barbie peeked through the long, thin window beside the door. She waved. The feathers she'd pinned in her hair bobbed with the motion.

Emmaline wished she had some feathers for her hair. Feathers were fun and adventurous. Sort of like she used to be.

She made a mental note to buy hair feathers. Then she squeed internally because, just like that, the morning did not suck. Yep, Barbie was her best friend in all of Denver.

All the world, really.

Barbie and Em met in middle school with their other besties—Cress and Lauren—and they'd been peas in a pod. Barbie with her long chestnut hair, warm brown eyes, and early-sprouting boobs that were surprisingly real given their size and the ratio to her tiny waist.

Barbie's mom always called her blessed, but Barbie said her figure gave her a backache. Really, boys weren't very respectful to girls who were blessed like Barbie. Girls either, for that matter.

Em stood entirely too quickly, banging her knee against the desk. Dammit. She finger combed her hair, getting as many of the little knots out as she could and wiped at the syrup spot on her lapel from breakfast.

She even pinched at her cheeks for some color. She hadn't exactly put on any makeup that morning since no one but Fiona was going to see her.

Working virtually was a good thing. Really, it was. She got an actual paycheck. She got to be home when Fiona got back from school. She could wear pajamas all day.

And also…okay, so she was only one day in, and it turned out she hated her job. But she loved her best friend.

She limped to the door and pulled it open. "Barbie!"

"Em!"

There was a great deal of hugging and "oh-my-gosh, this is really happening" chatter. They were opposites in nearly every way. Always had been.

Where Emmaline always said yes, Barbie had a healthy respect for the word *no*. And in a world where Emmaline searched for her new normal, Barbie stood out like a single pink toenail. There was not a lot of normal happening in the room when she showed up.

But there was something about Barbie—and Em couldn't say precisely what—that made everyone adore her. Always and forever, she was a favorite.

Except James. But he hardly liked anyone. He didn't count.

The truth was, Emmaline had a pretty good radar for assholes. And while Barbie didn't always understand when to stop talking, she was not a jerk. Not an intentional one, anyway.

Emmaline knew *all* about intentional assholes. That's why she'd decided to get away from California, so Fiona wouldn't have to live her life wondering if those around her were genuine or not. Sometimes the bold strokes of celebrity brought out the worst in people. Em used to find those bold strokes intriguing and, after feeling invisible in her own family, she craved that kind of life and attention. But that was before she saw what bold strokes could do to people.

That's why Emmaline was done with that phase of her life, for forever and ever and ever.

"You know anyone going by can see you through your window?" Barbie pointed at the windowpane. She sauntered in, tossed her purse on the sofa, and stretched like a Manx cat. "You're gonna need a curtain."

"Yep, and I probably should've set up my office on the other side of the house," Em agreed.

The little house she'd bought was in an older, established neighborhood. The place was cute. That's what the listing said, and everyone knew cute meant low square footage, but the opportunity for lots of character. The living room and kitchen area were linked by a small dining table and an island counter. The walls were taupe and beige with hints of cream. The previous owners had a whole kitschy nautical theme that wound throughout the house. It was…cute.

But not her.

The crisp pale paint palette itself was fine. Nothing intrusive, just walls. The space wasn't as big or bold as their former Bel-Air digs, but she and Fiona had both agreed that the deep mahogany cabinetry and hardwood floors—original to the house—felt like home.

Someday maybe they'd paint the walls a fun color, but that was more of a year three or four type of activity, she figured. Once she was solid in her new life and living the dream. Which was…not yet.

"I'm still figuring things out," Em said to Barbie.

Obviously. She gestured to her clothes. She probably should've put on daytime clothes instead of working in her pajamas. But, uh, why change when she'd just have to put them on again later?

Barbie only gave a cursory glance at Emmaline's PJs. "They're super cute."

Barbie was all about fashion. Honest as all hell, she wore one of the lowest cut shirts Emmaline had seen in her life. Not to say that she was judgey about what people wore. She didn't really care as long as they were happy and confident and the major parts were covered, but Barbie looked like she might have a nip slip at any moment. More so even than the lady Emmaline saw in Las Vegas that time who had electrical tape covering the important areas of her ta-tas.

"How's your first day on the job?" Barbie asked, punctuating each word as she set down her shopping bags. She flicked her hair back over her shoulder.

"I'm exhausted," Em said the first thing that came to her mind. She couldn't quite get back to sleep after the whole fire shebang.

They settled in and she told Barbie about lighting the neighborhood dumpster fire. That's what they did, as best friends. The talking, not the fires. Though, there was that one time—

"You lit a fire with the diddly-do you use on your vagoozlcookie?" Barbie asked, eyes huge and her expression frozen.

"Uh-huh." Em dropped her face to her hands.

She still had to face James at future family gatherings. That wouldn't change. But around four a.m. she had decided that the best course of action was to deliver Ethan some thank-you treats and then avoid him for forever and ever.

"That's not the worst part," Em said.

"James finding your scorched diddly-do is not the worst part?" Barbie asked, slowly.

"No. *Ethan Greene* is my new neighbor, and he was first on the scene," Em relayed the situation.

"Ethan Greene?" Barbie asked. "Used to do the save-a-restaurant show, and the barbecue show—the one where he made meatsicles?"

Em nodded.

"Holy shit. Holy, holy, holy shit." Barbie laughed. Stomped her feet. "Only you. Only you. Ethan-fah-reaking Greene!"

Why did the mention of his name give her a little zing in the nerve endings along her neckline? Avoiding him was way up at the top of the agenda. As such, her nerve endings had no business firing at the mention of his name.

Sure, Ethan was handsome—more handsome even than her ex. Not that it was a comparison. Ethan also had buckets of success and the ability to draw all the attention to himself.

A girl could not dazzle or stand out when she was on the arm of a guy like Ethan. No, when she was with a man like him, she dissolved into nothing. Ask her how she knew…

And, as though she needed an *and*, he'd already seen her in one of the most embarrassing moments of her life.

"He's only a person," she reminded Barbie.

"He is not only a person," Barbie corrected. "He's famous, and it sounds like he's into you. How do you always do that? I swear I need to take lessons."

"You mean how do I attract assholes with a strong social media following?" Em countered. For the record, her social media following was dismal and she liked it that way.

"I'm telling you. You are the total package." Barbie gestured from Em's head to her toes. "Embrace it."

"Which part? The uncombed hair or the syrup on my shirt?" Em asked.

It didn't matter if Ethan liked her or not. Before her marriage, Em had hobnobbed with celebrities—dated and…uh…slept with a few of them, too. During her marriage, she attended all the important Hollywood events. And if there was one thing she could count on with the famous and those who groupied with them, they were all the same: all phoney and all about themselves. All about shoving her to the side.

"I refuse," Em said. "Utterly refuse to be impressed by

anything other than uninspired ordinary. Bring on the small business owners or a plumber."

"Oh, come on. It wasn't that bad," Barbie urged. Though she had barely visited Em in California, and she hadn't seen the things Em had.

"I've missed this," Em said, gesturing between them. This was nice… falling back into the way things were.

"Well, there's no Tony here to interfere." Barbie rolled her eyes. "I sure hate that guy."

"I know," Em said.

Tony wasn't a fan of Barbie and Barbie *hated* Tony. Em was stuck in the middle so when Barbie stepped back from spending any time where Tony might be, Em didn't know what to do. There wasn't a right answer, it seemed, in those moments. That was the start of what Em thought of as the Christmas Card years. The years where she and Barbie texted a few times, forwarded memes on Facebook, sent holiday greetings, and otherwise lived their own lives.

But that was then. And this was now. And Em had already decided she would never make that mistake again.

"I'm sorry," Em said. "That I didn't fight to keep you in my life."

"Girl." Barbie nodded. "Same."

"These people like Ethan? Tony? The famous ones. They're toxic," Em assured. They would attempt to show that they weren't awful, but she'd been around this block more than a few times and she knew how it went.

"Okay, let's never talk about Tony again. Instead, let's talk about why I came." Barbie rummaged through her handbag. "I came because I actually got a gig and I need your help."

"You got a job?" Em asked.

Barbie was a trust fund baby and aside from a little

two-week stint at GAP when they were in high school, Barbie elected not to join the workforce.

"Well, I'm volunteering. Today I'm volun-told-ing." She danced a little in her seat. "They told me to figure this out. And I knew just the person to ask."

"Whatchagot?" Em asked, leaning in to get a better look.

"Well, you are a graphic artist and I need a logo for a local cat rescue." Barbie blinked her mascaraed lashes like she had a secret. "I need something unique and *super* cute."

When Em went to art school against her parents' wishes, she'd hoped to break out as a children's book illustrator and prove everyone wrong. She could be successful doing what she loved.

That hadn't gone to plan. Much like her life in general, actually.

She'd proven them pretty correct, unfortunately.

But Barbie knew about that history. Had a front-row seat to Em's decision to go to art school.

"I can do a logo, sure, but I mean, I have other work to do." She gestured to her laptop, though Barbie probably didn't really care about what she worked on. It's not like it was a fire truck, something seriously interesting to look at that got everyone excited.

"Oh, c'mon. Freelance?" Barbie asked, again with the heavy blinking. "I need you."

Those were the magic words, weren't they?

"Let me see what you need." Em took the piece of paper with a stick figure sketch on it.

Worst case, she'd have to say no. Best case, she'd get a reprieve from her current drag-and-drop.

Barbie tossed her hands in the air. "Okay, it's called Kitty's Cat House and—"

"Hold up." Emmaline squared her shoulders. "A cat house?"

Because there was only the one kind, right? The Vegas electrical tape on breasts kind? Yes. Definitely. But that wasn't entirely legal in Colorado. Unless…had things changed since she'd moved away?

But then why would Barbie be volunteering?

"A kitty cat rescue for cats…who need homes." Barbie tilted her head to the side and studied Emmaline like she'd just lit something else on fire with a sex toy. "The lady who runs it is named Kitty."

Em closed her eyes and screwed up her face. "I knew that."

She hadn't known that.

"We're a non-profit. We've got our tax-exempt status and everything," Barbie announced.

Actually, doing a little charity work wasn't a bad idea. It'd give her brain an opportunity to have a little fun without the worry of another full-time gig. Making something super cute sounded like the brain break she needed.

"Okay. I'm going to do this for you," Em said, because with Barbie involved, there would be nothing mundane about it.

"Yay!" Barbie rat-a-tat-tatted her long pink fingernails on the joggers she paired with heels. "Now here's what I propose. A little squid toe quota so everyone gets their happy ending."

"Quid pro quo…?" Because the other thing Barbie had said didn't make a bit of sense.

"Yep. Tit for tat. You do something for me, and I do something for yo-o-ou." Barbie sang the last note as she grinned wide.

"Or I could just do it as a donation?" Emmaline suggested.

Barbie made a *pf-shaw* sound. "You get something in return, sweet cheeks, I insist."

"But I don't need anything. I have you."

Barbie made a kissy face. "Oh, but there's still something I really want to give you. It'd be easier if you just agreed to the quo."

This was going to get interesting. Barbie loved giving extravagant and totally ridiculous gifts. Like the time she hired celebrity impersonators for Fiona's first birthday party as a surprise—which was funny because the actual celebrities were there. Or the time she sent a life-sized cardboard cut-out of herself to Em, so Em would feel closer to her.

Tony tossed it almost immediately.

"What is it you propose?" Em asked, ever so cautiously.

Barbie stood and pressed her palms together. Then she hurried to the bags and pulled out a garden gnome...a gnome that looked just like Em. Then she removed another smaller version from the sack—Fiona. "Ta da."

This was right up Barbie's ally. She gave good gifts, that was for sure.

"Oh my God." She took the gnomes, setting them on her coffee table. "These are amazing."

"Oh shit, Barbie made it here first," their friend, Cressida, said. Her voice was all muffled, as she peered into the windowpane beside the front door.

Emmaline should move putting curtains up to the top of the list of things that must be done right away. Right after buying the curtains, which would come after measuring for them.

Time to get on that.

Barbie went straight to the door, swinging it open and spreading her arms wide. "Welcome to Emmaline's! Prepare to party!"

"Barbie, we said no gnomes!" Cress said, leading the last of their crew—Lauren—into the room. Lauren, Cress, Barbie, and Em used to be inseparable. Before Em moved away.

Cress and her brown hair, tan skin, and subtle way of making things better was a contrast to Lauren who preferred not to spend any time in the sun, had strawberry-red hair and could be a bit of a hurricane.

Lauren held out a gorgeous basket filled with something that smelled really nice. Lavender? Yeah, that was lavender. Not the fakey-fake kind that came in a perfume bottle, but the real deal. And the basket was one of the handmade kinds Emmaline would expect to see at the galleries her ex took her to early in their relationship; back when things were good. At least, back when she'd *thought* they were good.

"We brought you a little welcome back basket." Lauren flashed a smile and held out the oversized, gorgeous basket. "This is the agreed-upon gift." She gave the gnomes side-eye.

Barbie lifted a shoulder, her shirt slipping a little and pushing the cleavage situation into seriously iffy territory.

"So…what have we missed in the past *decade*?" Cress asked, putting her hands on Em's shoulders and giving her a once-over. Like she was checking to ensure there were still two ears, ten fingers, two legs, all that. Lauren's presence was oddly settling against the persistent rattling Emmaline had gotten used to inside her own head lately.

"Well, it didn't involve the dumpster, last night's fire, and a faulty battery in her chick stick, that's for damn sure," Barbie said with a wink at Emmaline.

Oh, dear God. It was out there. Just like the all-day pajamas.

"Barbie," Em said between her teeth. "Filter."

Was it possible to actually feel the blood draining from one's head as one's cheeks heated? Just, you know, asking for a friend.

"I figured you might be involved when I heard about the fire in your new neighborhood." Cress didn't seem phased at all.

"Who told you about the fire?" Em asked.

Cress trailed her finger along the back of Em's sofa. "I have my ways of hearing things."

"But what's a chick stick?" Lauren asked.

Em shook her head faster than she'd done it before. "It's nothing. I was only playing with matches. No big deal."

"I think I know." Cress raised her hand and did a colorful dance.

"I've never been so curious about a situation since that time Emmaline let a bumblebee loose in Lance's bedroom. Remember? Because she decided she wanted a pet." Cress got wistful at the memory. "Stung him, right on the bum while he was…you know…"

"I apologized for that," Emmaline grumbled. "Now, I have new, more pressing issues."

"I know." Cress lifted her shoulders in excitement. "Isn't this fun? Somebody better spill."

"Barbie is exceptionally good at that, isn't she?" And they'd be having a little chat later.

Barbie gave a rather abbreviated explanation that involved unnecessary hand gestures.

"Oh! Of course, chick stick, that's cute." Lauren laughed.

"Could we not tell anyone else about this?" Em asked. "Pretty please." She looked straight at Barbie. "I'm mostly addressing you."

"This is girl talk. Cone of silence." Lauren mimed zipping her lips.

"But that only applies to us," Barbie said, making a circle motion with her fingertip.

"You'll notice Barbie is exactly the same as you left her." Cress pursed her lips and gave Barbie a sly glower. "That's why we love her. Who else keeps Viagra for their peonies?"

"Hey, it makes them stand up tall, and last longer," Barbie announced.

Cress and Lauren found this hysterical. Em laughed, too and covered her mouth with her hand because Barbie was being totally serious.

Barbie pushed her hands on her hips. "I'm not kidding. It works."

"She's not wrong," Lauren announced. "But it's fun watching her defend it."

"Haha," Barbie said. "Listen, I think we need to have another one of our special Tupperware parties for Em." Barbie said this like they'd done this before.

"I'm in," Cress said.

Em shook her head. "No. And also…*what*?!"

"Lauren hosted one of those parties last year and it was a hoot and a half," Barbie said.

"Hey, Em," Lauren said, holding up her index and middle fingers straight up. "Why can't you get yourself off with these two fingers?"

Now it was Em's turn to do the heavy blinking thing. Except her eyelashes were not as long as Barbie's, had no mascara on them, and therefore the effect was probably not the same.

"I have zero idea," Em said.

"Because they're mine." Lauren cackled.

Cress and Barbie both broke into hysterics again. Full on, bent over, laughing.

"Is this what it's going to be like now that I'm home?" Em asked, totally dumbfounded because nothing had changed with these women.

"Nope." Barbie popped the *p* at the end. "This is how it's been for ages. But you are back, so you're included. I promise, Em, coming back to Denver is the best thing you've done. Just watch."

Chapter Five
ETHAN

THE PULSE of jazz music played through the in-ceiling kitchen speakers, and Ethan was in his zone. His body felt lighter, and the worries of the world didn't matter when he was here in his happy place—the kitchen. The room where things made sense. Where science and chemistry could guarantee an outcome, but it was the art that ensured the outcome was brilliant.

Uh-huh, the one place he could rely on things to fall into place was the kitchen.

The timer on the oven beeped. One handed, he grabbed a gray kitchen towel and pulled the Mediterranean chicken off the rack and moved it to the stovetop. Grabbing a sample spoon and blowing at the concoction, he gave a quick taste.

Perfection.

Chicken, pesto, kalamata, a dash of spice but not too much, all served on a bed of spring greens with a touch of vinegar in the dressing. A little punch to the taste buds to complement the pesto.

Ethan let the flavors meld on his tongue, swirl together

in a symphony of delicious savory promise. He moaned because this was the stuff that made Michelin stars and he wanted others to experience the concoction, too. Live for the flavors like he did.

Call him whatever you like, but Ethan loved food, and that chicken was excellent.

He moved to the sink to drop the spoon, spiking the hand towel on the counter because he'd just scored a major goal with this dish.

"Dad?" Annie called from the front door, breaking his trance. "I'm back."

He turned. Huzzah, good food, *and* she was speaking to him once again.

"Welcome home." He grinned, untying his apron, and pulling it over his head.

When she came home from school earlier, his little one was mad as a Tasmanian devil. But she'd made friends with Fiona since they both avoided gluten and sat at the special lunch table together. That was good. And, after Annie cleaned up the house with her chores and tidied the cat box, he'd allowed her to go for a visit with her mate, Harmony.

He'd done this so they could catch a breather.

"Is Jack coming in?" he asked. Jack was Ethan's business manager, publicist, and good mate. He was also Harmony's stepdad. Jack was usually all business, all the time. But Ethan had some amazing chicken to get back to, and he did not particularly want to deal with business at the moment.

Annie nodded and lifted her index finger while she announced, "I'm telling you now that this is a good thing. It's not my fault you don't listen to what's good for you."

She started to bound up the steps and nearly made it to the top before he said—

"Hold it right there." He frowned.

She turned around, about halfway up. "Well, like, you know how people do the wrong thing, but they think it's for a good reason because you should be happy?" She didn't wait for him to respond. "Well, that's what I did."

She couldn't have posted anything online. He had all her devices. Bloody hell, tell him she didn't go searching for a new mum again with a new angle.

He kept his worry in check and said, calm as could be, "What happened?"

"Um. I think Jack is going to come in and tell you," Annie said, and the bright smile she flashed was a faker.

Then again, Annie was a bit pale, wasn't she?

"Are you feeling well?" Had she been sick at their house?

She was looking everywhere but at him.

The air in the room had a strange feel to it, as though everything was about to change, and he had no idea why or how.

"What. Is. It. You're. Not. Telling. Me?" he asked, hands going straight to his hips.

Whatever it was, they would handle it. They'd handled a load since they'd discovered each other.

"I didn't put you on a dating site," she announced, heading back up the stairs. "So you can't be mad at me."

"I know you didn't," he muttered to himself. He did know. He'd been there that morning to stop the events before they could take off. Then he took her access away.

"And I'm not sorry," she added as her door slammed shut.

Ethan was at the door as Jack made his way up the sidewalk to the house.

"Hey," Jack said. And the way he said it was the same way he said things before giving bad news.

"What in the bloody hell has happened?" Ethan asked.

Jack grimaced. "Annie, uh, somehow posted on your Instagram for you."

Ethan's mouth went dry, and his body got heavier with gravity seeming to work extra in his living room.

How in the bloody hell did she log in? He didn't even know how to login. He had a manager for that.

Crikey, but she was a smart one with the computers. Too smart for her own good.

"What did she post?" he asked, keeping himself as calm as he could.

"I don't want to tell you," Jack said. "But I'm going to, anyway."

Ethan's mobile was on the kitchen counter, so he couldn't look right then himself. He considered going after Annie and hauling her downstairs to explain herself, but this was one of the parenting times he wasn't sure what to do.

With a pained look, Jack held up his mobile screen for Ethan.

One reason Ethan had hired Jack as his brand manager was because the bloke was confident, smooth, and knew his shit.

But one glance at the screen and Ethan's world went a bit topsy-turvy.

There on the screen was his Insta page. He didn't manage it—Jack hired someone to do that. There on the post was Ethan from this morning, alone in his kitchen, still in his pajama shorts, cooking up banana pancakes for Annie's brekkie.

He wasn't wearing a shirt at all, and his hair was a right mess.

"Annie posted this?" he asked, standing still as a statue.

"Uh-huh," Jack replied.

Also…

"Why is this still up?" Ethan asked.

"Well, see, that's the thing," Jack said, stepping inside the door and closing it behind him. "Your daughter is really smart."

"Bloody hell, tell me about it," Ethan said.

"She created what has become a trending hashtag…to find you a wife." He said the last part so fast Ethan nearly didn't hear it.

"How?" Ethan pressed his hand to his forehead, because maybe now he was the one who would be sick. "And why did she do it before I got dressed?"

Jack gave him a look like he really should understand. Drat, Annie was too smart for her own good. Her marketing prowess was spot-on.

"The hashtag went viral really quickly, so I couldn't delete the post." Jack was in business manager mode. "At this point, if we delete it, that sends a message in itself. We have to be careful here. This could be a great thing for you with the prospects over at Nosh. Or…not." Jack pursed his lips. "I'm still working the angle."

"What did Annie say in the caption?" Ethan took the mobile back and sat on the sofa, rubbing his hand in his hair.

Ethan Greene is my dad! I think he'll delete this really fast. But he's super great. And he's lonely. He needs someone special, so he'll be happy all the time and I need a mum. Is that you? - Annie Greene #DateMyCelebrityDad

His heart kind of hurt reading that. A heavy weight sat in his stomach like he was the one who was going to be sick. He scowled, though he wasn't entirely sure what he was feeling right then.

Had he wanted this? Was that what this feeling was?

No, bloody hell, he didn't have time in his day for a girlfriend.

"I'm happy." He handed the phone back. "Why does she reckon I'm not happy?" He glanced up the stairs, but the door to Annie's room was still shut.

He was happy, dammit. His life was fine. He had his restaurants, his daughter, and the meeting today had gone well.

Hell, he saw women. He wasn't a monk. He had friends of the female variety who offered benefits that, well, benefitted them both. And he was perfectly happy with that setup. He kept it away from his daughter, of course.

All together, he liked his life just fine. Bloody hell, he *was* happy.

"I don't know." Jack shook his head.

"What does all this mean?" Ethan asked.

"You now have thousands of women messaging you privately." Jack gave a subtle head shake. Jack couldn't seem to meet Ethan's eyes. Then he seemed to come to a kind of decision with himself because he stared right at Ethan as he said, "The hashtag has already been used hundreds of thousands of times. It's impressive."

"It'll blow over. I've weathered worse." He was sure.

Jack ran two fingertips over his eyebrows. "Yeah, this isn't what you think it is."

Ethan scowled. "How can it not be?"

And why did he have a hunch it was going to ruin his week?

"Right." Jack held up his hands in surrender. "First thought: the way this is going, it would appear that you are going to need to prove that you are happy and probably paired up with someone, before it'll go away. Unless you want the attention?"

"Only if it'll get me back to Nosh," Ethan said.

He stood, strode to the kitchen to grab his mobile. Jack helped him download the app and login. Oh geez… his social media had blown up.

Ethan felt his jaw drop a bit. "I don't want to be ambushed by ladies every time I step out of the house."

"I'll start drafting a statement." Jack stood. "In the meantime, don't talk to anyone about this. And, uh, if you could keep Annie off your socials, that'd be helpful."

Annie.

Ethan needed to talk to her before he did anything else, then he could deal with the rest.

So Jack left and Ethan knocked on Annie's door before going inside. She laid on her pillow, staring at the ceiling like it was a really great movie.

But it was just the plaster, nothing special up there.

"I'm not angry," he said, stepping through the door. "But we need to talk about this."

Starting with posting photos of a person in their underwear without their permission. Then posting it on social media asking for a wife, and a mum.

But words seemed to stick in Ethan's throat. He opened his mouth to say something, but he wasn't sure what.

For the briefest of seconds, he saw the worry in Annie's eyes. Worry for him or that he'd be angry?

"I love you, Dad. And, well, you need to listen to me." She sat up and crossed her arms.

He didn't know what to say. Totally lost with how to parent in this situation. He'd never reckoned she'd have him wrapped so tight around her finger, but there they were, two peas in a pod.

Still, a heavy blanket of disappointment fell in the room.

"I'm very disappointed you didn't listen to me," he said.

"Well, I'm disappointed you didn't listen to me," she countered.

"I'm disappointed in myself that somehow I made you feel like I'm not happy. You make me happy, love. You do."

"You really don't want me to have a mum, huh?" she said, her face crumbling. "I'd really like a mum."

His entire chest hurt at that. He could be a lot of things for her, but he couldn't be that.

"You know?" he asked. "We'll both think more clearly with a full stomach. Wash up and meet me downstairs for dinner."

This was a right bloody mess and not at all how he'd planned his night to go.

Chapter Six
EMMALINE

EMMALINE SCANNED HER INSTAGRAM FEED. There was the usual mix of kitten videos and friend requests, but Ethan Greene had officially taken over the internet with his search for a wife.

Who would've thought he was so set on meeting someone? Her feed filled with women using the #DateMyCelebrityDad hashtag in an attempt to catch his attention.

I'm ready to take on your meatsicle!

Love a man who can cook!

Let's connect over lunch!

Em rolled her eyes because as popular as Ethan was during his prime Nosh Network show, his popularity now soared right past that. Which was great for him. Celebrities loved this kind of explosion. He must be relishing the attention.

And as much as Em appreciated that Fiona had made a best friend in his daughter, she sort of wished it wasn't *his* kid. But a week in the same class, living on the same street…well, the math pretty much mathed and Em heard all about Annie on the regular. Annie and her social media prowess. *Yeesh*. Wasn't that a whole thing? Such a little internet savant, that one.

And since Annie was Ethan's munchkin, it was going to make avoiding him long term a lot more of a task.

Today, while Annie and Fiona played together at Ethan's, Em finally unpacked the box with her Pyrex dessert pan and got down to business. The treats she owed him as promised. Once she paid up, she could officially move on from the night that *had never happened*. And she could start pretending he didn't live so close by.

"Hey, can you take these to Annie's dad and walk back with Fiona?" Emmaline asked Barbie as she brought in yet another box from the garage.

How many boxes did it take to move a person across the country with mini-me and the apple of her eyeballs?

A-freaking-lot, that's how many.

But they'd taken a mini-break to make an entire pan of gluten-free, salted caramel, Rice Krispies Treats. "I just need to wrap them in foil or something."

She'd tucked some elusive foil around this kitchen somewhere. Not where she checked in the drawers, but nothing was organized quite yet. The stuff was definitely here, though. She remembered unpacking it.

Barbie made gigantic eyes at Em. "*You* can take them."

Em rummaged through the last drawer, then closed it with her hip. There was no foil. Damn. Em stopped searching and closed her eyes so she could take a reprieve from the moving mess.

"No one can take them, anyway. I have nothing to wrap them in." She tossed her hands in the air too dramatically, but whatever.

"Just take him the pan," Barbie said, using that tone a person couldn't argue with because they'd lose. "I bet he'll even give it back."

That wasn't the issue. Not really. The main issue was that Emmaline wanted to drop and dash.

"I am avoiding him. For all the reasons you already know."

"So you can draw sketches of him instead?" Barbie asked, pure bullshit innocence.

"I have no idea what you're talking about." Em knew exactly what Barbie meant. Em's muse spoke to her and, when her brain had had enough drag-and-drop, she started sketching out a little story with a chef who only sort of looked like Ethan. Only sort of!

She thought she'd tucked those sketches away, but obviously Barbie saw them.

"Have you considered jumping him?" Barbie asked, as serious as Em was about getting the cabinets organized ASAP.

"No!" She couldn't tell Barbie that *of course*, she'd thought of it.

Look at him! He was precision gorgeous. But Em would have to get her eventual post-divorce benefits with somebody else. Preferably, someone who lived a completely normal life and who didn't live nearby.

"You need to spread your legs so you can spread your wings," Barbie said, all cheerful.

Then they engaged in a quiet stand-off. Neither said anything, but Barbie gave Em the look. The one that matched her tone from moments before.

"Not with him." Em stood firm.

Barbie continued giving her that same look.

"Maybe with someone else," Em conceded.

Barbie nodded, smiling like a villain.

"But I'm still not taking Ethan the pan. Because then he will have to return it, and it'll be a whole thing."

Barbie picked up the pan and held it out to her. "Take. The man. The pan."

"And no more talk about sleeping with him?" Em confirmed.

"I didn't say anything about sleeping. But I'll table the other suggestion. For now," Barbie assured.

Ugh, okay, Em would take the pan. He could drop it back on her porch. Or Annie could bring it the next time she visited Fiona.

Easy and logical.

Worst case, she wouldn't get it back. Of all the things she'd lost recently, the glass Pyrex didn't even make a slight dent.

Em nodded. "Fine."

She said that just like Fiona did when she couldn't get her way.

Dessert in hand, Emmaline held her head high and marched down the sidewalk to Ethan's house. Make the drop. Get the kid. No small talk. This was easy.

She paused because a sedan in the drive started to back out. A sedan with the principal of the girls' school in the driver's seat looking both ways as she backed onto the road.

That was weird. Did the woman make house calls often?

Em frowned, then moved the pan under her arm like a badass multitasker. She pressed his video doorbell.

Then she waited.

And waited.

Shifted on her feet.

Should she ring again? She'd just moved to press the button when the door cracked, then opened, and Ethan stood in his everyday sweatpants and muscle tee with a kitchen towel draped over his shoulder.

Yum-my.

She did her best not to stare at the tattoo sleeve along his right arm—swaths of black ink with swirls of blues and red. Slightly abstract at first glance, but all brought together in a tapestry of waves and clouds.

"Hi." She gripped the pan tighter, so she didn't accidentally drop it because she got distracted by the green flecks in his blue eyes or anything.

"Hey." He glanced at the pan in her grip, then back up to meet her gaze, his reflecting lots of questions. All the questions.

"I brought you treats," she announced.

He said nothing right away, and Em didn't like the way the silence itched. So, then, because she was oh-so-very slick, she added, "And I saw Annie's post. How's the wife hunt coming along? That is quite the little girl you have, huh?"

And with that, his face fell like she was a most unwelcome inconvenience.

She gulped, swallowed the dry feeling in her throat. "Uh…these are for you. As promised and delivered."

He stared at the tray entirely longer than necessary.

"Is something wrong?" she asked, glancing to the tray.

He shook his head. "No. 'Course not. Thank you."

He reached for the treats, but it seemed to be more of a task than it should've been, so she gripped the tray harder, not giving it up.

"You don't want my treats?" she asked, since it was clear he wasn't excited about the marshmallow goodness. And if that was the case, then she should take them back home and enjoy them with Barbie instead.

"You're very kind," he said. "Thank you."

"I owe you these. I'm not being kind," she confirmed.

If she'd been only kind, she would've grabbed the pre-mades at King Soopers grocery store and called it good.

His expression was one of odd neutrality. "Look, I have to be honest. The girls are great friends and all, but if you're here to audition for the missus and mum position, I've got to stop you there. I'm not… it's just not…"

She stared, waiting for him to continue on.

"It's not going to happen," he finished, gently.

Um. Okay, what?

"I'm sorry?" Em looked at the pan, then back at Ethan.

"You brought me sweets? You saw the hashtag? I get it. I've been getting it for a bloody week. Ms. VanRunkle just dropped a whole tray of brownies with her personal mobile number." He rubbed at his temples. "Every time I turn 'round there's another woman bringing me gifts. I can't do it anymore, Em. I just can't. I'm sorry. I don't mean to be so blunt."

Well, good thing, this was not that. Em pursed her lips and tried to think of the best way to word her reply.

"Um. No. I am not looking to do…*that*." Em glanced at the perfectly innocuous treats that did not anywhere say a thing about a desire to adopt him and his daughter. "I promised you Rice Krispies Treats…um…my first night in the neighborhood."

Were her words stilted? Yes, yes, they were.

He seemed even more surprised at that. Had he forgotten? Could she be that lucky?

"Righto, during your vibrational situation," he said with a cocky smile that wasn't necessary because he'd just turned her down for something she didn't even want.

Dear God, could she be any more awkward? She needed to hand over the treats and evacuate immediately. Then put the house up for sale and run, run, run.

"You're really not here because of the Insta post?" Ethan didn't seem to believe her, still clearly unsure what to do with that announcement.

"No." She shook her head, and she meant it. "I just owed you a tray of these, and now we never have to see each other again. Perfect, yes?"

That wasn't very clear. She should really explain further that—

"To be clear. There's no way that I would…" She gave him a head-to-toe once-over. "You know. If I was looking —and I'm not—but if I was, I'd be looking for someone way more not famous than you are." She paused. "That was a compliment, actually, because you are a handsome celebrity with thousands of women falling at your feet, and I'm just not into that." She gave a curt nod, pushed the treats at him.

He took them since he really didn't have any other choice.

"Enjoy your 'thank-you' treats," she said.

There. Done.

She turned on her heel and started to march back toward the sidewalk, head held high and shoulders square.

"You realize you're the first single woman in a week who hasn't tried to convince me to give it a go," he said, loud enough for her to hear.

She didn't even turn as she lifted her hand to wave. "Well, yay me."

"I'm sorry, I completely misunderstood. My bad," he said, sort of trailing off at the end.

She waved again and said nothing, just continued to march toward her house.

"Do you want to take your daughter along?" he called. "She's still here, eh?"

Dammit. Damn. Em froze right there in the middle of her grand departure.

Then she came back around and marched back up to his house. "Yes. That's the other reason I came by. Of course."

He gestured with his head that she could follow him into the house. Okay, fine, this is where her kid was, so this was precisely what she would do. Totally normal nothing-but-a-neighbor thing to do.

Ethan's foyer wasn't anything special. One might even call it typical. Average. Light yellow tile met beige carpet. The walls were white, but the furniture was colorful. Red and blue, clean underneath, but he and Annie clearly lived here without picking up often—what with the cups and bowls on the coffee table and a pair of Annie's socks dropped in the corner with a pile of shoes.

"Why don't you come in?" he asked.

She held her hands wide, then dropped them to her thighs, making a little smack sound. "I'm already in."

"I mean *more* in."

Did she want to be more in? Okay, fine. Sure.

"Kitchen's this way." He did the come-on-ahead-if-you-dare gesture with his head again.

Given the scents of garlic and salmon and…was that chocolate? She definitely didn't mind following him to the kitchen. The place smelled like a fancy restaurant she would have visited in her old life.

Where the living room was not-so-tidy, the kitchen was spotless. And while it may have smelled like a five-star restaurant, it felt like a home.

This space was comfortable and—

"I'm really sorry," she said, again, forcing herself not to wring her hands. "For before. I…uh…didn't mean to imply that I wanted anything other than nothing."

"Well, now I know we agree. It's nice. We can be friends," he said, absolutely serious.

Her body seemed to make a "ha" sound all by itself. "You think we can be friends?"

"My daughter and yours are getting on like a house on fire—" He stopped. "Sorry, terrible choice of words."

Em just nodded. "Maybe let's not talk about flames?"

"No dodgy stuff, just two parents getting along for the sake of the kids." This he said with a comfortable charm of a man who knew he was all that but didn't flaunt it. "Girls are up the top playing in the makeup."

Emmaline placed her palms on the counter, peeking over at whatever he had boiling on the stove. Looked like a raspberry sauce?

No.

Boundaries, Em, lots of boundaries. She demanded that her taste buds not salivate all over the man's counter.

"Want to join us for dinner?" he asked.

Her taste buds screamed that was a fantastic idea, demanding her new-wannabe-friend feed her. But her brain reminded her that arm's length was always the best choice with people like Ethan. And she should really work on practicing saying, "no, thank you." Like Barbie.

The bubble of his attention span apparently cracked because he pulled the towel from over his shoulder and went straight to the sauce. "It's nearly done."

He pushed the pan to the back burner and clicked off the fire on the front.

"My friend," Em said, just out of the blue when it popped into her head.

"What about your friend?"

"She's at my house. We can't stay for supper. We really have to go back."

"Annie," he called. "Fiona's mum's arrived. Come on down."

The girls called down their reluctant reply.

Meanwhile, he snagged two spoons from the drawer beside the stove. The first he dipped into the sauce, blew on it, and gave it a taste. That spoon got tossed to the right in the sink with a *clink*.

The other? He repeated the movement, chatting about something Annie had said about raspberries that was cute, but all Emmaline could focus on was the way his lips moved as he spoke, blew on the sauce, and then lifted that spoon across the island between them right up to her mouth, pausing so it wouldn't be weird because he was seriously cracking away at her personal space.

Was she supposed to take the spoon?

Or was she just supposed to let him feed her? They were friends and friends didn't feed friends, right? She was nearly certain. Especially because they'd clarified oh so very well where they stood. She should probably take the spoon and—

"Open," he said, his gaze affixed to her lips the same way hers fixed to his.

Going against her better instincts, she didn't say no. Instead, she opened her mouth. He slid the spoon through her parted lips and the move was somehow not invasive.

Holy hell. She closed her mouth around the smooth surface.

Her taste buds would not take any commands from her brain because the sauce was that good.

Then she actually reached for the handle, not even caring that her fingers brushed against his and the little nerve endings really liked that touch. She took the spoon because she was about to make out with his flatware like it was her first boyfriend and she didn't know what to do with her tongue, so she just put it everywhere.

Whatever he put in that sauce was pure witchcraft in raspberry form.

The grin he had was so much more than a half smile. The clarity that he liked that she liked his special sauce made her tummy flip right on over. In a super nice, flippy kind of way.

Bad Emmaline.

"Fiona," she called. "We have to go."

A kitten—probably a few months old, but not fully grown—scooted around the corner, batting at the air and having a great time with nothing at all. Oh, wonderful, a feline distraction.

And the only thing that could make Ethan actually *more* attractive. Dude in the kitchen making magic? Check. That he has a kitten? Holy all-the-checkmarks, Batman.

"Who's this?" she asked. Kneeling on the floor and putting her hand out to the cat.

"Annie and I are fostering this little guy," he said, apparently going along with the subject change.

That was fine by her because they were dipping into an uncertain and slightly scratchy territory with the other raspberry flavored chatter.

"Pepper." Ethan crouched beside where she gave the kitten a solid ear canoodle. "That's his name."

"That sounds about right."

"Say again?"

"Well, you're a chef. Of course you name your animals after food."

"Pepper's more of a spice."

But... "You eat it, so it'd be a food, yes?"

"If by food you mean spice, then yeah," he countered.

"Okay, maybe with pepper, but then what about basil?" she asked.

He stared at her funny. Yes, she was seriously arguing with an actual chef about what qualified as food or not.

"I should go up and get Fiona," Em said, so she didn't argue with him about salt next.

Ethan shook his head. "They'll be right down. Rule is that Annie has to wash off the makeup after. She's too young to be going out and about with it on."

Emmaline nodded, drew in a breath through one side of her mouth. She actually agreed with him on that.

"To answer your question, I s'pose basil would qualify as both, depending on the preparation. Food in a salad. Spice when crushed." Ethan looked at her then, as though this was the important part. Not a full assault with his gaze, just from under his lashes, as though he was ensuring she was listening.

Thank God in heaven, Fiona hopped down the staircase so they could stop talking about this. Or anything else.

"Can we stay for dinner?" Fiona asked. Really, it was a preteen plea.

Nope, they couldn't.

"Barbie's at our house." Probably snooping to find more not-actually-Ethan sketches. "We have to go." Em gave a pointed glance to the exit. "Right now."

Ethan chuckled, the sound trailing over the fine hairs of her arms in the same delicious way the raspberry sauce tasted.

That, right there, the way her body reacted? That was why they could never be friends.

Chapter Seven
ETHAN

THERE WAS an electric buzz in the southern California air surrounding Ethan. The air that was also thick with the scent of hairspray, perfume, cologne and even sweat from the glitzy celebrities who came before him, and a little also from those who followed behind. Others might not enjoy this type of thing, but it was definitely Ethan's bag. It wasn't the attention, mind.

No, it was what the attention *meant*.

He loved food and he loved sharing that love of food. For a time, it'd slipped through his fingertips. And now, *this* was the smell and the feel of his return.

So even as the California sun beat down on him in his pseudo-tuxedo, he didn't care about the discomfort of the heat. And he didn't wear sunglasses, but not as a style choice. No, he was there to show his face and scope out a possible fake girlfriend accomplice. That's exactly what he intended to do.

He'd had his hair professionally styled, which was silly since it looked exactly the same as when *he* styled it—if you asked him.

The rapid-fire sound of camera shutters clicked as paparazzi shouted names of the others on the carpet with him. A fair number of them were calling for him, too, which made a bloke feel good.

"Over here! Ethan!"

"Ethan Greene! This way!"

Ethan had no idea where the shouts came from so he turned one way, then the next. With one hand in his slacks pocket, he pivoted on his heel exactly as he was taught early in his career.

Smile plastered. Small wave. Cheeky grin.

Four steps forward and do it again.

"Ethan Greene! How's the wife hunt?"

That had him cringing inside. He did his best not to let it show on the outside, too. He wouldn't fuck up the last-minute opportunity Jack landed him to walk the red carpet for this premiere in Hollywood. He had no real idea what the movie was about. It didn't factor in the invitation.

So he skipped town for Hollywood and Annie got to do an impromptu sleepover at Jack's house with his stepdaughter.

"Date *Me* Celebrity Dad!" A woman shouted from behind the line of cameras.

He couldn't see her at first, not with all the flashes blinding his vision. But he caught sight of her as she tossed herself through the mayhem and managed to break through the barrier to the red carpet.

Damn, this woman was committed. This, right here, was why he needed to make this hashtag nonsense stop.

Cute as a button, she was, but he tended not to entangle himself with fans who shirked security and begged him for a date. Then again, he didn't entangle himself with anyone. And she wouldn't be able to handle the fake aspect of his proposal, that was certain.

She landed at his feet with a *thud* and while his instincts said to move away, he couldn't leave her there tumbled into a ball like that. He stepped forward to help her up with the security that had gathered.

Someone near them shouted about how he should show them his meatsicle. Hah, like he'd never heard that before.

"Gently, mate," he mumbled to the security team taking over with the woman on the ground now holding onto his ankles with a substantial grip. "She's a fan."

"I'll call you daddy," the woman said, breathlessly.

Security managed to pry her hands from Ethan's ankles, and he took the opportunity to follow his instincts this time 'round and take a step back.

"I'll date you, celebrity daddy!" the woman wailed.

What was a bloke to say to that?

Ethan didn't have a bloody idea, so he gave a curt nod. "Careful not to tumble again."

He missed out on anything that happened next because security swarmed between them, and he made it three more steps before two women flanked a group of paparazzi with cardboard signs announcing his hashtag. *#DateMyCelebrityDad*

Fuckin' hell.

The woman on the right threw a pair of her underwear in his direction. Well, he didn't know if they were her underwear since he wasn't privy to the removal. But he suspected them to be.

He glanced to the undies lying on the ground. Then around to the others nearby.

Right, well, he didn't particularly want unknown undies in his pocket, did he now? But it would probably be rude to leave them there.

He scratched at his neck, befuddled as to what he was supposed to do in this scenario.

Jack had never covered something like this.

Thank hell, someone with a broom and dustpan whisked the lace and fabric right off the red carpet.

He gave another nod in the woman's direction with a small wave. Then he was led through the rest of the melee, but he swore she'd pulled off her shirt as his escorts pressed him along to the next group.

Damn, that would buy her a trip to jail for indecency. He didn't want that for her. Then again, he also didn't want undergarments tossed at his face. This was exhausting.

"You are a popular man." Jack waited at the entrance to the theater, past the cameras, and smacked Ethan on his shoulder. "Ranking up there with Elvis and Bieber now that you've been pantied."

"When you say it like that it doesn't make it better," Ethan grumbled.

"Anyone you particularly like?" Jack asked, glancing around the room.

"No."

Jack smirked. He could. They were buddies and Jack understood that though Ethan loved his fandom, there were definitely boundaries that needed to be drawn. Those boundaries mostly regarding underthings and flicking them at him in public settings.

Jack handed Ethan a glass of champagne from one of the passing trays. Ethan downed it, brut that it was. Jack handed him another. Ethan didn't toss back that one.

"Ethan?" A woman's voice drifted toward him and he cringed because no unattached woman said his name in that tone without following it with a proposition since Annie's foray into social media.

Felicity.

They'd dated briefly before Annie came into his life.

"Felicity." He grinned and instinctively opened his arms for the incoming embrace. Felicity was a hugger.

"How long are you in town?" She didn't back away, but kept her body pushed right up against him.

"Not long. Headed back to Colorado after the show." He dropped his hand from her back, hoping it set the precedent for her to release him as well.

"The kid?" Felicity asked.

"Annie. Yeah," he confirmed.

"Postpone?" Felicity asked.

He knew that glint in her eye. He'd recognize her I-wanna-be-on-top look anytime. And the way she smiled was an obvious invitation.

"It's been entirely too long." She practically purred the words.

In another life he'd have tripped all over himself for a night with Felicity. But now he knew more. Understood there were better things in the world than a quick romp. He had a family now, and that's what he'd trip all over himself for.

"I really can't," he said.

"You know, Ethan Greene, I'm *also* looking for something more permanent these days." Felicity did the eyebrow thing again. "You've become very domesticated. It's... new. I like it."

That was his cue to move along.

Careful not to offend, he disentangled himself from her grasp. This wasn't easy, but he managed it with a little finesse. "Great to see you, Felicity."

She got the point and with only a small pout she faded back into the crowd.

"She's perfect for my pretend girlfriend suggestion."

Jack said. "I could reach out to her team and propose a mutually agreeable promotion between you? Or, you know, you can continue getting pelted with panties. Your call."

"No." Ethan shook his head. "She's interested. I need someone uninterested."

"Good luck with that," Jack muttered. He glanced around the gathering and there was a concocted vibe of those searching to find a reason to approach him without being shot down like Felicity.

Eyes all over him, people smiling warmly but with a nervous energy and a side of clear apprehension that they might face rejection.

And not because he was a celebrity—no, because here nearly everyone had a level of fame. Most of them greater than his own.

A woman to his right seemed to rally and headed his direction. He pasted on a grin and refused to give her anything but a shining Ethan Greene experience and memory. Unfortunately, this was the same story, different person.

Though, this time they'd never met and she didn't throw her knickers at his face.

They parted ways amicably and he rearranged his features into masked neutrality.

"No woman without a significant other owes you a favor?" Jack asked with that cheeky grin of his.

Of course, Ethan had told him that Em owed him something of a favor. They were mates, after all, and Em had a decent role in his life at the moment.

Though, he'd left out the bits she'd probably find embarrassing. He kept his word on that part.

"No." Ethan shook his head. "I mucked that right up with Em."

He gave Jack the run down.

"But you didn't *ask* her," Jack said. "You made it clear you are not interested in each other that way, which makes her the perfect person to not get the wrong idea, yeah?"

"No." Ethan cleared his throat. He couldn't quite put his finger on why he didn't want to make the ask, but call it pride? He'd already drastically misread that once. Didn't need a repeat.

But, then, twice more he repeated the same scenario with more women dressed to the nines like Felicity. Gorgeous women who wanted in his bed and in his life and who he knew deserved more than he could give them. They deserved a partner, and Ethan couldn't be that guy. There wasn't enough of him to be that guy.

Jack stared him down as the last woman walked away with a big smile because Ethan had ensured the letdown wasn't prickly and, really, didn't even feel like a letdown.

He clenched his teeth because… bugger him and call him stuffed… he'd have to swallow his pride and ask Em. There were no two ways about it. He was stuck between a rock and a hard place and he needed to make a decision.

Together he and Jack spent the rest of the evening crafting a plan that might actually staunch the bleeding of this hashtag storm, and the crux of it involved Ethan asking Em to play his girlfriend.

Em, who did owe him that favor she'd promised and who made it abundantly clear she had no interest in anyone famous. At all. Ever.

Chapter Eight
ETHAN

IT'D BEEN an awful few weeks, what with his social media storm brewing up right toward hurricane status. He hadn't asked Em yet. Though Jack was on his case about it all the bloody time.

"Ethan." One of the room mums for Annie's class—Tiffany—waved him over the second his sneaker touched the sidewalk at the park where the girls liked to hang out after school.

He gave a grin, but pointed to Em and the girls over on the soccer field.

That did nothing. Tiffany trotted over to him, huge smile, and a hope in her gaze he'd become entirely too accustomed to at this point.

"My sister didn't believe me when I told her you are a parent at the school. She's a huge fan," Tiffany said. "Mind if I snap a selfie with you?"

He nodded because of course he didn't mind. He draped his arm around her shoulder, and she took a snap.

"My sister's single," Tiffany said, eyes sparkling with misplaced mischief. "And she loves Denver. I know she'd enjoy visiting sometime. Maybe I can bring her over to meet you?"

"'Course," he said. "Love meeting all other food lovers."

Tiffany beamed. "You'll adore her. She's amazing. She's been single way too long."

He grinned and nodded since there wasn't much else to be done, but he knew this thing needed to be nipped in the bud before it really got out of hand. "I think I'm gonna take a break from the dating, you know?"

Tiffany smirked. "Yeah. Okay."

There were only so many times a guy could turn down a woman's sister before things did get prickly all 'round.

Ask him how he knew.

So he dropped it. Besides, given the number of letdowns he'd been tossing all over like confetti, he understood he walked on thin ice all day every day.

When he got back from Cali he had sworn to himself he'd ask Em straight away. But he'd been a chicken and he'd avoided everything. Hid out at home for a week, but that didn't work. Only stoked the social media fire.

And then today, Em had nabbed the girls after school, and he'd agreed to meet here. Since he needed to meet-up with Annie, and he had a pan to return to Em, this made loads of sense.

Neighbors returned pans all the time. And the returning of the pan was the perfect opportunity to make his pitch.

So, yes, he said his goodbyes to Tiffany and headed right to Em with a pan of brownies and his dick in his hand. Figuratively, of course. That wouldn't really work with the brownies. Not enough hands and all. Also, public park so…yeah.

"I sort of figured the statute of limitations on returning

my pan had run out." Em grinned a wry smile, taking the pan from him to set on a nearby picnic table with the rest of her stuff.

"No such limitations on brownies," he assured.

Ask her. Just ask her.

"They're gluten-free so the kids can eat them, too." On this note, he flashed a grin. A brownie-melting grin, he hoped.

She gave the brownies a solid sniff.

"Give them a try," he suggested.

She shook her head. "If I try to eat this, things could go badly."

"I doubt that. They're delicious." Why wouldn't she just eat one of the bloody things? Food tended to help sway others to his way of thinking.

She shook her head, wrinkling up her nose adorably. "I take a bite, then try to talk, then I'll probably choke and *then* you'll have to Heimlich me. It'll be a whole thing."

"Thank you for your caution," he replied, as cheeky as her. "I'd prefer not to provide any life-saving maneuvers today."

Ask her. Ask her.

He was going to do it. Right now. Right there.

And he'd approach this ask like any other business deal —with logic and a good dose of charm.

"How do you feel about that favor you mentioned?" he asked while their daughters ran around as girls did. Playing tag or catch the potato soccer or the like.

"The favor?" she countered, arms crossed, not even looking his way.

He crossed his arms to match hers. "Yeah. The night of the… you know."

"I feel like I'm not sure what you're talking about." She still didn't look at him. But her lips did twitch a tad.

Drat. He needed to get a read on how she felt about this when he pitched what was either one of his worst ideas or his best. No middle ground on this bloody mess.

But Em held the power to help him.

Gorgeous Em who came to the park with her hair pulled back, a couple of pencils sticking from the locks tucked up top. She looked a real mess. An adorable mess. The perfect fake girlfriend mess. An authentic pretend girlfriend.

"Look, this is where we are," he said. "You're not interested in me, and I have women wanting to be Annie's mum all day, every day. Jack—he's my manager—he said if I had a girlfriend, then this will all quiet down."

"You don't like the attention?" Em asked, eyeing him like he'd turned on the gas stove but forgot to light the flames.

He ran his hands over his hair. "It's driving me nuts. All the women all the time. I mean, in another life maybe it would've been a dream, but I can't even go to the pisser without my phone blowing up. I can't go into the restaurant through the front any longer. Drop off at the school is a right nightmare. Everywhere I go there's the stares—and not because they like my food and want to learn some culinary skills from a fun bloke. It's because they want to eat me."

"I could see that," Em agreed. "This Jack is a smart guy. If you want it to quiet down, then you should listen to him."

"Yes, exactly. So what do you say?" He pinched his lips together because he didn't want to say it. But he had to say it. "Help a bloke out?"

She looked at him now like he'd forgotten how to play toss the potato.

"Are you asking me to be your girlfriend?" she asked,

slowly like this wasn't possible. "Because I thought I made it clear, that's not—"

"Bogus girlfriend. Not real. For the pictures. That's all." *An easy experience for them both.*

"Are you feeling okay?" Em asked, her eyebrows pushing together.

"'Course. Why?"

"Because this is an awful idea," Em said. "Terrible. Like…bad."

Yes, he understood the possibility of that. "I said as much to Jack when he made the suggestion. But then I realized you and I trust each other with our kids. We live close. It makes sense for this to go down. So… what if it's not a bad idea?"

"I'm so sorry, Ethan. I cannot be your imitation girlfriend because…I'm divorced." She said this like it was a solid reason and not a wobbly one held up on stilts.

"I don't mind that you're divorced," Ethan said, hoping to smooth things over because *this* actually could work. "Better divorced than married to be my—how'd you say—imitation girlfriend?"

"I have a daughter," Emmaline said, not like she was out and out rejecting his idea, but going down some kind of list in her head.

"Me, too." He ran the pad of his thumb over his lower lip. "It adds a little something to the ruse, I think."

"And boxes." She gestured toward her house. "I have so many boxes in my living room. I'm not remotely unpacked from the move."

"Do you need help? Want help? I can help. Just a friendly fake boyfriend helping out his not-a-real-girlfriend."

"I would never ask a bogus boyfriend to do that. No one wants to unpack. Even me."

His eyebrows dropped together a little. "Well, I'm around and I'm good at lifting things. Bogus boyfriend or not. We are being friendly, yes?"

Her eyes fell to his biceps, and the apprehensive glimmer in her eyes only intensified as she stated, "You are *not* normal."

Uh…what? His eyebrows seemed to raise right up on their own a bit.

"Is that so?" He thought he seemed normal enough. He didn't collect toenail clippings or anything wicked weird.

"Okay, I don't want to say yes because this is ridiculous," she said. "I know I owe you. But I kind of meant… dinner or housesitting or lending you a cup of sugar."

"Grand scheme of things this isn't all that different," he assured her.

"The thing is," she continued. "I swore to myself when I started dating again it would be with a man who has stability. Someone stable with no sparkle at all."

Sparkle?

"Someone perfectly normal. Mundane even," she added. "You, Ethan, are definitely not normal nor mundane. Even if it's for pretend, I can't date you."

"Because I sparkle?" On that, he grinned.

She nodded, pressed her fingers to her eyelids.

"Assuming I were to agree, how would this even work?" she asked, talking with her hands. He had to watch out, so he didn't take an accidental whack.

Good. This was the good stuff where she was nearly ready to agree.

"Like a normal relationship, but without all the dodgy feelings and such." Just like that.

"There is no way this would end well for either of us…" She blew out a breath. A long one.

He nodded. "Yeah. It could be a right mess." He threw on as much charm as he could as he added, "But it doesn't need to be messy. It's not for very long and we are adults—we can handle this. Doesn't have to be a big deal."

"I haven't been on a real date in years," she said with a slightly hysterical laugh. "My first post-married date should not be phony."

She fidgeted with her hands, then clearly forced herself to stop, and slipped them in her pockets.

"You should know that about the woman you're asking. That's important information. You should seriously find someone else because I will be shit at this. Though…"

"Though, what?" he asked, carefully.

"Maybe this would be good for me. An introduction into the dating pool without any risk." She pondered that. "Actually…nope, still a horrible idea. Just mildly less."

He squinted because the sun was super bright, then remembered he did have one skill he hadn't used yet.

"Righto," he said. "What if I make you steak? Scallops? Chicken Marsala? You name it. I'll cook whatever you like for the duration of our time together."

"Are you trying to bribe me to be your fake girlfriend with your seductive culinary skills?" she asked.

"Is it working?" Because if it was, then he'd keep right on going.

"The answer is still no." She held up her hands. "It's just not going to work."

He bounced on his toes. "Bugger."

"I mean…what about the girls?" Em asked. "It's just a mess in the making."

Where *had* the girls run off to? He scanned the field. They must've tossed the ball behind the net.

"Annie!" he called.

Red faced, they came back 'round, still kickin' the ball back and forth, waving in their direction.

"We could be straight up with them. Let them in on the ruse," he assured. "That way, no one gets upset."

"By no one, you mean Annie?" Em asked, raising her eyebrows in that way of hers that made him question if this was the right choice. But, dammit all, he didn't want an actual girlfriend.

He nodded. "She's a wonderful girl, but she's got her head stuck on finding me a wife and herself a mum."

"I love that she's taken on Fiona as a friend and that means you and I are… friends. But we can't risk getting her hopes up with a ruse like this. She's already in a delicate place."

"Bloody hell." The weight of the damn hashtag pressed harder. "You're right, Em."

"I'd still like to order some of that raspberry stuff you made the other night," she added, like they were actually at a restaurant.

He sighed. "Consider it done."

"I'm sorry, Ethan. I wish I could help, but, this is… yeah… no." She shook her head. "I can't."

He'd have to figure out something else. "I s'pose it is what it is."

"I believe the words you're searching so hard for are, 'thank you, Em, for helping me see that this idea is not a good one.'" The little half grin made him sort of wish he could ask her to be his actual girlfriend.

But even if she wanted it, which she'd made it clear she didn't, *that* situation would definitely not be fair to anyone. Not at all. If all went to plan, he'd soon have network filming and the like to juggle with his schedule. There would be no time left for that kind of reality with her to work out.

"You make me raspberry sauce and I will go all out and fix you more treats," she said with big eyes. "And then I'll even check on your house when you are out of town again next time."

He chuckled. "I knew I liked you, Em."

She gave him a sidelong glance with a wry smile. "I mean, what's not to like?"

"Indeed," he agreed. "Indeed."

Chapter Nine
EMMALINE

THE THING Em forgot about living in a small community was how overlapped everyone's lives became. And how quickly it happened.

Like today at the elementary school Summer Splash Carnival—a PTA fundraiser. She stared at a formerly blank wall of the school as a new mural to supervise, her dad and all of her brothers brought a firetruck over for the kids to inspect, and Ethan manned the grill serving up fancy hot dogs for only five dollars.

Lauren and Cress got roped into serving at the bake sale table on the other side of Ethan's grill. Annie helped them keep things moving.

Barbie and a whole crew from the cat house had a fresh batch of cats and kittens all ready to be cuddled and, hopefully, adopted. Fiona had no problem volunteering to help snuggle all the animals.

Families scattered across the basketball courts for horseshoes and a bean bag toss. There were booths for face painting, balloon animals, and several inflatable bounce houses and huge inflatable slides near the playground. The high school jazz band even stopped in to play for everyone. It was lively... and surprisingly fun. There were kids everywhere and the vibe was filled with excitement.

"Oh, hon, careful," Em said to one of the kids as she knelt to clean up the paint splatters dripping off the side of a pink paint can. "Let the grown-ups get that."

For only a few dollars, kids could graffiti up the side of the school—under her supervision. They were calling it a mural, which was definitely a word...that's for sure. Lucky for them, they were already planning to repaint over the, well, mural, before school came back in session in August. Which was a solid choice given how it all didn't come together.

"You need a break, and some of that man's meat," Cress said, practically skipping over to where Em was supervising paint splatters.

Cress pointed to Ethan.

Em glanced over in his direction. He was serving hot dogs like they were free diamonds. His line was insane.

Hot dogs and signing autographs and...this was a charade. She couldn't say how she knew he wasn't enjoying himself. But he wasn't. He was great at putting up a front, smiling and being charming and patient despite the over-the-top manhandling by every woman in line, but she could tell that he was sort of miserable.

Somehow he seemed to sense Em's gaze on him. He glanced her way, waved a little with his tongs, and mouthed 'help', before getting sucked back into the fray.

Em had shared with her friends Ethan's request and her adamant dismissal of the idea. Which was, she was pretty certain, why Lauren decided to sell T-shirts at the carnival with Ethan's hashtag across the chest. And, also, why Cress wore one of those white T-shirts with the black block font right across her tatas.

"Skip the line," Cress said. "Jack has a plate ready for you and the other volunteers."

Em gave Cress a quick briefing on how the painting went and then she headed over to where Jack had plates all ready for volunteers.

It wasn't the usual carnival food that one would expect at something like this. No, this event was Ethanized and everything managed to look gourmet even on paper plates.

Gourmet with all sorts of toppings from cheese to jalapeños and even truffle oil. Freshly baked buns topped with seasonings—rosemary to garlic parm, and even a special spicy mustard version.

Em grabbed a plate and watched as Ethan scrubbed a hand over his face.

"He's losing his mind," Jack said, clearly talking about Ethan.

Em nodded. "I see that."

He was taking a ton of heat and Ethan looked to be a man at his breaking point. Which actually sat heavy on her chest because he was a good guy. The kind of guy who didn't want to hurt anyone and wanted everyone to feel important.

A guy who loved his daughter and adored Fiona, too. A guy who, in a few short weeks, had become Em's friend.

Em's mouth went dry because this sucked for him.

"This is my sister," Tiffany—one of the other moms—said with giddy gusto when she got to the front of Ethan's line.

Tiffany was happily married, as far as Em knew, so the enthusiastic giddy was new. The hashtag shirt was an interesting choice, considering her husband was over chatting with Em's brother, Blake, at the fire truck.

"She's the one I told you about," Tiffany said with a heavy, heavy wink.

Em sort of choked on Ethan's meat. Oh, right, there it was, the reason for the giddy.

"Hi." Ethan looked like he was ready to run.

"Jordan. I'm Jordan." Tiffany's sister flashed him a smile. "I would like to officially volunteer as tribute for your little hashtag project. Tiff has told me so much about you and all you do, and little Annie seems so sweet. I love kids. I want so many kids. I've always wanted a whole houseful of little kids. You know? So, hey, it's me. Your future right here."

"Ah." Ethan's eyes got big, and he seemed to stumble over his tongue. "I'm...uh... I'm..." He looked like a man ready to pop.

Em didn't seem to have control over her limbs. She couldn't say why she did what she did next. But she put on one of the damn shirts over her tank top and strutted right over to him.

"Hey, sweets." She draped her arm around his waist, lifted on her tiptoes, and pressed a chaste kiss to his cheek. "You ready for your break?" She glanced at Tiffany and her sister. "He's been working all day on this spread. The man doesn't stop. Even when I tell him how important it is to take time for himself."

Jaws dropped all across the other side of the table. Tiffany and Jordan and pretty much the rest of Ethan's insane line all made the same expression.

Em squeezed him and laid her head against his shoulder, really playing it up.

Jack seemed to choke on something and then cleared his throat over by the volunteer food table.

Lauren stared at Em from the bake sale table as though Em had personally set up a wet T-shirt contest for those who wanted to put on one of the hashtag tees.

But Ethan looked at her like she was saving his bacon.

Aw, that felt nice even though this whole thing was a really horrible idea.

Ethan's arm wound around her waist, and he rolled with it. "Jack, you got the grill?" Ethan asked with a chin-jerk to his buddy. "I'm gonna go eat with my girl."

The sound of hearts breaking all through the carnival seemed to be audible. That was probably the gasp that came from all the lines at the same time.

And the feel of Ethan's arm at Em's waist was actually nice. That was probably because she hadn't been touched like this in ages.

But then the gravity of what she had done seeped into her pores. That was probably just sweat from the heat.

All together, the trifecta made the whole day seem totally nuts.

Ethan snatched up a plate for himself, and Em collected her own. Then they headed across the grass to a sort of sad picnic table away from all the others. Sad, but private, so…yeah…it did the trick.

They sat across from each other. Em busied herself getting comfortable and avoiding Ethan's gaze. He set his plate down and didn't move. Not an inch.

Em squirmed. Then she fortified her position and stared Ethan straight in the eyes.

"That was unexpected, huh?" she said.

Ethan slow blinked at her, folding his hands under his chin.

"Hear me out," Em said, nudging her hot dog with her fingertip.

"I'm listening." Ethan didn't have any problem eating at all.

"One public date," Em said, holding up a finger. "You get *one*. I will hold your hand, but kissing outside of a peck on the cheek is out of the question."

"Bugger, why is that a letdown?" he asked.

Now it was her turn to blink heavily.

Then he grinned. "I've no intention of trying anything, anyhow. Promise."

"Okay good. It's settled." She smacked the table.

"Um… one date and an announcement here is hardly enough to prove you're my girlfriend," he said, pointedly staring at her.

Gah, he was right. Still, she held her ground with her own sharp stare as she amended, "You can post all about what we're not actually doing. I'll even let you cook for me and then take pictures. I'm nice like that."

Blah. The way she said *pictures* sounded dirty and she didn't hate that. Which was really bad.

"I'm serious, we'll do one more public outing to finish this off. After that, we can officially fake break up." She said this cheerfully, like they'd just picked out dessert. Nothing more.

"What changed?" he asked, genuinely.

"Call it understanding things a little better," she said. "I've been watching, and I…uh… I think I get it now. Why you aren't enjoying this. It's just…" She pinched her lips to one side. "Every other famous person I've known would love the attention. Love the constant reminder of how special they are."

He glanced down at that, his jaw ticking.

"But I think I finally see that you're not like the others. Maybe." She said it and truly wanted to believe it.

He nodded and ate in silence while she studied the wood grain pattern of the pressed plastic table.

"Hey, you two." Cress waved as she approached their table.

Em waved back.

Cress slid right onto the bench beside Em. "So, a thing happened—"

"Yeah, I was there." Em pushed her lips into a thin line.

"Not that thing." Cress poked at the table as she spoke. "Ethan's kid overheard the whole of your shenanigans, and I think you both need to have a chat with your girls because…that looked pretty real back there. Is it real?" She said the last part very quickly.

"No," Em said with a quick headshake.

"I'll talk to Annie," Ethan assured, nodding. "Clean up any mess this could cause there."

Crap, Em needed to tell her parents and her brothers, so they didn't all get their hopes up.

That gave Em a stomachache and all the reasons she'd held onto for why this was a horrible idea in the first place settled heavily in her gut.

"You know when you came to school and Lauren and Barbie and I were all friends? We took one look at you and knew immediately how awesome you are. I said to Lauren, 'Her. We need her.'" Cress let out a long breath. "We understood that what was missing in our lives was you. And, uh, I don't think we're the only people in the world to have that thought. If you get my drift." She slid her gaze across the grass over to where Annie helped at the bake sale table.

"I'm on it," Ethan assured.

"Sooner probably rather than later," Cress suggested. Then she eyed Em's hot dog. "You gonna eat that?"

Em shook her head. "All yours."

For the first time in a long time, she wasn't even a little bit hungry anymore.

Chapter Ten
EMMALINE

WITH THE CARNIVAL OVER, they'd explained the situation to the girls together. Annie hadn't liked the idea of staunching the flow of new mother applicants. But Ethan took her aside and somehow convinced her this was the right course.

Fiona used this opportunity to negotiate for a puppy. Em gave the prospect a solid maybe, and then Fiona announced that fake dating sounded like lotsa fun. Apparently, it helped that there would be cookies involved and probably a puppy, too.

Em had agreed about the cookies and, as a result, she'd put off her hope of breaking the seal of her divorce for a little longer. That is to say, finding someone also not looking for anything long term for a post-divorce…uh… she did not want to think of it as a hookup. Maybe just a liaison?

Anyway, that was all on hold.

"All right, Mr. Greene, what cookies are we making?" Emmaline rubbed her hands together, ready to get cracking so they could get to eating.

Excellent news, once the girls had had their chat and everyone knew the score, Em found her appetite again.

For their first photo op, Em and Fiona met up in Ethan's kitchen because hers was…well…still an unorganized wreck. There would be no magic making happening there. Also, he was cooking. So, yes, that, too.

"Annie has a request for a batch of her favorite oatmeal chocky chip cookies." Ethan draped his arm over his daughter.

Annie fought it. That much was clear with the way she rolled her eyes. But she totally loved her dad's hug. That much was even clearer with the way she leaned right into him.

"Yum," Emmaline agreed. "Excellent choice of cookie."

Ethan and Annie had matching aprons. Could they be any cuter together?

His read, *I'm the boss.*

Hers? *Lol. OK.*

Fiona's dad would never—not in a gazillion lifetimes—have worn something that silly. That fun.

"Mom's specialty is burned cookies," Fiona not-so-helpfully and oh-so-cheerfully added.

"She's not wrong," Em said, unfortunately having to agree with her little girl.

Ethan had set out everything ahead of time, like they were on a cooking show with cameras. But this time, the only camera was his cell. He had an air of excitement like he was going to teach them a new skill that he was thrilled about.

"Shall we?" He lifted his arm so Emmaline could get in closer for a selfie.

Right. Yes. This was exactly why they were there in this room together at this moment.

She shook out all of her reservations and, stepping in beside him, she smiled a big cheesy looking-forward-to-chocolate-chip-cookies grin up at the phone lens.

Darn. They didn't really look like a couple in the photo. Not that they didn't work together—she'd done herself up nicely. And he was Ethan-freaking-Greene. He could've had a paper bag on his head, and he'd still be gorgeous.

The way they looked individually wasn't the issue. No, their stance was just…meh. Two acquaintances taking a photo kind of blah.

"Here." Annie pulled off her apron and handed it to Emmaline. "So you match better."

"Kid's got a point." Ethan helped Em get the loop over her head without mucking up her hair.

His fingers trailed along the edge of her neck only because he had to straighten the clasp.

And the goose bumps she got because of his touch were only because she was a human female, and it was required when being touched by Ethan Greene.

Ethan went back to his spot. Emmaline got into position once more.

Ugh. Again, they looked so stilted. So…planned.

"Turn to each other," Fiona suggested. "Like you *like* her."

"I do like her," Ethan said, facing Emmaline. "We're great mates."

He smiled.

She smiled.

The camera was right there, and this was so very forced.

"Put your arm around him," Annie suggested. "So you can really get in there."

Em did as suggested. The first touch was slightly

awkward since they were right up in each other's business like this.

Annie held the camera for him this time, climbing up on a stool for a better angle.

"Maybe kiss him?" Fiona suggested, happily. "That'll convince *everyone*."

"Friends don't kiss," Em said, still face to face with Ethan. Still reminding her body she got to touch but not play.

"Thought you were playing pretend?" Fiona egged them on.

Em frowned at her daughter even as Ethan tightened his grip around her waist. And. She. Liked. It. Her stomach swooped and dipped as butterflies swarmed in her belly.

"You're not 'friends' in this picture," Fiona kept pushing.

She absolutely got that from her dad.

"You're boyfriend-girlfriend. That means you *have* to kiss," Fiona practically begged.

"Have you been hangin' out with Annie too much?" Ethan said, giving Fiona a sly look. "No, your mum and I agreed we won't be kissing in this charade. Messes with the long-term friendship and such."

"Put your heads together then," Annie suggested. "Foreheads touch, not lips."

Now that they could do. They took a few photos facing each other and another looking straight into the lens. The forehead touch was genius—more intimate than a kiss, really. Staring into each other's eyes, laughing because the situation was absurd, and knowing there would be no culmination to anything further. All the chemistry bottled in the tight space between them was sure to come through in the final photos.

Annie finally finished clicking so they could both peek at the results. With the girls' help, they confirmed they were ready.

Ethan sent the images over to his team for his online Emmaline announcement.

"We're gonna go make friendship bracelets," Annie announced, as Ethan got to work and whisked together the wet ingredients.

"Haven't you both made loads of those already?" Ethan asked.

He wasn't wrong. They both had two wrists filled with the beaded Taylor Swift style friendship bracelets.

"Can't have too many." Fiona was already halfway up the stairs.

"Fiona? You don't want to stay?" Emmaline asked, because since when did Fiona not want to help? She *always* wanted to help in the kitchen.

Both girls shook their heads in unison and bounced up the stairs.

"Is that concerning to anyone but me?" Em asked. Something was up with Fiona. She didn't know quite what, but a mom knows when her daughter is up to something—and she had a hunch, it wasn't bracelets.

"Don't question them too much," Ethan said, stirring away. "They're being good sports about the charade. Best not to shuffle those cards."

"Hey, I never asked. What did you tell Annie to get her to agree?" Em asked, leaning against the counter. She forced herself away from Ethan's forearm muscle porn as he whisked. Unfortunately, that adjustment only got her lost in his blue eyes.

Make no mistake, she had nice eyes, too. Those were one of her favorite features, even. But they were brown, and they were pretty standard—*nothing* like Ethan's blue.

"Told her this is a real mess. It's not bloody fair to all those ladies reaching out to me," he said, nodding as he spoke. "That she and Fiona will get to spend heaps more time together for the ruse to work." He paused his whisking. "That's the part that did it, I reckon." A lock of his hair brushed against the side of his ear. Slightly long, but not ridiculous.

More like…yummy long.

Gah. No. Cookies equaled yummy. Ethan equaled off-limits.

"It was the cookies for Fiona," Em said.

Ethan chuckled low in his chest. And that, ladies and gentlemen, was the only sound needed for all the women in Denver to drop their panties.

Except her because: long-term friendship.

Still, this was comfortable, actually. Him and her and a boatload of cookies headed her way.

Em folded her arms on the counter and lifted on her tiptoes to see just how he mixed the wet and dry ingredients together in a big wooden bowl.

"Why don't you use an electric mixer or one of those stand mixers?" she asked. It'd save a ton of time and it'd be way less work for him.

He thought on it for a second, staring fondly at the mixture he created, like it was super special.

How was it she actually had the passing thought that she'd like him to look at her the same way he looked at cookie dough? That was ridiculous.

She was not Ethan's cookie dough, and that was that.

"If there's a task I can do with my hands, I'd rather do it that way," he said, finally. "Appliances have their place, sure, but I like to do things the old-fashioned way. Something about it makes the experience more special, and the result more delicious. Y'know?"

He glanced at her from under his unfairly long eyelashes and the moment heated right up. Her heart kicked into gear because, with that smolder, it didn't feel like he was really talking about mixers in the kitchen.

No. No, it didn't.

"I prefer appliances," she said. "Saves the work. You know?"

His nose scrunched up. "But then there's electricity and batteries and the…risk of fire."

Did he wink? The guy winked at her.

"Oh my God." Emmaline's cheeks blazed. She dropped her face to her hands. "I thought we agreed that didn't happen?"

"What didn't happen?" he asked, the total picture of bullshit innocence.

"Don't even go there, mister." She pointed at him. "I came for photos, cookies, and maybe a life lesson. No reminders of when I've messed up or accidentally lit anything on fire."

"Life lesson, huh? Well…" He thought for only the briefest of seconds before he said, "How's this? I figure life is like an amazing batch of cookies—you can't force it," he said. "You can't rush it, and your only job is to do the mixing, wait, and enjoy the final flavors."

She gave him a golf clap for being able to pull that out on the fly.

"Good save," she said. "So sage."

"Help a bloke out." He handed her two spoons to shape the cookies. Then took two for himself. "Like this." He pressed the dough into a ball between the spoons before dropping it on the stone sheet pan.

She tried it. Made exactly the same motion he did. But hers somehow was square. Physics didn't seem to indicate that was possible.

"Yours is like edible art," Emmaline said, as he continued to mold the dough. "Mine isn't."

He chuckled. "You'll get it with practice."

"I'd rather do it with one of those scoopers. Get it over with quicker."

"Why rush when you can enjoy the full experience?" He continued scooping. "It's about more than the cookie at the end—it's about the journey there. The time spent perfecting technique."

Were they still talking about cookies? 'Cause it didn't feel like they were talking about cookies.

The air stilled, and she held his gaze, considering, the eye contact lasting a bit too long as the snap and sizzle of chemistry between them sparked palpably. A thin, invisible thread tugging them in the same direction like marionettes.

His eyes sparkled. They did not need that small enhancement because they were already stunning without that additional glimmer.

She shook off the moment and, since shaping wasn't happening for her, Em reached into the dough with her spoon. The puppet strings might push them together, but they'd already made the choice to clip the strings and move forward on their own when this was done.

She lifted the spoon to her lips. Gave it a test. "Oh my hell, this is divine."

She dipped the second spoon in and loaded it right up.

"I'd cook for you again just to get that same reaction," he said, way huskier than she'd expected.

They definitely needed to put a damper on that. No husky talk allowed. And no talk about anything that could be construed as remotely sexy.

"Can I ask you something?" she asked.

"Ask away." He radiated the confident charm of a

friendly neighbor. Not the guy with the husky undertone to his words.

She set the spoon down. "Okay."

"Okay," he replied, giving her his full attention.

"Why didn't you just pay someone to do this?" She gestured to herself. "The girlfriend schtick."

"Simple. Because finding someone willing to play along without attachment was harder than one would expect." He paused. "Also, I don't want Annie getting attached to someone she can't have." He pursed his lips, paused with the two spoons still in his hands. "I figure you're just up the street. She and Fiona are best mates. If she gets attached, she won't lose *you*." He gave her a deliciously warm look that rivaled the melted chocolate chips in his cookies. "We probably shoulda talked about that."

Uh-huh. "Yes. You should've mentioned that." She sighed a deep sigh, ready to clip any extra invisible strings. "We can't let this get any deeper than *this*." She gestured to the cookies. "We'll get the pictures. I'll definitely get a cookie. Then Fiona and I will head home."

"Mom," Fiona called, running from the living room, her cheeks flushed. The desperate way she called for Em made her words a splash of ice water. "I dropped my new bracelet in the gutter with all the yuck. I can't reach it." She heaved a huge breath. "Annie's still trying, but her arm's too short."

"Annie put her hand in the gutter?" Ethan stopped making the cookie dough balls. Dropped the spoons on the counter.

"Her whole arm!" Fiona said, nodding. "Hers are longer than mine."

Crud. Crud. Cruddy. Em headed out to the sidewalk, double time.

Chapter Eleven
EMMALINE

THE SUMMER SUN had pelted Denver after the morning's rain, so while it had once been wet, the asphalt was now freaking hot against the soles of Emmaline's shoes. She still hustled with Fiona to where Annie had her arm shoved into the grate, right up to her armpit. Emmaline flinched because that didn't look very comfortable.

"Don't put your hand in there," Emmaline said using her best you-have-to-listen-to-me-because-I'm-a-mom tone, and hoping it would work, as she hurried to the drain.

"Annie," Ethan called from beside Em. "Get it outta there."

"It's my favorite bracelet." Fiona threw her hands up like Emmaline should know this information.

"I made it special for her," Annie added. Thankfully, she'd pulled her hand from the gutter.

"It's getting ruined," Fiona practically wailed.

Emmaline knelt beside the drain like a mom on a mission and stared into the depths of the gutter grate thing where the muddy sprinkler and rainwater went. She'd never given much thought to these things, other than being grateful for their ability to ensure the water that came from the sky had a place to go. Never needed to think past that.

"I should call Grandpa. He'll know how to help me save it." Either Fiona was genuinely distraught, or she was seriously playing this up. A little tingle along Emmaline's spine had her questioning the authenticity of Fiona's distress.

Also, they didn't need her dad. They didn't. She was perfectly capable herself of dealing with this situation.

"Let's not bother Grandpa," Em said. Honestly, the last thing she needed was her parents involved in this fiasco. They'd bring along their opinions and—she, uh, hadn't mentioned the Ethan thing yet. She would, of course. But it hadn't come up and she didn't want to make a fuss.

Ethan pulled at the grate to pry it loose.

"Not working," Annie said, shaking her head.

"Crowbar?" Em asked, reaching for a solution. Any solution.

Ethan frowned. "Maybe? Dunno. You have a crowbar? I don't have one."

Like a badass, Emmaline pulled her cell from her pocket and flicked on the flashlight.

There, lo and behold, in all the yuck, was a floating, beaded friendship bracelet.

"It's right there," Fiona said, desperately, dropping to her hands and knees.

"We're coming for you," she assured the bracelet like it meant everything to her.

"Dad, save it," Annie begged.

Ethan scratched at his head. "Can't ya just make another one?"

Yeah. That. What he said.

"This one is special," Fiona said, softly, with reverence.

Perhaps Em had misread her daughter; it wouldn't be the first time. Because she hadn't seen that look in Fiona's eyes before—the desperation and fear of losing something important.

Fiona hadn't had that look when Em and her ex announced the divorce. Not when she and Fiona had hopped on the plane to Denver. Not as they'd unpacked. Not even as they'd argued about midnight marshmallows, or Fiona's wish to adopt a beagle.

That tone in her daughter's voice? Yeah, Emmaline would go after the bracelet.

She handed the cell over to Ethan, saying, "I'm going in."

Ethan raised his eyebrows and flicked his gaze from the floating bracelet to Emmaline like she'd forgotten how to use her brain.

"Well, it's not like *your* arm's gonna fit," Emmaline pointed out.

"Don't do it, Em," Ethan said, his lips twitching at the sides because they both seemed to know she was absolutely going to do it. "This is a bloody bad idea…"

Emmaline nodded, but that didn't stop her as she rubbed her arms, pushed her shirtsleeves up, and reached her hand through the grate to search for the bracelet.

The bracelet that slipped between her fingers in the hot gutter runoff water.

Water that did not smell good.

Emmaline gagged.

On a scale of boogers to vomit, this was a solid pukefest.

Ethan pressed his arm against his face. "What on earth dropped in the drain to make it smell so horrible?"

Emmaline wrinkled her nose and breathed through her mouth.

"I've got it," she said, finally getting a good grip on the bracelet and holding back any more gagging.

Fiona whooped with delight. And for the first time in a long time, Em actually felt like she'd done something good. Something right. Something to be proud of.

Was it rescuing a ten-cent bracelet? Yes.

Did that matter? No.

She removed her arm from the hot metal grate, making it to the elbow before things got tricky.

Reaching with the other hand, she tugged her arm. Then harder.

The grate was freaking hot, and her hand was freaking stuck.

"Oh, bloody hell," Ethan said.

Her pulse pounded, and she probably should stop holding her breath because being lightheaded wouldn't help. She pulled, yanked, and tried every other maneuver —but she could not get her arm out of the grate.

Oh no, no, no.

"C'mon, Em, you've got it," Ethan said, mimicking the movement that needed to happen.

"I'm stuck." Emmaline glanced frantically at him, hysterical laughter bubbling in her chest.

Fiona's jaw dropped way too dramatically, sorta like Emmaline's stomach. "You're stuck?"

"You're kidding, right?" Ethan asked.

"No." Emmaline tugged harder, but that only wedged her in further. "Any ideas? 'Cause I got nothing." She had exhausted all of her ideas with the pulling extraction method.

They were quite the pair there beside the road, her arm stuck.

What a mess.

Then she couldn't hold it in anymore.

She laughed. Laughed until her sides hurt.

She wasn't even totally sure what she was laughing at. Not really. Just of all the emotions that one popped right out.

"You all right there, Em?" Ethan asked, clearly not at all understanding why she found this whole thing as funny as all that either.

"No." She pinched her lips to stop the stupid laughter. "I'm not."

"Annie, run home and get the butter," Ethan said, jumping in and pulling at Emmaline's arm. But honest as all hell, it was stuck in the damn grate. Still, she kept a death grip on the bracelet. *Don't let it go.*

"Fiona, there's some butter in our fridge, too," Em added. "Go grab it, would you?"

She let out a breath through her mouth and closed her eyes. "This is fine. I'll eventually get used to the smell."

Annie hustled back with the butter and Em tried harder to pull at her arm, but it was well and truly caught.

"Move the torch," Ethan instructed, pointing at the flashlight as he rubbed the butter on Emmaline's arm where the metal held on to it. He did his best not to get it on her shirt, but this was a rag tag job they were both doing.

"I think that's enough," he said, sitting back on his heels.

He looked as though he was wishing he had something to wipe his hands on that wasn't his jeans. But she had nothing to offer.

"Are you ready?" he asked, catching Emmaline's gaze with his own and getting ready to tug.

He watched Emmaline extra carefully, seeming to wait for her signal. She nodded. "Do it."

So he pulled. Then he yanked harder. Harder still. He grunted.

She pinched her lips together.

The arm didn't budge.

"More butter?" she asked.

"Right, the answer in any situation is to add more butter," he confirmed.

He quit yanking, rubbed more of the mixture on the grate, and tried again. How had she wedged her arm inside so thoroughly? She wasn't entirely certain of the physics in this situation. The one thing she was certain of? Whatever they were, the physics of this situation sucked.

Ethan sat back on his heels again, thinking.

"I called Grandpa," Fiona hollered, running to them, with a tub of butter in her hand. "He'll bring his axe."

Emmaline said, "no," at the same time as Ethan.

Fiona raised her hands like she was giving up. "You said call him if it's a big problem. He said he's always close, anyway."

Oh no. Oh hell.

It's not that Em's parents didn't know she was a bit of a screw-up. It's just that she tried to hide it from them whenever she could. But they'd seen her through many episodes and brought them up. Often.

"If it helps, I don't think she meant he'll chop off your arm," Ethan assured.

Emmaline gave him a look like he was the one who had gone nuts. "No, I don't think that's what he would do, either."

There they were, stuck by the gutter with her arm thrust inside…and her dad on his way.

Worst case, her dad would bring up the divorce and how he had told her moving to California was a bad idea to begin with. Best case? He'd have laryngitis and be unable to speak.

"Bloody hell," Ethan said, wiping at his forehead with his arm.

"Should we play cards or something while we wait?" Em asked, attempting to be the picture of innocence.

"Em?" a male voice finally called from a truck, pulling up beside them.

Em glanced up to where James climbed out, eyes wide, with their mom and dad. Oh good, they all showed up.

Dad wasn't in uniform, so that was good. They hadn't called him from a shift. And Mom wasn't dressed up like she'd been at an important lunch or anything, either. Still…

"Hell," Em said under her breath. She let her head fall forward. "Hey Mom, Dad, James." She recovered quickly and waved jauntily with her not-trapped arm. "Got myself into a little pickle here." She followed this with, "Again," under her breath.

"Well, I don't know about anyone else, but I am appreciating the many opportunities to come to your sister's rescue." Ethan did the guy mind-meld thing with James, where they talk only using chin jerks and glowers.

Then James really looked at Em, puzzled.

Yeah, she understood that feeling, too.

"Ethan, you've met my brother, James. This is my dad, Jim, and my mom, Patty." Just to round out the embarrassment. "Everyone, this is Ethan, my…uh…"

Well, they hadn't discussed what they'd tell the parents. Shit.

"He's her boyfriend," Fiona said with a whole heaping of pride. "This is Annie. If they get married, she's going to be my sister!"

Fuck, fuck, fuckity fuck.

Annie waved.

Ethan locked eyes with Em, mirroring her own feeling of being paralyzed with surprise.

This was one of those times she wished she could vanish. Nope, no need to sparkle for herself. Ethan could have all the attention. Every single crumb. Where was some wallpaper to fade into when she actually needed it?

She could call herself a chameleon and blend into the background more skillfully and effectively than she'd ever blended before.

"That's not…" Em said, frantically pulling once more. "He's not…"

"It's a ruse for social media," Ethan announced. "Em's helping me out."

"I don't understand. What do you mean, a ruse? Are you dating?" Mom asked, nudging Dad with her elbow in a look-she's-doing-it-again kind of way.

"Yes," Ethan said at the same time Em said, "No."

"Yes and no," Ethan sort of clarified.

"Huh." James crossed his arms. "Did your new boyfriend call in a favor or something? Hold a little knowledge over your head to get you to agree, maybe?"

"James," Em hissed before Ethan could respond. "Stop. It's not like that at all."

Well, it sort of *was*, but not mostly.

"You're either dating or you're not." Dad kneeled to study the situation. "No idea how you do both at the same time. Doesn't matter, though, because you've got yourself good and stuck."

"Mom's saving my bracelet," Fiona announced. "She's being a hero like you and Uncle James!"

"I hope it's worth something to get your arm caught over." Dad frowned at the situation.

No, of course, it wasn't. It was cheap beads and embroidery thread.

"It's in my hand," Emmaline said, gritting her teeth so hard Ethan could probably feel it in *his* molars. "The bracelet."

Dad kneeled to check out what he'd be dealing with. "Rescuing things is in the blood. Good to see you did get a dash of that Eaton blood, after all."

Was that the pride of a father even when his daughter made a poor choice, or a little dig because Em's life hadn't quite gone as planned?

"Okay. I've got a plan." Dad held Em's gaze tight. "Patty, grab me the WD-40 in the trunk."

Oh, God. Dad used the stuff for everything. Honestly, it wouldn't surprise Em if he used it as a salad dressing sometimes.

Mom nodded and said to Ethan, "We stocked up since Em came back to town. Figured we'd need it."

Em dropped her forehead to her arm while Mom hurried off to find the blue-and-yellow can, and returned. Dad doused Emmaline's arm with the cold, oily solution and that scent brought back with it all the times in her childhood when she'd found herself in a mess.

"Here's what we're going to do," Dad said, keeping eye contact with her the whole time, like his goal was to keep her calm while he attempted to release her arm.

Of note, this did not make Emmaline calm.

"I'm going to pull. You're going to twist like this." Using his arm, he illustrated the maneuver with a confidence she did not have.

But she'd try it so perhaps Ethan wouldn't have to serve all her future meals out here on the sidewalk.

"Ready?" Dad asked.

Emmaline nodded.

Then she twisted as he tugged. The girls cheered, and Dad heaved until his face turned red. Meanwhile, her arm twisted further than she'd known it could.

She may have been in a mess and she may have *been* a mess, but she wouldn't give her dad any future ammunition for zingers at her expense, so she didn't say a word—not even a peep.

"I'm out." Emmaline fell backwards against Ethan.

He caught her and, was it only her, or did he take an extra moment before setting her to rights? Helping her sit on her tush so she wouldn't topple over, his hand lingered a little too long on her hip.

No chance to really consider that since her arm was finally free, Emmaline opened her hand. The poor bracelet hung there all wet, like a limp bag of sand.

"You saved it!" Fiona pushed in beside her.

Em went for easy breezy, but stood wobbly, like she was finding her footing for the first time. She tried to hand Fiona the bracelet, but her daughter wasn't having it. "Yuck."

"Uh…" Em didn't have time to say anything else, because Fiona bounded right over to her grandparents.

"Annie's my new best friend," Fiona said, pulling Dad's arm.

Then she raved to Annie about her grandma's garden and grandpa's firetruck. She went on and on about how Uncle James had a scooter he let her ride sometimes.

Annie nodded like mad, hanging on every word.

And there was that tickle again at the back of Em's neck.

"Bravo, Em. You made the right call going right on in for the bracelet," Ethan assured.

"Really?" she asked because it was super sweet of him to say that.

"Bloody hell, no." He shook his head. "But no need to rub salt in the wound."

She nodded because she agreed, but she still lanced him with her gaze. "Thanks."

"No worries." He flashed a sly smile and…*oh no, no, no.*

Something dormant inside her started to creak open. Something unwelcome that she tried to suppress because she didn't enjoy feeling this type of thing. Not with a man like Ethan.

The precise kind of man she'd sworn off.

But this was the kind of profound feeling a person had no power over. Like falling asleep—it's not something to control because it happened without any effort or consent. The kind of feeling that wiggled and nudged around her heart like a hug.

A hug that would eventually turn into a vice and a painful sort of pressure.

This was the type of thing that shifted the ground beneath her feet so she was stuck in a way that even WD-40 and Dad couldn't help.

She shook off the feeling. This whole thing was only pretend. There were no real feelings allowed with Ethan.

She needed to remember that.

Except…what if he *was* different? Could that even change anything for her? Or them?

Chapter Twelve
ETHAN

"I LIKE Fiona's gramma and grampa," Annie said, so close to the counter she was practically sitting on it.

"They look to be good folks," Ethan agreed. Though a bit hard on Em.

"Did you know that Fiona has cousins? A whole bunch of them," Annie continued. "She said maybe I'll get to meet them, too!"

Ethan pulled a finished tray of cookies from the oven. "Careful, love. Hot."

"Gramma and Grandpa say they can stay for cookies!" Fiona announced, skipping her way to the counter. "Uncle James didn't want to."

Well, Uncle James was a bit of a right ass, wasn't he?

After the bracelet debacle Ethan and Em were both ready to call it an afternoon—go their separate ways. But the girls invited Em's parents to his house to show off the rest of the bracelets. The grandparents didn't have much of a choice, honestly. Not with Fiona and Annie tag teaming them.

"Wonderful," Ethan said. "These are all ready. I've got another tray coming along."

The girls bounced to the living room to spread the news.

Ethan heaved a breath and went back to his work.

"So you're the man who doesn't know if he's dating my daughter?" Jim asked, hands on his hips at the kitchen entrance.

Silly question, if you asked Ethan, they'd already covered that bit out front.

"Em's helping me out with a problem," Ethan said. "Seems I have a need for a pretend girlfriend, and Em's willing to give me a hand."

"Well, I guess it always starts out pretend, doesn't it?" Jim laughed.

Ethan did not.

"Leave it to our Em to find one of the only famous bachelors in Denver," Jim said, shaking his head as he strode to where Ethan worked.

Jim was a big bloke—tall and clearly active.

"What do you mean by that?" Ethan asked. "Em doesn't care at all about my time on the telly."

"Em has a *history*," Jim said, pulling his lips to the side.

"It's different this time because it's not real," Em said from the little hallway between the living room and kitchen. "It's a friend favor. That's all."

She'd washed up and changed her clothes.

Jim alternated his gaze between Em and Ethan. Then he snorted. "Uh-huh. That's the line you're goin' with?"

"Jim." Em's mum followed Em into the kitchen. "If she says it's pretend, then who are we to question it?" Patty said the correct words, but she said them as if she didn't really believe them either.

Jim let out a disgruntled grunt.

"Have a cookie, mate." Ethan gave the tray a nod. Raising their blood sugar couldn't hurt, could it? "They're Annie's fave."

Jim picked up a cookie, and took a chomp.

Ethan waited to hear the verdict.

Jim snagged another one.

Not that Ethan had any doubts the treats would be delicious, but it always helped to have a bit of confirmation.

"Jim!" Patty chided.

"They're tasty," Jim said with a mouth full of cookie. "I like this one, Em." He jerked his thumb toward Ethan.

Was that a vote of confidence?

"Dad. Don't get attached because he's not permanent," Em assured, coming in once more as the voice of reason.

"Mom, can you show Annie how you draw a duck?" Fiona blasted toward her mum. "I told her you know how."

"I don't have any paper." Emmaline raised her hands like, *whatcha gonna do?*

"I have paper." Ethan pulled a notepad from the drawer beside his sink. The one he kept handy to track ingredients and such.

"My duck is probably more scribbles than she'd like." Emmaline sounded remarkably uncertain. Still, she grabbed the notepad and the pencil.

A smile tickled her lips as she drew what he supposed would be the feet.

"Most artists start with the bill or the body," she said as she finished one of the webbed feet. "But I like to start at the bottom and work my way up. No one thinks the feet are the most important part, but I beg to differ. I think they're the forgotten foundation of good animal art." She continued with the lines and loops.

Her slight smile was heaven.

Ethan caught himself gawking and quickly got back to work on the cookies, yanking another tray from the oven.

Annie and Fiona remained bewitched as Em moved to the tail feathers, then up the back to the head and the beak. She chucked in a couple of goofy eyes and a few strokes of shading.

"You try?" She held up the pencil to Annie.

Annie's mouth parted in awe. "Can you draw him a chicken friend?"

"Make him magical," Fiona suggested, doing a little jig on her feet.

Emmaline didn't seem certain, but he'd put his money on her crackin' this one. Her skills with the pen and paper were bloody brilliant.

He tried to keep focused on the cookies, but Em's drawing had him completely captivated.

She sketched the chicken on a pedestal, so he'd have room for his magical wand and hat. She'd even chucked in a bunny to pull from the hat. While she was at it, she'd added a little bear cub next to the ducky audience.

She didn't take extra time for anything too fancy, but she added some shading here and there for effect.

Everyone else might have been in a whole different world because Ethan didn't hear a peep while she worked, but had that vague sense that the world continued as he got lost in her imagination with her.

At last, apparently happy with the drawing, she showed it to Annie and Fiona. "Like this?"

A chunk of bangs tumbled to her forehead as she leaned forward over the paper.

His hand itched to fix it.

But she lifted her hand to her hair and brushed it aside.

Annie stared at her like she'd personally invented unicorns.

Fiona beamed. "Told ya she's good."

"That's not good." Patty leaned in.

Em started to cover the image.

Ethan was gearin' up to throw hands.

"It's not good," Patty repeated, staring straight at Em. "It's brilliant."

"Ducking brilliant," Fiona declared.

Em cleared her throat. "Fiona—"

"I didn't use a bad word." Fiona jumped right into defense mode. "I said it because it's a duck. Duck. Duck. Duck."

Em cleared her throat again. "Let's try a different word. Hmm?"

"But it's a ducking duck." Fiona tossed her hands up like no one in the world understood her.

"Can you draw a ducking duck?" Annie asked. "Maybe the magician chicken accidentally pulls a book out of the hat instead of the bunny and he throws it and the duck has to duck?"

Well, this was turning into a real party, wasn't it?

"Maybe he could throw it at the bear?" Jim suggested, gettin' right in on the action.

"Then it would be a ducking bear and that's even better!" Fiona declared.

"What about a ducking skunk!" Annie squealed. "All the animals are ducking."

"I reckon I might be keen to see something like that," Ethan said, deadpan. "For science."

Emmaline practically sliced him with her gaze, but he didn't mind. There was a glint of something behind her eyes. Something significant he wasn't in on.

"I've never seen a skunk ducking with a bear, and I've seen some pretty interesting art," Patty chimed in.

"I bet you could make an entire book about animals ducking from the magic chicken!" That gem came from Fiona. "He could throw all kinds of things that make them duck."

Emmaline straight up choked on air.

"How about I draw a skunk with an ice cream cone?" Emmaline offered, turning over the paper to the next page and starting in on skunk feet.

"I'm so glad we came for cookies," Patty said, all dreamy like.

That made Ethan's chest feel a bit odd.

In a good way, though.

Like he was witnessing something bloody important.

"After the feet you start around the belly," Em spoke as she worked, a dab hand at this type of thing.

"Then up around the tail." She glanced up at Ethan from under her eyelashes, like she dared him to make a comment about tails.

He didn't because he was a proper gent and there were parents and ankle-biters around.

"And voila," Em said, finishing the drawing with a flourish.

She was a natural at this. But he understood that making something look so easy took a heap of practice.

"This is a really good time," Ethan said, giving the counter a quick wipe since the cookies were finished. "You're great at that."

"She wanted to be famous with it," Dad said. "But that didn't work, so she took the next best thing."

Em had the look that she'd be arguing with him about it, so he asked quick as a bird—

"What do ya mean?" Ethan asked this as he broke open a cookie for himself and chucked it in his mouth.

"Her ex-husband is Antony Eaton. He's a *celebrity* attorney." Patty just tossed it on out there.

Em stilled and the air around her seemed denser.

"Em's Tony knows everybody," Patty said, eyes wide.

"He's not my Tony, Mom," Em corrected. "And he *doesn't* know everyone."

"Tony Eaton, huh?" Ethan asked. "I've met him." In passing and briefly, but his name was well known in the industry.

Em's face went completely blank. Shit. He didn't mean that he was tight with the bloke or anything like that.

"Before Tony she dated a couple of other famous guys," Patty continued. "Who was the one guy with the blue hair? Do you remember him?"

"Mom." Em shook her head. The air still dense around her. Her body rigid.

"I even met that guy from the pirate movies—the one with extra-long hair—at her old apartment," Patty continued. "He stood right next to me in the elevator."

This was all new news. Em looked as uneasy as Ethan felt. He found himself straight up scowling.

"Here I was, thinkin' Em wasn't into that sort of thing," Ethan mused.

"Because Em is not," Emmaline assured and the daggers she shot at her parents were extra sharp. "I've lived that life. I didn't enjoy it. I've had the handsome guy with the big-deal job and all the famous friends. And I was wallpaper in that situation. So, yeah, I want to meet someone with a normal job, who doesn't automatically demand all of the attention because he's a big deal. Someone who doesn't make me feel like…never mind."

He wanted to hear the rest of what she was going to say.

"You know what? Dad and I should head out," Patty said. "You two continue doing whatever it is you're pretending to do. Thank you for the delicious cookies, Ethan, and the fun time."

Jim grunted something that sounded like an agreement. Then he snagged two more cookies in his big paw of a hand and headed out with his missus. The girls followed right on their heels, glancing back to Em and Ethan repeatedly.

"Do the girls seem off to ya?" Ethan asked.

"I don't know. Change is hard on everyone," Em said, still not quite herself. "And…um…moving is hard. Finding normal is hard."

"That's the bloody truth," he agreed.

"I'm sure they're just feeling that. I mean everything's fine, and then it's not."

That was the honest truth.

Chapter Thirteen
EMMALINE

BESIDES EM'S distaste for her job, the imitation relationship she was actively avoiding, and the new puppy that kept chewing her shoes (Fiona's negotiation tactics complimented Em's perpetual motherly guilt perfectly), her life was actually great. Her parents may not understand her, but they were still fine parents. They spent loads of time with Fiona—including her with all the cousins. They included Annie, too.

They even bought the girls old-school walkie-talkies so they could still talk from their respective houses. Annie didn't earn her cell back yet, and Fiona didn't have one.

For everyone else, Em's parents were fabulous. They simply didn't understand Em or the life choices that had led her away from Denver.

And, really, she didn't know how to explain herself.

So she did what she did best—moved forward. She eventually got through a boatload of unpacking, organizing, and rearranging her furniture. Enough that the place finally felt like home. Even her new gnomes watched over the garden with a place of backyard honor.

Also, she adored that Fiona and Annie spent loads of time at her house. Loved how they made everything loud and fun. The girls chose Em's backyard most because it came with a treehouse, a play structure with swings, and a slide, and this tube thing that led to a secret spot behind the bushes that could only be accessed from above or from the tube.

Em had always wanted a loud, busy house like the one she'd grown up in. At their old house in California, running was absolutely not allowed. Her ex-husband—Tony's—art collection was too precious to risk even a tiny dose of fun.

"Gramma and Grandpa will agree," Fiona said, tromping up the stairs with Annie.

"It's almost too late," Annie countered. "They're gonna break up."

"Gramma will help. I'll ask," Fiona assured. "Double promise."

Em stilled, made her breaths shallow so she could hear better. But the girls slipped into Fiona's room and spoke in whispers.

She could put her ear against the wall, that wouldn't be weird.

Gah, yes, it would be totally weird.

She was still gonna do it.

"I don't want my mom to date someone else," Fiona said, a little seepage of concern in her voice. "Your dad's nice. I like him."

Emmaline's breath caught. She pressed her ear more against the wall.

"Dad needs this." This was Annie.

Why were Em's palms sweaty against the paint of the wall?

Oh, right, because she was listening to things that weren't meant for her to hear.

Things she should really bring up with Ethan. Because even if they were upfront with the kids about what this really was between them, the girls clearly didn't believe it.

She scooted Sketch, the new beagle puppy, off the mattress in her room and started to remake the bedding. He jumped right back up, practically daring her to try that again.

"Sketch," she said pointing to the floor. "Down."

This was a work in progress, and he didn't know this command yet. Or any.

"Down," she said again, pointing to the floor.

Nothing.

She sat cross-legged on the carpet. "See? It's fun down here."

A slight shift in the corner of her vision had her turning that way. Annie waited in the hallway outside with her hand on the bathroom handle.

Annie watched Em with a reverent gaze. Not obnoxious like, and not with a lot of frustration or concern. There was a quizzical look in her eye that made Emmaline want to scoop her into her arms and give her a hug.

She wouldn't because Annie was a preteen and Em was fairly confident anything like that would embarrass her.

"Hi," she said instead. "You okay?"

Annie nodded, her expression softening. "I'm okay."

Em got up and moved toward Annie. "You sure?"

"Mom?" Fiona asked, then she stopped Em before she could step into the hallway. She rolled her eyes, exasperated. "Can you go somewhere else? We're talking. C'mon, Annie."

Fiona gestured back to her bedroom.

Annie scooted right inside.

Em didn't move because she didn't exactly know what to do when her ten-year-old caught the attitude virus.

So she followed them to the door of Fiona's room to find out what was so important they were kicking her out.

"This is *private*." Fiona made enormous eyes at Emmaline in an impressive imitation of how her grandma looked when she asked Fiona for a minute so she could chat with Emmaline. "It's important."

Oh. Well, in that case Em needed to know even more what was going on in their world.

Fiona closed the door. Right in Em's face.

She did not.

Emmaline opened her mouth. Closed it. Opened. Closed.

The doorbell chimed, saving Fiona from any further motherly embarrassment via her presence alone, and immediate consequences. Which was good, since Em had no idea what the punishment for this kind of thing would even be.

She checked the doorbell video-app on her phone and her breath whooshed right out of her lungs.

Ethan was waiting outside for her. Or Annie.

Definitely Annie. He was only waiting for his kid.

Em pulled open the door wide so he could come inside. She shoved a hair behind her ear. "Hey."

"Em." He said her name and then seemed to be waiting for her to say more.

So here's the thing. All the stuff that happened at his house with her parents? The whole bit about Tony—and him knowing Tony? It'd wiggled under her skin and she needed a minute to work through it.

One moment turned into another and a minute had morphed into days and then…well…the picture pretty much painted itself, didn't it? But he hadn't reached out to her, either.

Maybe that's how a fake breakup for a fake relationship went. This was all new to her, so she wouldn't have known.

"Do you want to come in?" Em asked. "The girls are upstairs in Fiona's room. I can get them."

"Why do I feel you're avoiding me?" Ethan asked following her inside and cutting right to the point, not even answering her sort-of question.

His question was an easy one to answer.

"Because I am," Emmaline said, going with the truth because at this point in the day, it was just that much easier.

"You are?" He seemed surprised at her quick acknowledgment.

"You weren't supposed to notice, though." She lifted one eyebrow. "I was blending."

"Em." He said her name in such a way that it totally made her pause.

She glanced up. She sorta wished she hadn't because he held her still with a molten stare she felt all the way to her toes.

"I…" He didn't stalk her way, but the look he gave made her feel like he had. Like he moved forward to blow right through her personal space bubble. "Noticed."

Oh. Dear.

Her body seemed to purr in complete opposition to her dedication to avoidance.

So she wasn't as good at avoiding and blending and becoming one with the shadows as she'd hoped. *Good to know.*

"You don't have to." He pushed his hands in his pockets in that adorable way that made her consider opening herself up for real.

"You don't have to avoid me," he clarified.

Which was why, "I've been taking some space after everything that happened with my parents," she admitted. "They really got in my head."

There, now he knew. Could she puh-lease go back to blending now?

That announcement had his eyebrows raising and his head ticking a little to the right in question.

"About all that…with your parents. That whole bit got in my head, too," he said as though it was no big deal.

To be clear, admitting *that* had taken a lot from her. But the way he said it?

It cost him nothing.

"I brought you a little something," Ethan said, holding out a white paper sack.

"You brought me cookies." Cookies she had no problem accepting.

"You didn't get any last time, if I recall." Ethan's eyes sparkled with wit and…this was super-duper sweet.

Her chest heaved with humor and the weight of that sweet.

I don't want my mom to date someone else…

"Thanks." She picked at the edge of the bag with the serrated edge. "Really, thanks."

He leaned closer, not super close, but just enough for her to notice the scent of expensive tea leaves and mornings at the beach. "You're welcome."

She held out a cookie for him.

He took it from her and slid it right on his tongue in a move that made her squirm.

In a good, non-blending way.

"Do you want something to drink?" she asked. "Water? Soda? Beer?"

He nodded. "Water."

Phew, because she didn't actually have the others, but it seemed like she probably should've had something more than water and boxed wine.

She poured him a glass, sliding it across the countertop like a bartending pro, which she wasn't.

He took this invitation and moved to one barstool—counter-height chunky squares she'd found at a yard sale right after they moved in. She'd refinished them to just the right shade of gray, and loved the way they worked to help distinguish the space between the living room and kitchen.

Things got quiet then. Neither of them speaking.

Not a comfortable silence either. This was one of those silences that reached right under the skin and itched.

"Even though this isn't real, I liked that—" he said at the same time she spoke, "I left my world behind—"

They both stopped speaking and the scratchy silence descended again.

"You go first," she said, going for breezy.

Easy peasy breezy.

He nodded. "Even though this isn't real, I liked that you didn't see my celebrity as all that I am," he said. "That's why I asked you to help instead of paying someone."

"Sometimes I do forget who you are," she said, crossing her arms and squeezing. The trend of forgetting he was Ethan-freaking-Greene could easily become a habit and then it'd be dangerous. Very dangerous.

"No." He tucked a chunk of hair behind her ear.

Her throat got thick, the air heavier in the room.

The touch wasn't an invasion—there was still a whole lot of space between them, and it was platonic. But the move was more than comfortable. Like his hand was supposed to brush against her skin, and she was supposed to get goose bumps.

He seemed to realize what he'd done and pulled his hand back.

"You see me," he continued. "Not just Ethan Greene the chef, but Ethan the dad and Ethan the neighbor and Ethan the guy. Y'know?"

Okay, now it was her turn.

"Even though this isn't real," she said. "I still left my world behind because it was awful. And I know you used to run in those circles. Like I did get that. But I didn't really understand it until I found out you know Tony and—"

"Brief meeting," he said. "Nothing heavy."

"Since this isn't real, I should not feel so relieved at that," she said.

He crossed his arms, too. His forearms flexing with the movement.

She'd noted the ink there before, of course. One didn't have tattoos like Ethan's and have them go unnoticed. But now, really looking at them, they were made of an intricate design of leaves, flowers, and words—all coming together in a canvas of truly inspired artwork.

"Hey, listen," she said. "I heard Annie and Fiona chatting and…I think they don't understand what this is between us."

He pursed his lips. "Go on…"

So she told him what she'd heard and then finished with, "It's probably best we get on with the ruse so we can get broken up."

His mouth pulled down briefly before he recovered. "How about dinner at my restaurant on Friday? We'll get pictures. Post them. Then you can officially knock me back, and we can all move on." With that he grinned, but it was definitely forced. "Hopefully, enough time has passed I won't be inundated with new prospects again… Assuming I can keep Annie off my socials."

He lifted his water glass to his lips, his Adam's apple bobbing as he swallowed.

She couldn't seem to pull her gaze away from the column of his throat. A few steps and she could be right there sharing his air, moving to him. Getting rid of all the pesky space between them and let her mouth brush his. Ethan and ice, and she wouldn't care less that he would upstage her at every turn.

What mattered would be the way this Ethan in her mind took over the kiss, parting her lips with only a slight movement of his mouth. He'd have no issue sweeping his tongue against hers.

Oh yes. That would be a wonderful kiss. Maybe the best kiss she'd had.

"You've got a whirly bird swirling in your head," Real Ethan said. Which was the truth because Ethan in her mind had a wandering hand going to her waist, bunching the fabric there and sliding lower…

Reaching for a cookie, she took a bite so she could focus on something other than Pretend Ethan and his wandering hands.

Of note, the cookie was delish.

Chapter Fourteen
EMMALINE

"C'MON," Emmaline said, the words under her breath as a prayer, and a wish, and all the hopes as she searched through the bin of clean laundry she'd pulled out of the dryer.

This was a *situation*.

Not a horrible situation, but she did sort of prefer to wear full-coverage panties to fancy restaurants with her fake celebrity-chef boyfriend before their real breakup.

She'd gotten caught up with an extra batch of business cards for agents in the greater Cincinnati area, and Sketch discovered a love of pulling—and eating—the clothes from her laundry basket.

She loved him. She did. He would someday be a wonderful addition.

But—unfortunately—today, thanks to Sketch, the only underwear she had left was her you-haven't-done-laundry-enough thong. The pair she kept as an emergency fallback in the dredges of her underwear drawer.

"Yoo hoo," Barbie said as the doorbell announced the front door breach.

Well, it didn't say the word *breach*, but it gave the gong sound that announced it'd been opened.

She'd agreed to hang out with Sketch at her house, until Em was finished with the not-a-date date.

"Hey, Barbie," Emmaline shouted back. "I'm in the laundry room."

Barbie sauntered through the kitchen to the laundry room, blowing on her fingernails. "Have you tried these sticker things?" Barbie held up her fingers. "They're paint in a *sticker* you just press right on the nail bed. Can you even believe it?"

"I tried those once." Emmaline hadn't been super successful, and they'd all peeled off within an hour. "They didn't work for me."

"I keep blowing on them, but they're already dry. Strangest thing." Barbie tapped each of the front of her fingernails against her bottom lip, tongue, and teeth, all while making a unique facial expression that Emmaline couldn't quite describe. If she were to try, it would be the look of someone tasting fingernail polish and not enjoying it, but then going back for more.

"I'm going to give you a manicure if I can figure out how to make them stay put. I give the best manicure. I don't even need a license because I'm that good." Barbie pressed her hands on the hips of her leopard print pants. She'd cinched them tight with a belt and paired them with a bright yellow bodysuit top.

The kind of outfit Em would never have the courage to wear. Yet, Barbie pulled it off in spades.

"Ethan's going to be here any second." Emmaline gave up on her hunt for not-a-thong undies and checked her purse to ensure she had extra cash and a credit card just in case.

Lip gloss. Check.

Mascara. Check.

"Oh, I hope you get some bedroom attention tonight." Barbie did a little shimmy shake. "In that dress, he'd be stupid not to."

Em had gone with an easy-breezy sundress with a white bodice that she would never wear around Fiona because things. Would. Get. Spilled. The dress flowed beautifully into a pastel yellow skirt that cascaded to just below the knee.

Lauren had helped her pick some white strappy sandals to complete the look.

Em had even used the spray tan in a can stuff Cress recommended, so her legs wouldn't blind any random strangers. Or Ethan.

"It's not like that at all." Though Em was sort of missing the idea of intimacy like that. She didn't think she would…and yet.

"You, my friend, need to get laid." Barbie stopped poking at her fingernail stickers with her tongue and reached into her cleavage to pull out a folded paper.

"After Ethan and I break up, it'll be first thing on the agenda. Trust me," Em agreed.

Also, maybe not the first thing…but it was something she'd thought about lately. Now that she'd gotten settled.

Barbie spread out the paper. Ah. The mock-ups of logos Emmaline had e-mailed over earlier in the day. "Since he's not here, yet, and you're not on Nocturnal Cupid so we can't pick you a new guy, we've got time to talk about this." Barbie pointed to the center of the page.

There were five gorgeous, streamlined logos all in a column.

"But he's coming any minute." And Emmaline needed all those moments to convince herself not to run upstairs and hide under her bed so she could become one with the carpet, and stay home with Sketch.

If she was quick enough to get there before Ethan showed up, she'd have the entire night to herself—since Fiona and Annie were with her parents for the night at a sleepover with some of the cousins.

She and Ethan had, one more time, explained to the girls about the "date" and that it would be the end of the ruse. The girls shared a look that Em couldn't quite decipher.

"Other than all those sketches of Ethan you're hiding in the drawer beside your desk, he's not here now, is he?" Barbie glanced around. "Nope." She answered her own question. "So. Logo." She pointed to the page holding five illustrated kitty cat infused logos.

Emmaline hadn't drawn them by hand. She'd used a vector-based computer program, so they'd look more realistic than her…scribbles.

More realistic. More professional. *Blah. Blah. Ugh.*

They were precisely the thing National Insurance drilled into her head in the many, many—oh, so many— branding meetings.

"Right track or no?" Emmaline asked, glancing at the logos.

They were precisely in line with what was the rage these days for big corporations and other not-for-profits. Clean lines and only a hint of color. They'd look great against an ivory business card or embroidered on a sweatshirt.

Barbie extracted another paper from her other bra cup. This one was blank.

Emmaline said nothing because she had a hunch Barbie would fill in the details lickity split.

Barbie extracted a pen from straight in the middle of her cleavage. One of the fine tipped Sharpies.

"I want you to draw me a cat," Barbie said this with a nod of sly acknowledgment that she knew Em would fight it. "With a pen."

"You want me to *hand draw* your logo?" Emmaline asked. Why did the thought of that make her heart speed up and her underarms sweat?

She held her elbows out a little just in case she really got to perspiring. That way, she wouldn't totally wreck her dress and then have to go change into something else that might not match white strappy sandals.

"I know your talent." Barbie handed over the marker pen. Emmaline took it, boob sweat notwithstanding.

"And I know that if you can make Ethan a cartoon, you can make a kitty a cartoon." This she said with utmost assurance.

"Okay, so if I were to hand draw you a kitten, I'd probably actually do several in a row, connected by one long thread of a horizontal line that loops together." Emmaline started at the feet, then moved her way up. The first cat was wandering to the left, the second sat regally, and the third was licking his little tootsies. He came out a little wonky, but Emmaline kinda dug him. She continued with a few hashes of shading.

The doorbell rang.

"Ethan's here." Emmaline stopped sketching, but before she could even look up Barbie was at the door opening it. "I'll finish this late—"

Emmaline lifted the marker, so she didn't smudge the drawing. Not that it was truly a concern because this was not the kind of logo Barbie would actually want. Way too whimsical and…how would Tony have said it? Like something a kindergartener would draw.

She shook away the thought. *No. Tony isn't here.*

And she got to go eat yummy food and end a faux relationship she didn't want to be in anyway. Everything really was coming up Em.

"Don't you look like a handsome guy." Barbie said this like Ethan was five and he was ready for the spring pageant at school.

"Thanks," he replied.

For the record, he looked like a *very* handsome guy.

He sort of exuded the confidence of the man Em had always envisioned in Carly Simon's "You're So Vain" song. Though he didn't have an apricot-colored scarf, and there wasn't a yacht anywhere close to downtown Denver.

At her invitation, Ethan strode through the door looking quite delicious.

Em did the introductions.

"Hey," he said, all low and rumbly and yummy.

"Hi." She capped the pen. "I'm ready when you are."

"No." Barbie sauntered between them. "She's not ready. She's been holding out on me." With that announcement, she pointed to Emmaline.

"I'm ready," Emmaline repeated as she set the pen next to the drawing, before she moved around the counter. But Ethan had already come inside, and he eyed her kitties.

"You did this?" he asked, turning it with one finger in his direction.

"She did do this, because she's amazing," Barbie said.

"Well done." Ethan's gaze caught Em's.

She blushed. "I had to." Emmaline grabbed her purse, holding it against her palms. "Barbie didn't give me a choice."

"This is excellent." He lifted his gaze from the paper to hers and her cheeks immediately burned. But not in a bad, scorching way. In a way like sometimes happened when she'd get an art teacher who liked her work.

Not everyone said she scribbled.

"That fancy California art school paid off." Barbie tapped at the drawing with her fingernail. "Even though art school led to the douche canoe of her ex, I think she learned a few things."

"Right, well, some might say I make illegible illustrations." Em cleared her throat and ticked her head toward the door.

"And those 'some' are now lonely in California without you. Aren't they?" Barbie countered.

Honestly, Em's parents weren't super supportive either, and her siblings, and a few teachers here and there who were jerks to everyone.

But it was enough people all at once that she switched gears and married a man everyone said was brilliant instead of aiming for that herself—even James and her parents thought Tony was the bee's knees.

And, of course, Tony thought so, too. He had no issue telling everyone how good he was.

At everything.

"Yeah-nah, this is *really* good, Em," Ethan said again to apparently punctuate his point.

Warmth and fuzzy goodness bloomed in her chest at the compliment, but she tamped it down.

"It's three cats in a row." Emmaline started to the door, hoping they might follow.

"She can't take a compliment," Barbie said. "She doesn't have a lot of flaws, but the girl can't take a compliment."

"That's a shame," Ethan agreed. "Maybe we should practice with her?"

"Yes. Let's do it." Barbie settled her hands on her hips. "Love your hair, Em."

"I grew it myself." Em tried to be silly, but it landed funny.

"Wow, bloody awful acceptance." Ethan let out a low whistle.

"Let's try again?" Barbie asked. Then she started straight at Em as she said, "This time start with thanks before you say anything else."

"Righto, I believe in you, Em." Ethan grinned huge.

"The drawing is spectacular, wouldn't you agree, Ethan Greene?" Barbie asked turning to him.

"I would," he said. "It's fab."

They both stared at Em expectantly. Waiting for her to say something.

"Thanks." Em said and then she glanced back at the image. "I mean it's not awful, but I could probably do better with her markers and a scrap of paper that hadn't snuggled Barbie's boob."

"She's got work to do, for sure," Ethan said to Barbie.

"Uh-huh." Barbie nodded.

"Don't we have reservations?" Emmaline asked.

Ethan handed the image to Barbie's waiting hand. "Pretty sure they'll hold our table."

"Hah," Emmaline said, and the lightness in her chest was really nice. Comfortable.

"This is what I want." Barbie held up the paper. "How much?"

Wait, Barbie wanted it? *This* is what she wanted?

A little crack broke through the creativity cocoon wall Emmaline had formed around herself. That tiny fissure felt like taking her bra off after a long day. That good.

"You can have it after I clean it up a little." Emmaline

held up her one-second fingertip. "No arguing with me about that. It's my artwork, I get to fuss with it."

"Just a little?" Barbie confirmed. "Not too much?"

"Not too much," Emmaline agreed, but she'd already had an idea for the wonky cat on the side to make him less wonky.

"Because it's really good," Barbie said, and she did the wide-eye thing again.

"Thanks," Em said. She didn't add anything else.

Ethan stood there taking the whole thing in with a funny look of pride sketched on his face while he stared at her. That look of pride? It made her feel like she popped right out of the wallpaper.

"Well done, Em. Well done," he said.

Another good feeling. An 'I-matter-too' feeling.

The kind she wished she could bottle and hold on to forever.

But, no, this feeling had to be as fake as the date itself.

"Don't you bring her back early!" Barbie called as they left. "Keep her out late. Heck, keep her out all night; I'm going to sleep here anyway!"

"Sorry about my best friend," Em muttered.

"I like her," Ethan said cheerfully.

Em rolled her eyes. Everyone loved Barbie.

ETHAN NEEDED the ruse to last a touch longer.

Nosh actually loved the schtick with him having a girl-friend. And in a few weeks the president of Nosh was gettin' married up in the mountains only an hour out from Denver. He wanted Ethan to attend…with Em.

This was his problem as the maître d' met them at the door, greeted Ethan with a quick rundown of restaurant business—as he did whenever Ethan stopped in during operating hours—and then wasted no time snapping a few photos to send to the social media team. The staff would take more pictures and send them along all throughout the evening.

The hairs on his neck tingled and raised with the stares coming at them from the dining room. There were cameras on them already; he could feel it without even glancing that way.

Ethan reached for Emmaline's hand as they moved along the edges of the restaurant to be seated. This was part of the deal, discussed and agreed upon. But it didn't feel forced the way Em's hand molded to his. It just felt normal. Natural.

She linked their fingers together. Then she glanced at him from under her eyelashes and the subtle smile radiated all through his bones. The urge to kiss her came out of the blue, and he was keen on the feeling of wanting and not having. Something about it made the chemistry between them crackle.

The little sizzle at their touch wasn't half bad either.

Bit funny, though, that would happen now. For some reason, the timing made the back of his neck itch.

"Your restaurant is fantastic," Em whispered to him, but all he could focus on was the curve of her upper lip and how her mouth moved as she spoke.

His restaurants received praise regularly from some of the best in the industry. Yet, when Em gave her stamp of approval? Well, his chest puffed up and he got weirdly warm inside. "Thank you."

He liked that she liked his space. Wished he could take credit for it. But here's the thing, Ethan was a chef—exceptional with all things cuisine. He was not good with décor. Didn't particularly want to be, either.

So he'd hired that part out in the restaurants he'd opened. He was fussy when he chose the interior decorator, but once they came on board, he gave total control over the dining space. One might expect they'd go with contemporary chic.

They didn't.

They'd picked blue velvet and twinkle lights, white accents with cream undertones, along with chairs they'd called Queen Anne inspired. He did not know what that meant, but they were comfy and looked good. He figured nothing else really mattered when it came down to it.

For tonight's charade, Ethan reserved the table in the

center of the main dining room. If this was a real date, he would've taken Em to the private tasting table in the back. But this was not that. This was the time to be seen. To get social media traction since she was the one to #DateMy-CelebrityDad.

He released her grip so they could sit. She lifted an eyebrow as she took a leather-bound menu.

Why did this feel so different tonight? There was no reason for it to be different.

They neared the end of their sticky situation so no one would #DateMyCelebrityDad publicly, ever again. But he needed to ask her to hang in there a little longer.

A dose of courage and then he'd ask.

So, why did havin' her in his restaurant feel like more than a ruse? Why did the spark between them crackle like it was charged with electricity?

"I can give suggestions if you'd like?" He scanned the menu out of habit. "But since I created the menu, you won't go wrong with any of it."

Her cheeks went rosy at that. Pinked in a way that made the twinkle lights seem to be only shining for the two of them. She snapped her menu closed with an efficiency he expected from his sous chefs.

"I've already decided." She folded her hands under her chin and smiled his way.

So he'd been correct, after all.

A gut feeling Emmaline would prefer to pick her own meal bothered him the entire time he tried drafting a special spread. Finally, he chucked in the towel so she could choose for herself.

Didn't seem that in her previous life she'd had much of a choice in things.

Right away, he decided he detested her bloke of an ex. Anthony Eaton had already dated two new starlets since

Emmaline moved to Denver. Everything about him screamed extravagance. No wonder she was searching for more normal in her life after being married to that wanker.

Do it, Ethan. Do it. "Em, there's something—"

A woman at the table next to them gasped and said louder than bloody necessary, "That's *the* Ethan Greene."

He glanced up at the mention of his name, gave a head nod in acknowledgement to her, and then immediately regretted it because she seemed to take that nod as an invitation to come over for a yarn.

Ah well, maybe he could get her to post a selfie with them on her socials. Jack called that social media proof. He liked it when Ethan did stuff like that.

"Hello," the woman said, moving between tables to get to them.

"Hello," he replied, hoping though he was annoyed, his tone held enough warmth to relay his gratitude for visiting his establishment.

"You're Ethan Greene," she said, as though he didn't know who he was. He got a right kick when people told him who he was.

"I am." There wasn't a lot he was always certain of, but this was one thing he held confidence about. "And this is my girlfriend, Em."

"We had the bisque," the guest gushed, not even giving Em the slightest bit of attention. "Absolutely delicious. Though, the breadsticks were a little too crunchy for my liking. The crunch"—she pulled an ick face—"is a bold choice if you ask me. It didn't quite work out as you'd hoped."

"I'm so glad you enjoyed the bisque," he said. Words he'd said billions of times over his career. "I think Em would enjoy the bisque as well."

Em nodded with a wry smile. "I'm certain I would."

"I'll relay your message about the bread." He'd relay that message to Pepper the cat, because those breadsticks were meant to be crunchy, and the kitchen staff didn't need to worry about it.

This was not a chain restaurant where one could get fluffy breadsticks and a bowl of reheated soup for five dollars. Not that he was judgy, just his breadsticks were perfect as is.

"I didn't catch your name," he said, holding out his hand.

"Mary," she responded. "This is my husband, Walter." She waved to Walter to come say hi, but Walter was hiding behind his hand.

With that, Mary was off to the races once more with her in-depth critiques. Critique of the candlestick holders, the linen used for the tablecloths, and her hope that the herb-crusted lamb would knock her socks off more than the breadsticks, which barely blew at her feet.

Emmaline used her chameleon powers so no one noticed her.

But he noticed.

Which was why he pulled his attention from Mary's gushing about the viscosity of the bisque and laid his gaze on Emmaline.

At that, she startled a bit. Only a small jerk of her head in surprise.

Was this surprise that he'd noticed her attempt to slide away into nothingness?

He gave her a soft wink he hoped would bring her back, even as the other woman continued to chatter on about the décor.

Thank hell Mary stopped long enough to breathe because he was a bit tired of all the comments.

"Would you believe that Em here is an artist?" Ethan asked. "A damn fine one, too." He gave Em a subtle nod.

"Thank you," Em said. "That's very kind."

Righto, she was going to get the hang of accepting praise yet.

Mary went into a slew of questions about Em's art. Ethan sat back, happy to let Em have the spotlight.

"Mary, would you help me with a problem I have?" he asked conspiratorially when she finally wound down. He tossed on a dash of the charisma he sometimes—rarely— used when he needed something to go his way.

Eager as all get out to help, she nodded emphatically. "Anything."

"Em is special to me." He gestured to Emmaline.

Her cheeks pinked again, and that eyebrow lifted once more. He'd never noticed her do that before, but tonight she'd done it twice in the span of moments. Noted.

He continued on, speaking to Mary. "I was wondering if you might take a picture of us?"

The woman nodded emphatically.

"I don't mind at all." Mary stood taller, apparently pleased to have marching orders straight from Ethan Greene himself.

She snapped the photo. Then one with her and agreed he could post it as long as she could, too.

"Thank you." Then he said lower, "Dessert is on the house tonight."

Her eyes lit up like a sparkler. "Oh, Mr. Greene, you don't have to—"

"I insist." He gave Walter a wave and, thankfully, Mary marched straight back to him.

Poor Walter was in for it the rest of the night now that Mary'd had the chef's ear. Ethan doubted she'd stop the chatter until she finally fell asleep.

"That was inspired." Emmaline lifted the crystal water glass to her lips.

He laid his elbows on the table—a faux pas, sure—but it was the only way he could reach for her hands and hold them in his own. "Gotta make it look real, yeah?"

She gave his hands a squeeze, but did not pull them away. "How long do I have to hold your hands, again?"

"I figure just long enough for people to notice."

She seemed to chew on something she wanted to say, but hadn't come up with the right words.

He waited.

Finally, she said, "That was nice, the way you pulled me into the conversation like that. But how do you do it so easily? Just be all—"

"Sparkly?"

"Uh-huh."

Of all the things she could've said, this was the most unexpected.

Um. "The first thing I do is moisturize regularly."

She snort laughed.

"I mean…" She cleared her throat. Reached for her water and took a sip, rattling the silverware a touch when she replaced it on the table. "What I mean is, how do you keep the confidence? It's like you don't even think about it. It's just there."

"I guess I just decided a lot of blokes—and Mary's—aren't gonna like me no matter what I do." He cleared his throat this time. "So I try not to care."

That got him a small trace of a grin. "I wish I didn't care what people thought about my art, but I do. I need the reassurance because…"

"Because?" he asked, gently.

"There was this time when I actually painted a whole watercolor for the living room at our old place. Spent loads of time on it. I loved it. It was gorgeous, I thought." She closed her eyes as though trying to look at the art in her memory. She opened them and continued, "I gave it to my ex for his birthday. And, he…well, he unwrapped it and he looked like he was waiting for a punchline." Her voice cracked a bit.

"Em?"

"A punchline that didn't come." She swallowed, hard.

"I'm sorry," he said, since it's all he could say.

"He hated it." She toyed with the stem of her wine glass. "He didn't say it out loud, but he didn't hang it up on the wall, either. I found it in the garage when I was packing up our stuff to move here."

Ethan wanted to throttle the idiot.

"He didn't even re-wrap it before putting it on the shelf, so it was all ruined and warped." She pushed the wine glass away and pressed her palms into the tablecloth. "You know, this type of conversation requires more under-wear than my I-didn't-do-enough-laundry thong."

She announced this bit to him, cheeky as hell.

Luck was on his side, though, because his jaw did not drop into his just-delivered soup. But he was pretty damn sure it came close.

"That is an interesting visual." Ethan chuckled and spooned his bisque to his lips. "And you deserve better. I'm glad you're finding your better."

"I'm going to have to work harder on the whole don't-say-everything-that-comes-to-mind shebang," she said.

Emmaline went in for her own soup. Tasted. Paused. Tasted again.

Set down her spoon.

Dammit, he wanted to know what she thought. But didn't want to ask.

"This *is* amazing," she finally said. "Mary is correct. I

would totally eat this again. And, truly, I think the crispness to the sticks is a bold choice," Emmaline declared. "A deliciously bold choice."

He chuckled again. Deep and low in his throat. "You approve."

"I totally approve." Emmaline stirred her bisque with one of them.

The bold bread sticks had nothing on the coq au vin she ordered. *That* dish would have made even Julia Child weep.

Ethan didn't date anymore, but when he had, it was usually work to ensure the other person stayed happy and had a good time.

Em didn't seem to need any of that from him.

Which was…different.

Chapter Sixteen
EMMALINE

THEY'D MOVED ONTO DESSERT, and Emmaline had barely pushed her fork into the tiramisu when her purse buzzed.

Seeing as she'd set her phone to silence with one exception, she immediately reached for it, mouthing "the girls" to Ethan.

"Hi, Mom. What's up?" she asked, phone pressed to her ear.

"Everything's fine," Mom said, which every mom on the planet understood meant that everything was *not* fine.

Emmaline's mouth went a little dry.

"What's wrong?" She turned all her focus from the tiramisu to the call.

Mom said, "Oh, yes, well, Fiona takes after her mother and we have a little issue…"

Em was a mother, so the mandatory invasive thoughts took hold. An entire menagerie of things that could go wrong flipped through her brain: swallowing a button battery, ice skating on the trampoline, sticking her fork in the plug-in, accidentally swallowing the whole fork, testing the flavor of laundry pods—

"Everything all right?" Ethan asked.

She looked to Ethan, hoping he might send her some soothing energy, but Mom was still talking, "The kids got a little kooky playing the piano with their toes, and Fiona took a tumble—"

"Repeat that?" Emmaline said, holding up her one-second finger for Ethan.

She what?

"We finally got that sorted, she's fine," Mom continued. "I'm actually calling about the gum stuck in her hair. The cousins chewed it to look like barrettes. They did a good job, too, and Fiona was happy to be their model. I wanted to be sure she doesn't have a problem with mayonnaise before I put it on her scalp. Annie said it's fine, but she's ten. The jar doesn't say it has gluten. The google had several opinions. Dad suggested I call to be sure there's nothing in it she can't have in her hair. That's all. We'll get it settled, and you can go back to your da—whatever you're doing on your night off from responsibility with your…whatever he is."

"Mayonnaise is fine," Emmaline said, frowning. "Why don't I head over?"

She'd have to forgo her tiramisu to ensure her daughter still had a full head of hair come the morning. But that was parenting, in a nutshell.

Ethan was already standing as Emmaline snatched her purse.

She adjusted the cell against her cheek. "Do not let her eat a button battery or laundry soap or magnets…"

"Oh no, no, no," Mom said. "Bask in the bliss of your utter freedom from any obligations. Just…needed to know about the mayonnaise. You think Miracle Whip works better?" There was some rustling in the background. "Oh, or I found that makeup remover with the mineral oil that makes me break out. I can use that. I bet that will work."

Phone still held to her ear, Emmaline looked at Ethan. "Fiona's got gum stuck in her hair."

"Oh, the google came through!" Mom declared. "Miracle Whip is just fine. We'll try that before the makeup remover. Don't worry about a thing. We've got it all under control. She's having a Popsicle while we sort the details."

"Don't let her eat the Popsicle stick," Emmaline said, pressing her fingertips against her temple.

"Why would she eat a Popsicle stick?" Mom *pf-shawed*. "I swear you make no sense sometimes." A muffled sound came across the line. "Jim, you don't need cheese; we're not fixing sandwiches."

Mom hung up, and Emmaline stared at her phone. Then she glanced to Ethan, who waited patiently. She licked her lips.

"Should we head over?" he asked.

"I think we should go and just do a well-check. Make sure the Miracle Whip works, you know?" Because even though she trusted her parents, she really should put eyes on her kid. Just for everyone's sakes.

"I have no idea what that means," he replied.

"I'll fill you in on the way."

Ethan scooted them out of the restaurant, lickity split. He didn't ask questions after she relayed the issue and her parents' address. The GPS did the heavy lifting while she ranted about why her family couldn't at least pretend to be normal for an evening.

She'd made it nearly through all of her bullet points when he parked the sedan right out front of the house.

No police or ambulances. That was reassuring. They

already had the firefighter with her dad in the house, and the nurse with her mom.

She didn't hurry to the door, but she didn't lollygag, either. Ethan stayed right at her side.

This was her childhood home, so there was no need to ring the bell or anything. She pushed right on in. "Fiona?"

"Well, that was sure quick," Mom said, emerging from the kitchen with a half-full jar of Miracle Whip, white goop all over her hand, and a bag of frozen peas. "Hi, Ethan. Good to see you again. Annie's just the sweetest. She fits right in with the kids." Mom beamed at him and, yes, she totally checked him out. Head to toe. Then she grinned as though she approved of every morsel of him.

"Fiona's doing much better," Mom went on. "I shouldn't have worried you. It's just a sprain. She just really took us for a loop when she went ass over teakettle like that at the piano. I swear that girl got all your genes and none of Tony's. I forgot what it's like to have a mini version of you in the house. One second she's twinkle, twinkling with her tootsies and the next she's splayed on the tiles." Mom was moving to the backyard. Emmaline followed, Ethan staying right at her back.

"I thought it was the gum?" Emmaline asked.

"Oh, we're soaking that with this." She held up the jar as she walked. "I think we're close."

"But she's got a sprain, too?" Emmaline confirmed. No one said anything about a sprain on the call.

"You know, I told your dad he needed to put carpet in that room. The tile's just not good for kids. But he's"— Mom whispered the next part—"getting to it." She continued right on to the patio. "I swear I don't know how many grandkids we have to break before he"—She whispered again— "gets to it." She turned to Ethan. "Can I get you anything? I'm sorry I interrupted your special time together."

Ethan stared at her wide-eyed. As one would do when entering the energy field of her parents' home for the first time.

"I'll go ahead and grab you a Fresca. Emmaline? Do you want one, too?" Mom asked.

But Emmaline had her eyes on her girl, and that was all that mattered. She strode right there with purpose.

She knelt to Fiona and gave her a once-over. "Hey, Fiona. Hi, Annie."

The girls sat together, knees dangling and their hair covered by a shower cap filled with what appeared to be Miracle Whip.

"I tried the barrettes, too," Annie said.

"How much gum did each of you end up with tangled in your hair?" Ethan asked.

"Not even a lot," Mom dodged in that special way of hers. "We're working it out, and it's looking good."

"Do I have to come home?" Fiona full court whined.

"I don't want to go home, either," Annie announced.

"I thought I got to stay at Gramma and Grandpa's?" Fiona said. "You said I got to spend the night!"

If it was possible for a little girl to stomp her foot while dangling her feet, she would've done it.

"I want a sleepover, too," Annie said, eyes on Ethan.

"What muscle, exactly, do you think she sprained?" Emmaline asked her mom, because if she was going to leave Fiona there for the night—everything that happened notwithstanding—she should probably ensure that the child didn't need an x-ray or anything along those lines.

"Oh, gosh." Mom fluttered around, lifting Fiona's arm, and pressing the bag of peas to her elbow. "Just a little tap to the funny bone. She'll be right as rain tomorrow. Kids are pretty bendy like that. And we'd love Annie to stay, too."

"Please, can I stay?" Fiona asked, practically begging.

"Me, too!" Annie added.

"I…uh…" Emmaline glanced at Ethan.

"I'm okay with it," Ethan said. "If Em is, too."

"*Mooom*," Fiona used her special super nails-on-chalkboard tone.

"Oh, gosh, c'mon, Em," Mom said. "The girls were looking forward to the sleepover. I promise we'll wrap them in bubble wrap. Not to worry, we're also done with the gum and piano portion of the night."

Emmaline pursed her lips. "Fiona, no more using your feet for things meant for your hands."

Fiona nodded. "I promise."

"That goes for you, too, Annie," Ethan added.

"And no more sticky things near your head," Em continued down the list.

Fiona nodded again. "Double promise."

Annie agreed as well.

"And do not eat things that aren't meant for eating. Agreed?" Em kept going.

"Triple promise." Fiona made wide eyes at Emmaline like she was the one embarrassing everyone.

"I promise, too," Annie said.

Fine. Then Emmaline would just go back home. By herself.

"I'll see you tomorrow." Emmaline sighed and pressed a kiss to Fiona's forehead, below the Miracle Whip line.

Chapter Seventeen
ETHAN

EM'S FOLKS took a real shine to Annie. Ethan appreciated how they slotted her into the family fun easily, even if it did end with her hair caked in sauce and she reeked of a picnic sandwich.

He backed out of the drive and turned left onto the street in front of Em's family home.

"Annie fits right in with your lot," he said. "Your family is—"

"Different? Odd? Not entirely a full box of crackers?" Emmaline seemed like she could keep going. "My mom is…my mom."

Ethan slid his gaze from the road to her. "I was going to say how kind it was of them to take Annie tonight and add her to the mix. They're nice folks."

Em scrunched her nose, and she shifted so the yellow skirt hitched up a tad, revealing her thigh. His body took notice, even as his mind reckoned it shouldn't. "Nice is not a word I would use," she said. "Though they have their good points."

"They're great with the kids." This, he said with a load of certainty.

"I'm glad to be back where I can see them a lot. Don't get me wrong. I just…I just struggle to fit."

"I reckon under all of the nonsense…well…I think they're keen on you," he assured. They were parents and there was a heap to be proud of with their daughter.

"I doubt it." She stared out at the traffic, her profile mirrored back in the window.

"You don't believe me?" he asked.

"I believe you are trying to be extra nice to me because our daughters are currently bathing in Miracle Whip." She paused. "That is a sentence I never thought I'd say."

Also not something he'd thought he'd find in his life, either.

"I reckon your family was stoked to have you move back." He kind of switched the convo when he should've just asked her, already.

She continued staring at the cars waiting alongside them at the traffic light. "They are. They were. Mom and Dad didn't like that I moved away. They had six kids and I'm the only one who moved away. I guess I'm the problem."

"You wanted to do something different." Nothing wrong with that.

"I thought I did. I didn't know what I wanted." She lifted a shoulder and shifted in the seat so her skirt hiked up a smidge more.

His cheeks got a bit toasty. He cleared his throat.

"It takes a brave person to try something new. Something as big as moving to a new state. New city."

"New country?" she asked, sliding her gaze to him.

"New country," he agreed.

He had her number on that subject change she was working on. Turning the conversation to him.

"Is your family nice, too?" she not-so-subtly asked.

Exactly like that.

"My family is my family. They also didn't love that I moved away. Loved it even less when I didn't hurry home with Annie." He couldn't—or wouldn't—do that for heaps of reasons.

"Did you consider that? Because Australia is a helluva long way away. Way further than Los Angeles."

He nodded, chest tight even after some time away from making the decision. "After talking to some pros who understand kids a lot more than me, I decided that in a world where everything's gone topsy-turvy for her, any stability I can give her is worth it. In this case, gallivanting around the globe seemed like it might push her ability to cope with life's curveballs a little too far. She has rellies in the States—uncles, aunties, and grandparents—from her mum's side. They all enjoy seeing her. She likes to see them. We're close enough they can drop by regularly without being at our front door every other night." The last he whispered, as though the words were secret and not something he shared with anyone else. Because he didn't.

There was more to him not nickin' off to Australia, too. Annie was the priority, no doubt, but the Nosh Network was here in the States. His future was here with Annie, and he still hoped it'd also be on Nosh again.

Fiddling with the bottom of her skirt, Em couldn't quite look at him. "I guess this is the part where we break up."

He needed to ask. *Just ask her already.*

He turned right when they should've gone straight. This was not the direction of home. This was the direction of dessert.

Was it a bribe? Some might call it that.

"Do you want a big 'to-do' from me? A whole scene?" Em asked. "Or are we good to just be done and move on?"

Ethan gripped the steering wheel. He had to say it. Put it out there. Stop mollycoddling himself.

"Here's the deal." Ethan gulped down a huge lump in his throat. "There's a wedding up in Estes in a couple of weeks. I need us to stay together until that's over. They think we're a couple, and it'd be awkward to go alone. Reckon you could stick it out 'til then?"

She stared at him like he'd announced he'd decided to turn the restaurants into a croc rescue. That wasn't hopeful. He didn't like that.

But she didn't say anything straight away. That part held promise. So he waited.

"You're serious?" she asked, finally.

No doubt he was.

"Not like I can find another pretend girlfriend in that time. At least one who isn't really looking to be a missus." That was the honest truth. "It's just one more time, then we're done. Promise."

"Tonight is the *one* time. That's what we agreed." She was still pursing her lips.

Yes, that was the initial deal. Now he needed to chuck in a bit of a tweak.

"Is this leading it on for the girls?" Em asked. "We'll get their hopes up."

Bloody hell, he hadn't given much thought to that. But they'd already been playing pretend, what was a bit longer in the grand scheme?

"Children have built-in bulldust radar," he said. "They'll know it's not a true relationship just as we've told them from the start."

He waited. Waited for her to say something else. But

neither of them said anything for about a block. The silence stretched between them.

If he could get back in the good graces of the Nosh family, he'd be sitting pretty.

"I could really do with a hand," he said, hoping she'd understand how much this meant to him.

"And I could really do to get laid," she countered under her breath, totally serious. "Looks like we both have issues."

"Sorry?" He'd misheard her. He was certain. "Did you say?"

"Ethan." She pursed her lips. "Fine. Okay. Wedding. Let's do it."

"I knew I could count on you, Em." He gave her a cheeky smile. "Now, what's this about getting lucky?"

"See? Why couldn't I say it like that? It sounds much better when you say it. Yours sounds so reasonable. Mine just sounds dirty."

"You didn't answer the question, love."

"I just figured when we ended things I could finally… post-divorce…you know?" She tilted her head from side to side. "Not only by myself."

He did know, but for some reason he couldn't put his finger on, he didn't like the idea of Em with another bloke.

"Okay. I'll do it." Ethan took a left into the King Soopers' parking lot.

"You'll do it?" Em asked. "I didn't ask you to."

"Right, but I'm a good friend. You're doing something for me. I'll do something for you."

Emmaline turned toward him in her seat. "Gosh, Ethan, I wouldn't want to put you out."

"Believe me, this is not a hardship." *Not in the least.*

He let himself think what it would be like to undress

her. Kiss her. Pull her on top of him. His mouth went dry and his donger said hi.

"We'll leave the option open, then," Em agreed. Staring at his mouth like it was raspberry sauce.

"We're here for dessert," he said, looking toward the grocery store.

She still stared at his lips like she had a craving. "You're going to make me dessert?"

Too right he was. "I wasn't gonna grab a frozen pie, if that's what you're thinkin'."

Nah, Ethan wasn't a frozen pie sort of bloke. Not by a long shot. He never slipped when it came to food. A bit like having a woman in his bed—he gave it his all.

His hand dropped to hers for a friendly pat, all casual-like, as if it was a completely normal thing to do. But this time there was some kind of static charge when their skin touched. "You didn't get to enjoy dessert after dinner, so I reckon I owe you one."

"All good," she assured, her breaths coming quicker. "You don't owe me."

"Then do you want to fix dessert?" He twined their fingers together again as though it were just a natural part of life. Nothing out of the ordinary, when it really was. It didn't have to be more, but they both understood it did.

She let out an adorably soft cackle. "I suppose it depends if you are okay with Krispies and s'mores, because those are the two things I know how to make well."

"If we go s'mores, I'll handle the fire to toast the marshmallows," he said, deadpan. "It's not that I don't trust you, it's just…" He pulled a yeesh face.

"Hah." She started to push open the door to the sedan so she could head inside, but he gripped tighter, snagging her hand before she could extract it from his. He gave her a little tug back in his direction. She turned, and he removed most of the gap between them.

His mouth hovered in the air over hers. "I can do the other part for you, too. If you'd like."

The air in the car went from light and funny to holy crap, bloody hell hot in the blink of an eye.

Her pupils dilated and her lips parted.

"I can come up with an ulterior motive for bringing you back to my home so we can have dessert," he said, stroking the top of her hand with his fingertip. "If that'll help."

Her breaths came quicker. "That's going to—"

"Complicate things?" he asked, finishing her sentence for her. "Nah. I help you with what you need. You help me with what I need. Everybody wins."

"Do you even know how long it's been since anyone had ulterior motives with me?" she asked, a touch squeaky.

Apparently, it'd been way too freaking long, that's for damn sure.

"Ethan." She dropped her forehead against his, keeping a space between their lips. He reveled in the vanilla scent of her perfume and the peppermint on her breath. "Are we still responsible adults?"

His hand shifted to the column of her neck, tracing it with the tip of his fingers. "I'd say responsible adulting is not an issue for us."

His lips were drifting a hairsbreadth over her lips and every nerve in his body seemed to fire as he spoke. Each nerve ending in his body attempted to convince him to erase that bit of space and take her mouth. Because he wanted to, and she clearly wanted it, too.

She leaned into him, but he backed off the slightest bit so she could ask for it. She had to ask for it. He moved his hand to her shoulder and fiddled with the spaghetti strap there.

"Why haven't you kissed me already?" she asked.

He grinned and smoothed the fabric on her shoulder, but since it was only a thin strip of cloth, he mostly touched her skin.

"Waiting for you to ask me to," he replied, the words gravelly.

"Kiss me already." This she said a bit too loudly and with a little too much assertion.

"That's not asking nicely, is it now?" He trailed his finger down from her temple to the edge of her mouth, parting her lips with the pad of his thumb.

"Ethan. Would you please kiss me?" She squirmed. Practically moaned.

He moved and pressed a light kiss to the edge of where her neck met her shoulder. "Like this?"

She groaned low in her throat. Oh, that was an Em pleasure spot. Good to know.

"Not there," she said on a breath.

He paused the light kisses, but his lips curved into a grin against her skin.

"Here?" he asked, moving to her earlobe.

She shivered.

"Not there." Of note, she did brush her hair aside for better access.

He kissed lower, along her collarbone.

"Wrong direction," she muttered.

"Is that so?" His words were husky.

"Maybe I should help," she said, moving her lips to his earlobe and kissing him where it met his jawline.

He shivered. "Now that, I like."

She moved in, and he arranged himself carefully so as not to chip anyone's tooth because that would totally wreck the mood. He seemed to surprise her with his maneuvering, but she was apparently okay with it because when his mouth got close to hers, she let him take control.

Their mouths met and he handled the teeth check thing, and the pressure thing, and—well, he just handled it all.

"God, it's been a long time," she said against his mouth. Still squirming in her seat. She made erotic sounds in the back of her throat, and he countered with low rumbles as he held her mouth hostage.

When they finally came up for air, she had been well and truly kissed to smithereens.

"Any particular brand of chocolate?" he asked, hand on the car's door handle.

"Huh?" she asked, totally confused.

"For your dessert." He paused. "Chocolate. Marshmallow. Graham Crackers," he continued, husky and craving more of her mouth.

"Oh, I'm very picky about my chocolate for s'mores."

"Good, me, too."

The cat's-had-his-cream-and-was-going-to-have-the-whole-carton-of-milk expression on her face made him shiver and his donger hard as steel.

He stepped from the car and met her at the hood, taking her hand in his as they moved inside the grocery store.

"Mostly, I'm particular about how my marshmallows are toasted," she said.

"I just bet you are."

She nudged him with the side of her arm. "I'm serious. If you're going to run the flame, then you should know that I like them toasted all the way around so that the center is properly mushy and the outside is crisp, but not in any way burned. Just on the cusp of it, but then you pull the marshmallow away in its perfection."

Clearly, she'd given this loads of thought on more than one occasion.

He stopped moving to give her his full attention, not even willing to use any of his thoughts for walking, moving. No, every morsel of his awareness pinned to her.

She shivered again.

"Noted," he said.

These s'mores were going to be the best s'mores in the history of toasted marshmallow goodness. He'd be sure of it.

Chapter Eighteen
ETHAN

THEY DIDN'T GO STRAIGHT to dessert.

Groceries were purchased. They drove home without any drama. Em checked in with Barbie and the pup. And then they hurried to Ethan's place for "s'mores."

But they weren't making dessert. He'd barely dropped the grocery sack on the counter before they went right on in. He kissed her again. She kissed him right back. This one was different, urgent, with his hands in her hair taking charge.

"Bloody unreal. You kiss like a legend," he said, cradling her head in his palm.

This wasn't anything. Not really. It wasn't. It couldn't be. So why did it feel like it was only the two of them in the whole world?

Why did it feel like it wasn't pretend?

And why didn't that scare him?

"Quite the compliment." She bit at her bottom lip.

He nodded, staring at her lips. "You're practically a pro."

Her eyes widened slightly.

Bugger him, that wasn't what he meant to say.

Her cheeks pinked.

"I didn't mean that." He pulled back. Gave some space between them.

"Oh no." Her grin was intoxicating. "That's quite the compliment. Keep them coming."

He was still feeling the buzz of their kiss, as if they were still in the middle of it. The same fluttering in his belly and hardening below the belt. He wanted to savor every inch of her.

"What are you thinking?" she asked, touching his cheek.

"I can't say what's on my mind," he said, with confidence.

"Now I have to know."

"Emmaline." He said her name low with a subtle head shake.

"Spill it, Mr. Chef." Ah, there was the bit of cheek he got such a kick out of.

"I was thinking…"

She gestured for him to continue.

"That I'd like to show you what I can do with my tongue between your legs. Listen to you cry out when you're done."

"Did you?" Her mouth fell open. "You just said that. Yes, you totally did. In your *kitchen*."

"I did," he affirmed. "The kitchen didn't seem to care."

"I think we should go ahead and do that." She gave a nod before flinging herself at him. He caught her in his arms.

With the visual of his mouth between her thighs, his body cooperated fully with heaps of spark and a massive dose of chemistry happening between them.

There was loads of mouth on mouth, hands everywhere, and sounds that probably scared the cat away with how wild they were.

He pressed her chest to chest, body to body, against his…fridge. His leg slipped between her legs, and she groaned.

Right.

"The locale doesn't make much sense, but it's what we have to work with, so onward," he said against her mouth.

"I like the location," she said, breathy, between kisses.

He'd make it happen. *Happen* being the most inappropriate word ever because he was enjoying the hell out of this happening.

As was she, given the sounds coming from her throat.

Her hands traced the line of his throat and moved up his jawline.

"You're sure you're good with this?" he asked, pressing his mouth against her mouth. Pressing wasn't pushing, yeah?

He allowed, for the briefest of moments, his hands to roam down her body, along the edges of her breasts, to her waist and hips, stopping before he made it to the edge of her skirt.

"Totally good," she murmured against his mouth, pressing her ass right into his hands.

"I want to undress you," he said between the frantic kisses. "Lay you on the counter and eat you until you come."

In response, she moaned and gripped his suit jacket by the lapels and slipped it over his shoulders, roaming her palms along his biceps and somehow around, pulling until the jacket was basically cuffing him, and he had no use of his hands. No use at all because those hands were stuck behind his back, and he was the one against the fridge with no space in-between.

She did things to his mouth he'd forgotten could be done.

His blood was pounding hard and his breaths were uneven as he tried, and failed, to control his excitement. Tried to keep up with her kisses as his erection pressed against her belly through his slacks.

If a donger could wish that someone would let him out to play, his made that wish right then.

"Ethan," she sighed against his lips, still with this crazy make-out sesh against his fridge.

"Right here, love," he replied, keeping up with her mouth as she trailed it everywhere.

The mewl that came from the back of her throat was feral and feline and...the thin strip of a rubber band holding his self-control in check seemed to snap clear free.

"My turn," he said.

No longer able to keep his hands from her, he took hold. An odd thought about marshmallows and dessert nagged at his subconscious even as he pushed the suit jacket to the floor and reversed their positions, letting his hard length press against her core through the layers of cotton and polyester, allowing the hardness of him to plea-sure the softness of her—even though they were fully clothed.

"I've never put the kitchen to this use before," he said against her mouth.

The kitchen was a sacred space for him. A place for only him—not a spot for a quickie.

Sure, he knew there were chefs who got it on regularly in their kitchen spaces. Even a bloke with no skills and a decent béchamel could make the kitchen a panty-dropping locale. That's what he'd heard, at least.

Not his game.

This place was special.

Skin pressed on skin, lips against lips, the length of him against—and between—all of her.

Her breasts heaved against his chest, the air filling her chest and releasing in quick bursts that matched his.

"I can't even…" She gripped at his sleeves, adjusting her stance just that tiniest bit so the long, hard length of his erection slipped further between her thighs. The fabric was nothing. Also, everything.

She moved against his hardness and made a small, but audible, "Mm-hmm."

He kissed her then and let his lips talk with no words.

She responded, her body screaming in the affirmative as his blood heated just to the edge of perfection. The spot where the bubbles formed around the rim of the pan without anything getting burned.

His hands were in her hair. She gripped the lapels of his shirt again. Gripping them like they were a lifeline to something neither of them knew possible.

A look of hesitation crossed her features.

"What is it?" he asked.

"I don't know what I'm even doing. God, it's been forever." Her voice cracked as she spoke.

"Don't worry, then. I've got you." Gentle, like she was the fussiest of soufflés, he moved her to the floor. He laid her on the tile. Putting his jacket under her head and keeping their gazes locked while he began lifting her skirt.

"Ethan…" She said his name with such significance, as if it held more weight than just a couple of syllables and a few letters.

"I'll take care of you," he said, holding her there, his face right above hers, her eyes holding him steady.

He moved his hand to lift the edge of her skirt, going higher along her thigh. His eyes never leaving hers.

The recipe for the evening needed a dollop of care, a bloody lot of attention, and flames that only burned for them.

"I'll start by taking off the wrapper, peeling through the layers to get to the center. Then I'll have a taste," he said as he worked.

Except.

"There's barely any wrapper," he murmured. Then again, that's what she'd said at the restaurant, wasn't it?

His hand moved higher to her hip, his fingertips moving the scrap of fabric there. Pulling it away from her center.

He leaned forward, kissing the stuffing out of her while his hand grazed along the line of her waist.

"Emergency thong for the win," she said, pulling her lips in a *whatcha gonna do* line.

"Sketch's been eating my laundry," she clarified.

"I don't know what to say to that." The truth was the only thing that came to mind.

She pulled his hand lower, to between her legs. "Then say nothing."

Occasionally, he stumbled upon a fussy soufflé that refused to release from the edges. The trick was to change tactics.

He trailed a light movement to her core. She moaned against his lips and pulled her ankles up, letting her knees fall apart.

Did his mouth part? Salivate? His eyes grow wide? Yes, all of those things happened. He tested the softness of her, allowing the heat to stoke between them. Link them together.

His erection strained against the cloth at his fly.

"I am so hard for you," he said as he touched her.

She gripped his wrist, moving it to the center of her and lifting only the slightest bit so his fingers found her opening.

"Please," she said, warmth at the tip of his fingers. "Don't you dare stop."

That's all he needed before he slipped a finger, then two, inside this woman who lifted her hips to welcome him into her heat. Allowed him to stoke the fire.

He lazily trailed around the edge of the bundle of nerves outside her opening with his thumb while he worked her with two fingers inside.

Her gaze had gone glassy, and they were both basically still wearing most of their clothes. And he was about to finish in his trousers.

"My God," he said, unable to stop himself from allowing the beauty of the moment to envelop him. "You're so bloody gorgeous."

"I'm there," she said with a gasp. "Don't stop. Please. Don't stop."

There was not one chance in hell he would stop this movement that had her panting and making those sounds just before her internal muscles flexed around his fingers. She inhaled deeply as the muscles flexed and released, flexed and released.

His erection followed that same movement, even though it wasn't inside her. He took a touch of relief by pressing against her thigh.

She made the sound she'd made the first time she'd come to the kitchen and tasted his raspberry sauce. That subtle moan of delight.

This time she followed it with a sound he could not describe—bliss and pleasure and pure Emmaline in the space that was all his, and his alone.

Chapter Nineteen
EMMALINE

HIS BREATH BRUSHED against the nerves of her earlobe. "Emmaline."

He said her name with a trace of possessiveness to it, like it was more than just a name of an imitation girlfriend. Like it was the name of someone immensely special to him.

She swallowed, not wanting to allow any sort of feelings to come through but realizing that sometimes—like now, after coming like a Puffle Yum cherry tart after 30 seconds in the toaster—there was not one thing she could actually do to prevent them. But she would try. Of course, she would. Mind-numbing orgasms didn't have to get all emotional.

Not to put a name to it, but her ex—while totally show-stopping—wasn't exactly attentive. He'd been more of a two-seconds-in-the-microwave-toaster-tart kind of guy.

But that was not this. The past was not the present. That future wasn't today.

Today, the only thing that mattered was the way Ethan's breath ignited the little sparks along her neckline.

She moaned again because she couldn't help it. There was only one moment, and that moment was now. No responsibility because it was just the two of them.

His lips trailed along her collarbone to where her bra still kissed the edge of her dress.

"Ethan…" She said his name because, honestly, no other words would form. "That was…"

"Amazing? Fantastic?" he asked, with a chuckle.

This was one of those times when she should just hand over the controls to someone who knew what to do.

Gently, oh, so gently, Ethan pressed his thigh between her legs, opening them, even as his mouth continued to do marvelous things to the swath of skin between her neck and her nipples.

"Say something," she murmured, unable to stop herself. "I like to hear your voice."

"What do you need me to say?" he asked, genuine and husky.

"I…" Well, she wasn't entirely sure.

But he'd stopped. Given her his full attention while everything they'd been working toward came to a standstill. Dammit, that was just not going to work. Not when he'd got the pulsing ache between her thighs pulsing again, and the desire for him was increasing by the second.

"I don't know what I need from you," she whispered, her mouth only millimeters from his. "I don't even know what I need from me." She didn't, not really. Honestly, life at the moment was a big ol' question mark.

"Em…" He said her name with the same reverence as his mouth worked along her shoulder. "Let's find out together." His hands both threaded her hair on each side of her head.

She grinned. Let out a deep—massive—lungful of air.

His lips found hers, pressing quietly there. "You are the

most beautiful, the most delicious, and the most wonderful person, Em. Know that."

He studied her face. Her heart softened because it wasn't lust in his eyes. This was something else. Something…more. Something else entirely. Something different…dangerous.

His mouth was against hers and his hands were urgently pulling the cloth from her chest, up and over her head, only breaking the seal of the kiss for the briefest of seconds.

He seemed to have sensed her hesitation and didn't want it to fester. To go further. Which was good, because she'd never felt this urgency of desire laced with a helluva lot of craving.

"I'm going to take you to the sofa, now," he said.

"Okay," she muttered against his mouth.

He moved her to the sofa, stopping at the door to flip all the locks and even the chain thing.

She wasn't sure where her clothes went along the way, but it didn't really matter in the grand scheme of his tongue tracing lines along the line of her breasts. Mulling over the tip of her nipples and diving deep into the valley between her breasts before moving down to her belly button.

He stopped there, lavishing her with attention while one hand held her ass.

"One sec," he said. "Protection."

She nodded and he stood, jogged up the stairs, and left her naked on his sofa.

But he came right back with the condom in his hand. Aw, look at him so prepared!

And then his mouth was at her center, coming in from the side into a sensitive space she didn't even know existed.

"Delicious, I told you," he said.

This wasn't a full-frontal attack—this was a sneak assault from the side that left her trembling and making sounds she was certain she'd never made before in her life.

A life lesson probably developed from Ethan's brilliance at going down on her, but she wasn't in the headspace to evaluate that just now.

But then his mouth disappeared from between her legs.

"Emmaline," he said, his lips now against hers. Not kissing her, just talking. Talking like he hadn't nearly brought her to the edge and dropped her there.

She cleared her throat at the earnest look in his gaze. "Uh-huh?"

"I'm going to get off here." He pulled her closer, the evidence of his desire to, ahem, "get off" excessively clear between her thighs.

"Okay, good." She wanted him to have that, too.

"You're also going to get off here…again." He pressed the long, hard length of him right at the apex of her thighs. "Be sure to give a yell about what you like. What works for you." His mouth met hers then. "I'm a bloody good student, but you've got to tell me what you like. What you need. No holding your breath."

Was she holding her breath?

Okay, yeah, she had totally been holding her breath.

He sat up on his knees, unclasping his pants and pulling them down.

Here's the thing—she didn't particularly find male anatomy below the belt supremely attractive. And yet…his was nice.

Honestly? Fine. She straight up gasped.

"I won't hold my breath," she heard herself say, even as her hand reached for his shaft, stroking up, up, up to the tip of all that was him.

Yep. She'd breathe just fine for an all-access pass to *this*.

"Fuck me," he said, as she moved her hand over the head of his manhood back down the shaft to the root.

She gave him two swift strokes before he took control once more.

Her legs were parted. Thankfully, everyone was naked, and his mouth was—once again—against her core. There was an active amount of tongue work, a decent amount of groaning—from both of them—before the coil inside her belly started cinching in that way she knew would bring her to her knees.

There was a crinkle of foil. Honestly, she probably should've been more aware of what was happening given the gravity of having not-fake sex with her very-fake boyfriend, but she truly just wanted to give him a high five for remembering to protect them both from what they were about to do.

Were. Doing.

She groaned a long exhale as he slipped inside her.

Did she clinch around him? Yes, yes, she did.

Was it an orgasm? Yes, yes, it was.

Would there be more, given the way he moved inside her? Uh-huh.

She rode the wave of the first climax, her eyes fixed on him as he thrust inside her. There were lotsa noises made that were not living room appropriate.

But then as she drifted down from orgasm mountain, Ethan's gaze held hers and this was so much more than a trip up and down the mountain. This was…something else.

This was a bold paintbrush of red with chocolate and marshmallow.

What could she say? The panic started right there because she wanted to do it again.

"I think we should make this a regular thing," she said

with a considerably more nonchalant tone than she genuinely felt.

"Same, Emmaline. Same." His forehead fell to hers as he said the words and a shudder ran through his body.

"Ethan?" she asked.

"Mm-hmm?" he pressed kisses along her jawline.

"Thank you."

He tilted his head to the side, studying her. "Thank you?"

"For making me feel like I can do this."

He grinned then. "Em?"

"Mm-hmm?"

"Thank you."

"Thank you?" she asked, mimicking his question from earlier.

"For showing me how much I needed this."

She laughed. He nuzzled her neck. Then he dealt with the things that needed dealing, and she dealt with other things that needed dealing.

After everything, they finally got to eat dessert. He did not disappoint with the toasted marshmallows.

He even made her the raspberry sauce he promised.

It was divine.

Chapter Twenty
EMMALINE

EMMALINE DIDN'T SLEEP OVER.

Not that Ethan didn't extend an invitation.

Her cheeks heated at that memory. Hoo boy, he'd extended that invite and included a hefty dose of tongue. But that was a little too…uh…real. She declined, also with a hefty dose of tongue.

But that was last night. Last night was not today.

Last night was a sundress exchanged for his shirt. Today was capri pants and a slouchy, pink summer sweater with no bulk at all. Really, the thing was practically see-through. But it looked nice when Emmaline paired it with a white camisole.

Make no mistake, sleeping over was a commitment to morning breath and funky hair and…things that were all too real.

The night before was not reality. A total fantasy. Her whole body gave an appreciative shake at the memory of how Ethan had worked that fantasy.

But that was then, and today was today.

The rundown? Today, after Fiona got home, Em

invited her parents to stay for a late breakfast. Then she invited Annie and Ethan over, too. A totally normal, neighborly brunch so the girls could play together.

Barbie took no time sniffing out the makeshift party, and she brought along Cress and Lauren, and that was the end of that. Cress brought the orange juice concentrate. Barbie brought champagne. Lauren brought a bag of supermarket ice because, well, she was Lauren.

Ethan brought the bacon. Emmaline supplied the eggs and the waffle mix. Then Ethan scoffed at the waffle mix, choosing to make his own instead.

Clearly, there was some kind of cardinal chef rule about using a waffle mix when there was flour and baking powder in the house. She didn't get it, but whatever.

James was the first of her brothers to show. He'd only recently gotten off work, and he was actually relieved to have Ethan's waffles and eggs before he crashed for the day.

James was appreciative. Who would've thought?

It probably wouldn't be long after that for her other brothers to start showing up, too—if they weren't on shift, and found out there was free food.

For now, it was a garden party—given that it was in Emmaline's garden.

The kids were playing in the playhouse, going up and down the yellow slide and through the blue tube connecting the little area in the back that was theirs alone.

There was laughter. People were happy.

No one was criticizing the curtains. Uh-huh. This was nice. *Nice* being the wrong word, but the one that seemed to fit.

Whatever, it was pretty kick-ass to have a little morning shindig at her house after the phenomenal evening before.

Things did not suck.

And things had sucked for a long, long time. She'd just appreciate that it blew for a bit instead of sucked.

Wait. That wasn't right. Scratch that.

Whatever.

"Somebody got some," Cress sang as she pulled the plastic tie from around the lip of the can for reconstituted orange juice.

Cress was a jeans and t-shirt person, but thankfully she hadn't worn her hashtag tee that morning.

Lauren did a little dance to the song Cress freestyled. She was in a summer dress and looked like she might have someplace to be later.

That was food for thought to ask about when they were alone.

"Somebody smashed some cookies last night," Barbie continued, singsongy.

Barbie also wore a semi-see-through sweater like Em. She'd just gone with a bra underneath, not a camisole. Luckily, the bra covered enough that the kids could still be in the room.

"Girls," Em hissed. "Stop it."

Lauren bumped Emmaline with her hip. "She didn't say *you* got lucky. She said *somebody* has that lucky glow."

Cress dumped the concentrated orange juice into the pitcher, where it slid with a slushy *thunk*.

"Well, I'm not talking about it." Em lifted a shoulder and handed over a wooden spoon so Cress could stir away at her concoction.

Barbie continued humming Cress's little ditty. "I wish I had stuck around to see what time you got in because *some-body* has a special cookie-crunch glow."

"Fine," Emmaline said, quietly and only for her friends' ears. "I didn't *not* get some." She raised her eyebrows to punctuate her point.

Barbie let out a screech that probably made the puppy pee himself and find more laundry to munch.

Not subtle at all.

"Everything okay?" Ethan asked from across the kitchen.

"Fine. Totally fine," Em assured, lancing Barbie with her gaze.

Lauren and Cress found this hysterical and had no issue at all cracking up.

Ethan was in his zone in her kitchen, which added to her happy bubble. He had on jeans, sneakers, and a black T-shirt with a beer logo on the front.

This wasn't his kitchen, but he seemed completely at home. Heck, her appliances may not have been as top of the line as his, but they did the trick.

The best part? As he moved behind her to grab a kitchen towel, he touched her waist. Not where anyone could see or notice, just so she knew he was there, and he wanted that. Wanted that with her. Specifically, to touch her.

Her cheeks were probably red as all hell because she was so smitten with the guy.

The way he brushed against the edge of her hip had her mind turning with some truly naughty things that involved him, lifesavers, her mouth, and alone time.

Somewhere, deep down inside, she understood this whole get-lucky-with-Ethan thing was a bad idea.

But bad ideas were still ideas, and sometimes they got to come out and play, too. Besides, the space between a bad idea and a good idea was nothing more than perception.

Speaking of...inspiration struck, and Emmaline grabbed a Sharpie.

"How about this?" She sketched out another kitten on

one of the disposable napkins she'd put out for the shebang.

Along with the champagne, Barbie had arrived that morning with loads of ideas for her logo. Unfortunately, now that she understood Emmaline's skill set, she had no qualms about manipulating it and squeezing it for all it was worth.

Emmaline didn't mind. Stretching her creative brain turned out to be pretty fantastic, too.

"Mmm." Barbie pulled a face and said nothing else. She didn't have to because her face said it all.

The drawing was good! Emmaline had finally figured out how to make the cat on the far right not look so lopsided.

She turned the napkin toward her, frowned, and sketched out another option at the corner.

A flit of a memory from her previous life tickled her brain. Not one of the icky memories, like she'd become used to. This one was the time she'd chatted with Dr. Paul at one of Tony's holiday party things. Dr. Paul was a celebrity but, she realized, he was more like Ethan—a reality show celebrity who wasn't high on himself and was actually a super nice guy.

He and Emmaline had sketched out an entire napkin-filled story about his son and Hanukkah.

It had not impressed Tony.

At all.

Emmaline was not there to doodle. She was there to hold his cocktail while he schmoozed.

She shook off the memory because that was then. Today was today.

Ethan slid a plate in front of Emmaline's sketchy napkin, breaking the train of the memory before Tony could wreck that, too.

She looked up because he'd made her eggs and a waffle. He'd even added a pad of butter and a drizzle of maple syrup. Honest as hell, he practically styled the plate for a food magazine.

The breakfast was simple, no doubt. There was nothing fancy about the egg or the waffle—other than their aesthetic perfection. But as she lifted a bite to her mouth, the realization hit that this was probably the best egg she'd ever eaten. In. Her. Life.

"How did you do this?" she asked, savoring the flavor.

"Do what?" he asked. But the sly grin on his face did nothing to convince her he didn't know. This guy understood precisely what he was up to.

"These are the best eggs I've eaten." She went in for a second bite.

"High praise." The lopsided grin did it all for her. Every little single thing. Done. Done. And done. All with only that trace of the edge of his mouth.

"Share your secrets." Because she'd been eating eggs wrong her entire life, if they could taste like this.

"The secret is a hot pan, salt, pepper, and take your time." He went back to another batch, cracking with one hand and tossing the shells into the trash.

"No." She shook her head. "There's more to it than that."

"Let me show you?" he asked, the question an invitation.

Well, yeah. Because she had to see this. There was no way that was "all" there was to it. If her kitchen could produce eggs like this, she damn well had a right to know how.

She snagged her plate and moved closer, so she had a better view of the stove.

"Low heat," he said, turning down the flame on her stove. "Then you let it do its thing. Add a little salt and pepper." He did this with a quick movement. "Wait some more." He stared at the eggs in the pan as though they were a serious test, and he was not about to risk failure.

"Still waiting," he said, the timbre of his voice low and husky and—

He flipped the egg in one shocking swoop, the muscles in his forearm flexing with the movement and the egg sliding clean off the spatula to cozy right back up with the pan.

"I think I want eggs." Barbie raised her hand. "Those eggs." She pointed for good measure.

"I'll take some eggs, too," Lauren agreed, holding her hand up.

"Count me in," Cress added, hand also in the air.

"We all want eggs," Em agreed.

"I'd like an omelet if we're placing orders," Mom said from the doorway.

Em gave Ethan a sly look. "Cooking lessons for everyone."

"Ladies." Ethan held up his spatula. "There's plenty to go around."

"I should've gone to cooking school." James moved beside Barbie, shaking his head.

"Don't worry, James," Barbie said. "I'm sure you'll find some other talents someday."

Lauren snort laughed at this.

Cress just frowned and glanced between the two of them.

"Dad!" Annie burst through the door, Fiona right there with her. "My hair came out."

Her French braid was more than a little lopsided, as

though she'd climbed out of the tube slide straight into the rose bushes, rolling around for a bit. Annie skidded to a halt when she caught sight of Emmaline standing so close to her dad. Her smile stretched across her face.

"Hey, Annie." Em suddenly had an intense urge to scoot away from Ethan just to avoid feeding Annie's hope.

"You think you're ready for this?" Ethan passed the spatula to Emmaline with an intense reverence.

Well, no. Not at all. She wasn't ready for any of it—the eggs or the sticky daughter situations. But he hadn't waited for an answer, so she didn't have a choice. Ready or not, here she came.

"I'll supervise her," Cress assured.

While Em poked at the edges of the eggs, Ethan lifted Annie until he got her to giggle. He firefighter-carried her to the sofa and took no time in pulling the wonky braid from her hair, finger brushing the locks and leaves, and then starting a new French braid.

"The man knows how to braid his daughter's hair," Lauren said on a gasp. "I think I want to date this celebrity dad, too."

Emmaline's mouth parted at the sight of Ethan braiding his daughter's hair.

Hell, she was done having kids. She was a one and done. But her ovaries perked to attention at the way Ethan made a braid. Over and under and…shit. He even understood how to make it work at the neckline so there wasn't a funky bump there.

She shattered her focus of his braiding skills and turned back to the eggs. A little too brown. Ugh.

"I thought you were supervising," she muttered to Cress.

"Shh," Cress replied. "I'm busy."

Em slid the eggs onto a plate and practically threw them in Barbie's direction before flicking off the fire so she could pause and take a breath. Or four. All while she observed Ethan in his natural habitat.

"Do mine next?" Fiona asked, plopping right next to Annie.

"Ohhhh-varies in overdrive," Cress muttered under her breath.

Uh-huh. That. Also, hold up because for the record? Emmaline tried to braid Fiona's hair often, but Fiona would have none of it. Sometimes she'd go for a ponytail. On a special day, she'd let Emmaline curl it.

But she never let her mother braid her hair.

Then again, Em didn't have forearms like Ethan's. Forearms that flexed and bunched with muscles under the ink. Twisting the hair in perfect proportions and not looking perturbed at all about any of it.

"Sure thing." Ethan pulled the elastic from his teeth—Yes! His teeth!—before he twisted it at the end of Annie's braid.

Fiona handed him her own elastic—where in the world had she Smurfed one of those into existence?

That's the moment Ethan Greene braided her daughter's hair. The moment Emmaline might've limped unwillingly over a line—a line that marked something more than lust with him and scared the pants off her.

(Figuratively, because they had company.)

All that to say, a woman did not watch her pretend boyfriend braid her kid's hair without falling a little in real love with him.

Nope. Dammit all. That wasn't possible.

"Somebody get some popcorn or something," Barbie said.

Hoo boy, yep, because Ethan put on quite a show.

Em pulled her lip between her teeth.

Watching him with her kid, she was feeling all kinds of conflicted about their charade. Because she wanted to hide again, slide into the invisible.

But, also, she didn't want to.

That didn't make any sense, but there it was.

Chapter Twenty-One
ETHAN

BY THE TIME everyone finished eating, the sun had risen higher in the sky. It was beating down on them with its rays, giving them a healthy dose of vitamin D. Ethan couldn't complain because he had a plate of waffles in his hand.

Sketch trotted over to him with fabric hanging out of his gob and clenched between his teeth.

Em wasn't gonna like that.

"Ethan," James called from the backyard. "Come on over."

To not head over to James would've been rude. Ethan walked over to where the guys were hanging out, watching the kids outside in Em's backyard. There was more furniture back here since the last time he came by. The grass was looking lush from being well-watered on a proper schedule. Emmaline had gone and added buckets of flowers along the porch's edge—red and yellow and pink with a few orange ones thrown in the mix.

He appreciated that in just a few weeks, the place felt like a proper home, not just a house.

There were two of Em's brothers over today. Lance came late—and he brought along his ankle-biters. James arrived after his shift. The others—Sam, Blake and Patrick —were all at work at various fire stations throughout Denver.

"Look who finally gets to play," James said, taking his eyes away from the scrambling kids and looking toward Ethan.

He didn't seem as crotchety as the norm.

"Do my playin' in the kitchen, mostly," Ethan said, grabbing the chair beside Em's dad to join their party.

The whole gang of kids ran wild, taking turns on the slide, playhouse, and tube. He caught Annie out of the corner of his eye scrambling inside the tube.

"Oh, don't worry, he was playing inside." James didn't even bother to turn towards Ethan. Just stared straight into the sun as if he wasn't afraid of burning his eyes. "Every woman within a five-mile radius is craving eggs right now and wanting their hair braided."

Jim snorted as he chuckled. "I make a mean brisket, and I can put out a fire, but I don't mess with anyone's hair."

"Had to learn for Annie," Ethan said. "When her mum left. Annie struggled, and it was something I could learn for her. Y'know?"

Jim gave him a long look like he was trying to make a decision about Ethan.

"We have a question," Lance said, pulling down his sunglasses a smidge as he pinched his gaze on Ethan.

Lance was a mammoth of a guy who clearly spent most of his time at the firehouse gym. Today, his tanned skin contrasted with the vibrant colors of the tropical shirt. Bald by choice, not genetics, Lance had a wicked gleam in his eyes. He was lounging in one of the Adirondack chairs in Em's garden area, looking as though he had nothing to worry about other than making sure the kids didn't hurt themselves. But Ethan knew that couldn't be further from the truth. Lance seemed a bloke with his mind constantly working, running through different scenarios to make sense of things. That's what Ethan figured, anyway.

"What's your question?" Ethan asked, cautiously.

"When did it become 'real' with my sister?" James kinda asked, kinda probed. "And do you plan on breaking her heart, too? Like all the others?"

"Because then we're going to have a problem," Lance added.

Ethan didn't fancy the way "all the others" sounded like there'd been heaps of guys. That was ridiculous, though, because he had no claim on her.

"Yeah-nah, we're only holding on to the charade a bit longer. Through an event I've got to get past. Still, nothing serious," Ethan assured, though he'd begun questioning where the line between real and fake was himself last night. "We're on course with the original plan. Just had to drag it out a bit."

They'd made some tweaks, is all.

"You're making her food. Feeding her family. Braiding her kid's hair." This was James, still staring directly at the sun. "Doesn't smell fake to me."

Ethan frowned. Was that giving the wrong idea?

"I just don't understand how you can pretend to date, anyway. It's all just a bunch of nonsense if you ask me," Jim said, giving Ethan a thorough once-over, clearly trying to assess his intentions. "You're not seein' anyone else. She's not seein' anyone else. It doesn't matter if you decide to call what you're doing unicorn wrangling, it's all the same."

"Em's finding her footing. She doesn't need anyone

tripping her," James added. "You tell us here, man-to-man, that you'll catch her if she slips? Well, welcome to the family, bro."

"I think you're misunderstanding the whole thing," Ethan said, his stomach turning itself over. He wasn't feeling hungry for waffles anymore. "We're still neighbors. Still friends," Ethan said. "She's only helping me out. I like her." Ethan stared at the uneaten portion of his waffle. "Like her, a lot. Wouldn't dream of…tripping her."

"Given the way she looked at you while you were braiding hair?" James made his eyes get big. "I'm thinkin' that's mutual. And I'm worried you've taken her way off course."

"I promise, it's not the case," Ethan assured.

"I give Em a heap of shit because that's what we do," James said. "It's the way it's always been between us. But she's a good mom and a good person and she doesn't deserve to be dicked around by a guy braiding her kid's hair. You get me?"

Annie had messed up her braid, then Fiona asked for one, too. No one needed to rag on him for it.

"I get you," Ethan assured.

"Em's had a lot of letdown, lately. I'd appreciate it, if you watched yourself so you don't get added to the list of asses I have to kick," Lance said. This time he looked right at Ethan.

Ethan didn't want to be on the list. But he did feel… something last night. Things shifted inside him. A clock that hadn't ticked in a long time ticked and tocked in his chest. Figuratively, at least. Unfortunately, he wasn't sure himself if the game was still the same as yesterday.

He didn't bloody know.

But they hadn't changed the rules, so he had to stick with the original plan.

"We tripped her," James said.

That got Ethan's attention.

"When Em decided to go to art school. We tripped her. The whole bunch of us. Didn't want her to go," James continued.

"It wasn't a good look for us," Lance said.

"You made her question herself?" Ethan asked, but mostly pointed out.

Lance nodded, pursed his lips.

"Shame, mate, because she's got some serious skills," Ethan said with a nod. "I've seen her work and it's amazing. She should definitely keep creating without the hit to her confidence."

"For what it's worth," Lance said as his throat worked. "I believe you. I think you do care about my sister."

Well, that was progress, then.

"But the kids…" Lance tilted his head toward them. "I think they're getting the wrong impression."

"We've been upfront with the girls from the beginning," Ethan assured.

The last thing they wanted was to let them down.

"They're still pretty hopeful they'll get to be sisters," Jim added. "Something to keep in mind when you're done with this whole thing. It's more than just Em we're worrying over."

"That's good to know," Ethan said. He and Em could keep telling the kids this was all a ruse, but they saw their folks playing along and that had to give them a bit of hope.

Especially Annie, who was fair keen on having a real mum.

They'd need to be a bit more careful with that.

Chapter Twenty-Two
EMMALINE

PHOTO OF A GUY in a red tie selling insurance. Yup.

Point to the photo. Click the photo. Drag to the template. Release.

Confirm the spelling of his name.

Export to PDF.

Send to the guy in the red tie.

Photo of lady in a red blouse selling insurance. Yup.

Point to the photo. Click the photo. Drag to the template. Release.

Confirm the spelling of her name.

Export to PDF.

Send to the lady in the red blouse.

Emmaline rubbed at her eyes. Only twenty more to go.

This was a good stopping point. Then again, every spot in this job was a good stopping point. Ugh. She wanted to enjoy this so much more.

Like the time she saw *Phantom of the Opera* at The Buell? Everyone raved about it. Said it was the best thing ever. But she'd been recovering from the stomach flu and, honestly, she just wanted to vomit all over the chandelier when it fell on cue.

Fiona and Annie had started summer break at a day camp with their friend, Harmony. So even they couldn't keep her entertained in Em's downtime.

Of course, the girls still asked her to doodle a lot. She appreciated it. The mini-not-Ethan-chef series had also become her secret refuge, a place where her creative spirit could roam. The sterile font that seemed to dominate her work life didn't belong there.

In these stolen moments, she could breathe, she could dream, and her imagination could soar. Scribbling wasn't confined to uniformity in those moments.

Last week, she'd suggested matching a sans serif font for variety in one of the branding meetings, but the higher-ups at the insurance company shot that down faster than a Top Gun fighter pilot.

Given their unwillingness to consider another font choice, one could easily imagine how her suggestion of adding a pop of yellow to the tedious red color scheme went over.

She should go see what Ethan was up to. That was an acceptable thing for a counterfeit girlfriend, right? She was still sorting out the nuances of this artificial romance.

They'd agreed to keep a good distance when the girls were around, so they wouldn't get their hopes up any further.

But…the girls weren't there, and seeing Ethan sounded like way more fun than her alternate project of futzing with Abraham Maldonado-Fumagalli's photo so his entire face would fit in the little box, and his name would fit on the billboard.

There was no reason she couldn't head on over and say hello while she still could.

Thinking anything about the upcoming ending of their shebang made her feel as though Cress had dumped a can of frozen orange juice in her stomach.

Her brain actually hurt from staring at the screen for so long. An aching pulse that only going outside and getting an Ethan friends-with-benefits hit could fix.

So she'd do that.

She'd go outside.

What happened next? She'd just see what happened.

First things first: she checked in with the puppy and leashed him up to tag along. Good news, Sketch and Pepper actually liked each other. He didn't even try to eat her.

Sketch on the leash, she headed outside.

She had a relaxing space in the backyard, but she wandered down the sidewalk since Sketch needed a little walk, and she needed outside air and, well, this *was* the direction of Ethan's place.

They hadn't had any alone time in the past few days, so there hadn't been any more hanky-panky or crushing cookies, as Barbie said. Which was a complete bummer because she sort of wanted the hanky-panky part of their…whatever this was…to be a bigger part of…whatever this was.

She walked quickly up his front walk, Sketch trotting beside her, his little tail bopping with excitement at seeing Ethan.

Or Pepper.

Anyway, she lifted her hand to knock.

No answer.

She sighed. Glanced to Sketch as he sat staring up at her like she was the one who had to solve this problem all by her lonesome.

She rang the bell this time.

Nothing.

Dang. She deflated a little, standing there on Ethan's stoop.

She could text him. He'd been responding to her messages. So she could do that. And say what? "I'm here for my booty call."

She was a woman. A woman who had been through quite the drought downstairs, and Ethan was a talented man who had showed her what she was missing. Now she was missing it even more because she knew what she was missing.

Okay, this was silly. She had twenty more drag-and-drops to finish. She'd just head home and do that instead.

"C'mon, Sketch." They made it all the way to the sidewalk when Ethan's door opened.

"Em?" he asked.

She turned. While he was fully clothed, he had wet hair and… Okay, so it'd been a late shower for him.

"You were in the shower," she said, as though this wasn't already obvious. Not that she had any place to judge there. Sometimes she didn't even get in a shower every day, so…yup.

"You came by," he said this, and the way he said it all husky and rumbly made the little hairs on her arms perk up and stand at attention.

"Hi." She did a quick walk to him. "I needed a break. I thought I'd say hi since I've already done sixty business cards and the Abraham Maldonado-Fumagalli project isn't going to be fun. I mean, would it kill the photographer to get a bit more perspective and more of his head in the image?"

Ethan looked at her kind of funny.

"I wanted to see you. In person. Right here." Okay, she could be so much smoother than this.

He nodded. Scratched at his neck. Grinned a little. "I'm glad you're here."

See? He was so smooth. Why couldn't she be smooth like that?

"Come inside?" he asked low and husky and freshly showered.

Oh, yes puh-lease.

She nodded. "Thanks."

Following him inside, she stepped around Pepper and into the foyer. "I hope it's okay Sketch came, too."

"I'll lock up my laundry." He stood with his hands looped around the drawstring waist of his athletic pants.

"I've been thinking about something." She followed him farther into the room.

"Yeah?"

"Maybe we should have a schedule," she said, unclipping Sketch's leash. "I mean, I guess since we're doing this, maybe we should be organized."

He grinned a slow grin. "Organized?"

Sketch and Pepper were done with their initial sniffs of hello and just went at it, playing like they'd been deprived of time together for more than a day.

Maybe they were onto something?

She stepped forward. Totally normal. Reached her hand to his chest because she could and that was allowed.

He glanced down at her hand on his chest, a question clearly forming in his expression.

Instead of doing what she told her brain to do—which was to remove her hand—she gripped the fabric and pulled him two steps to fill the gap between their bodies.

And then she went in for it. Went for him. Let all the frustration and inability to be breezy just go. Let her mouth talk for her without words, and her tongue do that thing that made him moan.

Good news, he seemed to have missed this, too. Because he was all about the kissing and the touching. Things were…uh…frantic.

"Upstairs?" he asked, unfortunately having to pull his mouth from hers long enough to speak.

Well, the front door was locked, and the girls were at camp. One of the other moms was on slate to pick them up.

Maybe this time they should actually try to make it to a bed? That would be more comfortable than the sofa.

Ethan tethered them together with their hands linked and showed her the way. Second door on the right was his. He hadn't made his bed that morning, which wasn't a big deal for her because she didn't always make hers, either. Seeing his bed a mess and his nightstand cluttered with books, he wasn't Ethan Greene, the famous television chef. This was Ethan, her fakey-fake boyfriend with benefits.

He did the neck and jaw thing again, and oh boy, that worked.

She kicked up on her toes and planted a kiss on his mouth, the kiss a grown-up woman gave her grown-up pretend boyfriend in his bedroom.

He continued kissing the thoughts right out of her head, moving her to the bed and placing her there.

Then he went to the window and sealed the curtains. The bedroom door and closed it.

He turned to her and held her gaze with his as he pulled his shirt over his head, revealing his abs and biceps and oh, that landscape of tattooed clouds and waves.

She wanted to trace the ink with her fingertip. Follow the lines of the artist.

Striding to the bed, he crawled in alongside her, laying his hand against her thigh so everything inside her buzzed with heady awareness.

The intricate ink along his biceps wound around, up and over his shoulder to his neck. She traced it with her mouth, her lips parted as she followed the lines of artistry. He leaned back on the bed and let her do her thing, his erection clear—pressing through his pants.

She straddled him, right so her intimate place was against his.

Who am I?

Whoever she was, she liked it.

He groaned and, honestly, so did she. The hard length of him an enormous distraction, but one she wasn't about to succumb to, yet.

Instead she studied his ink, traced it like she wanted.

"You like ink?" he asked.

She leaned back so his hard length was more aligned with her core and studied the canvas of him.

"Uh-huh." She traced along the edges, pausing only briefly at his nipple where it pebbled under her touch.

His hands were on her hips, and he was totally rubbing against her in a way that felt deliciously divine.

She let her head fall back a little because he'd found her sweet spot with his thumb, and they practically had sex right there between their clothes.

Okay, enough was enough of that.

She moved from him. It took a whole lotta effort, but she did it and pulled off her shorts and her top. She wasn't smooth or breezy, but she got her big-girl panties off and barely got her bra unclasped before he finished shucking his pants and boxers.

Now, with all that nonsense out of the way, they could have some real fun.

"Condom?" she asked.

He lifted his eyebrows like he wasn't entirely sure they

were at the condom stage of the event, but she had some ideas and they required she not have any surprises after.

"If you're sure you're ready." He reached to his nightstand, removing a fresh box of Trojans, and cracking the seal before pulling out a foil packet.

He held it between his index and middle finger.

She reached for it, opened the seal, and—she could do this, it'd been a while since she needed to, but it's like riding a bike, right?

"I think I remember how to do this," she said to herself, and to him, and to the condom. "Tell me if I get it wrong?"

He nodded. "'Course."

Carefully, she covered him with the latex. Giving an extra tug at the root when his dick jumped in her hand.

"That is delightfully empowering," she said, glancing to the smirk on his face.

"By all means, keep empowering yourself," he suggested. "I'm enjoying it quite a lot."

Then she took control and straddled him, letting him fill her and take control of the moment.

"You okay, love?" he asked as she sheathed him slowly with her body.

"You're not small," she said as she adjusted herself over him.

"Can't do much about that, I'm afraid," he replied and then hissed as his eyes seemed to roll back in his head.

Ethan wasn't small, and thankfully she was super turned on, because she was ready to take him in all the way.

That settled, her body filled with his, she went back to the ink, this time tracing it with her tongue and riding him all at the same time.

"Bloody hell," he said as his hands fell to her waist, and he moaned.

"Noises like these are exactly what I need in my day," she said as she rocked forward.

Funny thing, she gasped as he rolled his hips up into her and found the bundle of nerves with his thumb again.

"You are so pretty," he said, as he took control. "I've been waiting for this. I need you, Em. So, so badly."

Now she couldn't focus on the ink because he was the one taking her for a ride. Bucking up and gently coming down.

"You are so strong. So pretty, love," he continued.

And then the heavy lids of his eyes opened all the way, and he stared right at her.

It wasn't the thumb or the sex or the words… He saw her and she…

"Ethan," she said his name as she came, falling forward to his chest because there was no way she could sit up through that intensity. Ethan didn't even pause after he just lazily moved in and out of her body, continuing to whisper over and over, "You feel so good, Em."

He kept saying her name, and honestly, she'd never been with a talker before. But there was so much to be said about the reassurance when she was at her most vulnerable.

He built her up again, and she came once more before he followed, gripping her against him and making it clear that she was the one he was with.

"Em," he murmured. "So good, love. So good."

The one he wanted to be with. With his words and his body, he made that epically clear.

Breathing hard, he rolled her to her side, pulling himself from her body and kissing the end of her nose.

"Thank you," he said as he pulled away.

"Thank you?" she asked.

"For letting go with me." He traced her lips with his thumb before he rose and strode to the en suite and handled all the things that needed handling.

She pulled the sheet up and over herself because she might be ready to trace his ink with her tongue, and ride him like a bull, and even call him her boyfriend and not get sick over it. But she wasn't entirely ready to be so brazen as to just hang out naked with the man.

He, apparently, had no problem with this. Because he sauntered out of the bathroom, climbing into bed beside her and kissing her again. Not like it was leading anywhere, just because he wanted to, and he could.

That was…rather real.

And that's when things got dicey because the front door chime rang. Ethan's expression turned horrified, and there were footsteps in the foyer. Lots of footsteps.

"Oh my God," Emmaline whispered. "How long were we up here?"

"Ethan?" Harmony's mom, April, hollered. "It's Wednesday. Camp gets out early on Wednesday. Did you forget?"

Oh, dear God.

"Why's Sketch here?" That would be Fiona. Her Fiona. Sketch yelped in his way of saying hello.

And the dog was there because mommy was having a booty call.

"Dad?" Annie called.

"Oh my God." This Emmaline said out loud. Not even quiet.

If they were trying to keep things simple and easy for the girls, this was not the way to do it.

"Dad, where are you?" Annie yelled. "Is Em with you? Dad?"

"Hey," April said super loud. "Looks like your dad's not available, *Annie*. I bet he's with your mom, *Fiona*." Apparently, she'd put two and two together, which wasn't too hard given Sketch's presence and the locked front door. "Let's go to Fiona's house and wait for them." Again, she said this entirely louder than necessary. "But I hope they hurry because Harmony has ballet in thirty minutes."

"Why are you yelling like that?" Harmony asked. "Sketch doesn't care they're not here. Moms are so weird."

"I'm not yelling," April countered, still totally yelling.

"Oh my God." Emmaline covered her face with her hands. They were the only words that seemed to work for her right now. Just going on repeat in her brain and right out of her mouth.

"Emmaline," Ethan said, holding her face between his palms. "Take a breath."

Nope, that was a bad idea because she'd just nearly gotten caught naked in his bed. Best to go right on and pass out from lack of oxygen. That was the easier option.

Chapter Twenty-Three
ETHAN

THIS SITUATION WASN'T IDEAL.

Ethan got that. He wasn't a complete idiot.

"They're going to figure it out," Em whispered. But at least she was breathing again.

Em had gone from gobsmacked to dead-set terrified. Honestly, she was sort of cute when she was naked and holding on to him like this, but he would not say a peep about it because he was also naked and his crown jewels were right out there for the squeezing.

There were lots of things he figured out in the few minutes spaced between the kids coming home early and the current bout of Emmaline's panic.

He'd considered perhaps they drop the fake, pretend, and imitation part of their titles. Give it a go? He could be upfront about what he could and couldn't give. They could move forward with a new understanding.

They'd take baby steps toward a potential future. He could be gentle with Em and with Annie. Understanding that Em didn't want to mess up the future she'd started and spent heaps of time preparing, and that Annie had a load of baggage when it came to mum figures. Annie could help Fiona as much as Fiona helped Annie.

He'd be honest with Em about not having much time to spare for her.

"Em…" He said her name, trying to get her to refocus on him because her eyes were darting from one side to the other. She was overthinking the whole kit and caboodle.

He got it. Really, he did. Because at first, he'd felt a solid dose of that, too. Being butt arse naked in bed with his fake girlfriend slash daughter's best friend's mum? Yeah, not a good place to be found.

But once everyone left, his worries had eased a fair bit.

Meanwhile, Emmaline's went through the roof.

"Why is my dog here?" Em asked, her eyes still frantic. She gripped his shoulders and gave a little shake. "Ethan, we have to figure out why the dog's here."

"Em." He shifted so his body was right against hers, hoping the reassurance of his touch might help with the total meltdown she was having.

"The dog's here, and you're not and, presumably," she went on, working this out with words. He was cool with that because maybe she'd come up with a ripper solution for them.

"I'm not," she went on. "Because I didn't answer when they came in." She started talking with her hands, which was sort of a hazard, given how close he was. But, hey, now her eyeballs weren't darting around. This was a step up.

"April has it under control," he said. April was Jack's wife and mum to his step-kids, so she was good with finesse. "She *gets* it. If you get my meaning. She knows things happen." He gestured between them. "Things like this."

"Like I shirked my responsibilities to boi-i-ing you in the middle of the afternoon?"

Okay, for real, that was pretty damn cute.

"It's not even lunch," she wailed at this last line. "I hate Wednesdays. Nobody remembers it's Wednesday. Nothing happens on Wednesday. Except the kids get home early."

She was totally not herself, but her rant against Wednesday while naked in his bed was a total turn-on. Probably not her intention, so he'd stay quiet.

"What if I had accidentally cut off a toe or something?" She was actually serious.

Annnd that killed his mood. Also, he would not let her near his kitchen and the knives.

"I cut my toe because I'm me," she went on. "You had to drive me to the ER, and the dog got left to be watched by the kitten, and now they're reattaching my toe—a doctor, not the cat"—she held up her hands between them —"and everything's going to be fine because I had the best care. But that's why the dog's here, and we forgot it's Wednesday."

There were times a bloke knew when to step in and times when he understood it wasn't the go. This was a time to step in. Change tact.

"Your toe is fine," he assured. It'd stay all good, because he liked her with all her toes. If she were going to give up a digit—fictional or otherwise—then it should be for a better reason than they forgot about early knock-off from day camp.

"I'll just wear a bandage and limp for a few weeks?" She chewed on her bottom lip. That innocent expression while after that rant? He forced himself not to come onto her for a—how did she say?—boi-i-ing. Crush some cook-ies. Whatever.

No, he wouldn't because that would be inappropriate timing. However, the next time they got naked together, he was totally going to ask her to rant about the days of the week again.

"I have a plan," he said, hoping his assured confidence would catch her attention.

"Is it better than mine?" she asked.

Seeing as any plan was better than hers, he said, "Yeah."

Much better than missing toes.

"Okay, shoot." She made a *c'mon* motion with her hands.

"You had to go into the office to see your boss. I agreed to watch Sketch." He nodded as he spoke.

"That's it?" she asked.

"Yeah. That's it." Simple was good and required no doctor visits.

"You shirked your responsibilities?" she asked, clearly not buying it. "You weren't in here and you wouldn't do that."

"I ran up the street to talk to Mr. Davidson." See? Way better than losing a toe. "I shirked nothing. The dog and cat were fine for a time on their own. Just like they were fine while we..." He'd let that one sit there.

"Oh." She nodded. "I like that one. You're good at this."

"Good news." He leaned in and pressed a light kiss to her mouth. "Your meeting's over, and you're on your way home."

"I wonder what my meeting was about?" she asked, frowning.

"Probably that Abraham guy with the long last name." Seemed good to him.

She let out a long breath that sounded like she released the pressure valve on the Tower of Terror. "Okay. My meeting's over. We've got that sorted."

"Let's get dressed?" he asked.

She nodded.

"Would you and Fiona like to come over later for dinner?" He pulled away, moving from the bed to grab his boxers and his pants. "I'm thinking homemade chicken nuggets. Maybe a bottle of Pinot to go with them?"

"Oh wow. Yum." Em was back to herself, which was good. "But I think we should keep the distance thing going."

He'd thought that, too.

But after this romp? After she rode him into oblivion?

He didn't want to anymore.

She finished getting dressed, and he finished getting dressed, and everyone was finally wearing clothes. He lent her a comb because he'd messed up her hair and she looked proper disheveled.

"I'll go grab the girls so April can get Harmony to dance. I'll walk Fiona back and you can slip on home. That'll give you time to"—he gestured to her—"do whatever you need to do."

"You're good with plans, aren't you?" She smiled, and it reached her eyes. Then she leaned in and gave him a quick kiss.

He hoped so. There was still a lot he had to work out.

They headed downstairs, and as he put his foot on the landing, he stepped into the prickly reality.

The reality of their girls, Harmony, and April all looking right up at them from his living room.

April's eyes went extra wide. Same as he felt, really.

"Hey," Em said from behind him, all happy and what-are-you-doing-here cheeky.

"We came back for my better shoes," Annie said, eyeing Em carefully.

"I did my best," April said, flinching a little.

"Why is Sketch here?" Fiona asked. "Why are *you* here?"

"Oh…" Em was floundering. "Uh…"

"Why are you back so early?" he asked, glancing around conspicuously.

Yeah, he was going to play possum and pretend he knew nothing about anything.

"It's Wednesday," Annie said, hand on her hip, her eyes little slits, and her head tilted to the side.

"It's Wednesday. We got done early," Fiona said doing a pretty solid impression of Annie's expression. "We were just here. You didn't say hi."

Her child-approved bull dust detector pinged.

"Oh my gosh." Em made a very unrealistic snap motion with her hand and her elbow. "Wouldn't you know I got called into the office?" She licked at her lips. "And then I stubbed my toe." She pointed to her perfectly fine toe. "And then…"

"I was showing her the new rose bush I put in the backyard over the weekend. The one Annie picked out," he said. *Please work. Please work.*

"Is your toe okay?" Fiona asked, looking down at Emmaline's feet.

"Just a little broken. Totally fine. Toes break all the time. It's a tape-up-and-go kind of thing." Em made a *go, go, go* motion. Like this was a good thing. Though, given the alternative, it was. "I love the rose bush, though. We should buy one just like it."

"Mom?" Fiona frowned. "We have like three already."

"Oh, right?" She gritted her teeth so hard Ethan practically heard her dental bill going up. "I meant—"

"She means the same one, like we got, so they'll grow at the same speed." No one could say he wasn't trying. "That way you'll have best friend rose bushes."

"Can we get one for Harmony, too?" Fiona's eyes brightened.

"Of course." Em gave a laugh that was not at all convincing and even made him uncomfortable. "Everyone gets rose bushes." Em scratched behind her ear. "Let's go home, yeah?"

Annie shook her head. "I looked in the backyard. You weren't there."

"That's probably when I was at the doctor, getting my toe taped up." Em scratched at her neck again. Turned out, when Em wasn't telling the entire truth, she scratched at her collarbone a bunch.

"I don't see any tape." Annie was a bloodhound on the hunt for truth and he should take notes for when she was a teenager and he needed to quiz her.

"It's clear tape," Em said. "Everything's good now. And we're heading home."

"We've gotta jet," April announced, clearly ready to escape. They did the goodbye schtick and then Fiona and Em went home with Sketch, too.

Annie gave him some odd looks as she stalked up to her room. Side-eye, like she wasn't buying anything he was selling.

"Em is a really nice person," she said, carefully. "And she likes you."

"She's a great friend," he agreed.

Unfortunately, he wasn't sure that's what he wanted anymore. And that stuck like a toothpick in his ticker.

Chapter Twenty-Four
EMMALINE

"I'LL GET IT," Fiona announced, bouncing from Em's bed, eager to get downstairs and greet Ethan.

Annie and Fiona had helped her curl the heck out of her hair. With their encouragement, she elected to wear it down for the wedding event and embraced the fact that she sort of resembled Medusa with all the curls.

Em was all dressed up in her little blue dress, accented with pink heels. She'd tossed a towel around her shoulders while Annie worked her preteen magic on Em's makeup.

Fiona helped with the 'fit. Annie helped with the glitz.

This was fine, everything was fine. She and Ethan had agreed that this entanglement would be done after they attended the wedding and reception. They could both move along with their lives as nothing but friendly neighbors with best friend kids.

That day? The wedding day? That was today.

Tomorrow was not about them, but today could be.

Today *would* be.

Em didn't really want their entanglement to end.

Which was probably the main reason why it had to be nixed. That was the rule. No attachments, no heartache. It was the perfect plan...at least in theory.

So she focused on the girls instead of the impending fake-but-felt-real breakup. The cherry on the crap sundae of the day was that weddings were *not* her favorite. She had the same visceral reaction to weddings as she did when Fiona popped homemade slime between her fingers.

Ack. That sound? No thank you.

Because in her experience nothing good happened at a wedding. (Like marrying Tony.) There were lots of weddings where good things happened, probably. Where the couple stayed happy.

Emmaline had to ditch the divorcee mentality. Her experience was not everyone's. Her hurt was not the norm. Her marriage was not the status quo.

So good for her for facing this straight on, changing her perspective, and powering right on through.

Also, there would be an open bar. So...Emmaline was headed to the wedding. Her semi-secret boyfriend had ordered a limo to take them up the mountain.

Emmaline was meh about it. Limos weren't her favorite. She'd lived, and left, that life.

But today, the excitement of the girls was well worth the price of admission. They were both helping her get ready. Annie was in charge of picking the perfect shade of lipstick and Fiona played shoe stylist.

"Okay, open," Annie said, brandishing the lipstick tube.

Em did as instructed, trying not to flinch as Annie went to work. Annie took her lipstick application very seriously. Her little forehead scrunched up in concentration.

"All done," she declared triumphantly.

Em took a look in the hand mirror. She couldn't have done a better job herself.

"You're really good at this," she said.

Annie practically beamed. She was definitely a kid who thrived on compliments and helping out. Em loved having her around. Annie was a fantastic friend to Fiona—always there for her. And even Em had found that Annie wiggled right inside of her heart.

Em had become attached.

Plus, there was the added benefit of spending time with Ethan...and all the, uh, *perks* that came with that.

But it wasn't just about the physical stuff—

Ethan cleared his throat at the door to her bedroom.

Annie turned to him, a mischievous grin spreading across her face. Without a word, she hurried down the hall to the staircase, her feet thudding against the hardwood as she rushed away.

Em glanced from the mirror to Ethan and immediately appreciated the view. He'd gone with a tailored gray suit, black shirt, and matching tie with polished wingtips.

Her breath caught in her chest.

The look of Ethan in that suit? *Oh, my, my, my.*

Dang, but he looked good enough to lick.

She said the first thing that came to her mind: "Hi."

"Hi," he replied, using his bedroom voice and his bedroom eyes and that little husky note he only tuned into when he dirty talked to her while they were...you know.

He said "hi" so much better than she did.

Ethan lingered in the doorway. Likely because they avoided being in the same space with a bed whenever the kids were nearby because they tended to just, uh, go at it.

Even with the distance between them, he wasn't subtle about the eye caress over her body, specifically pausing at her cleavage. Oh, yes. His gaze roamed over her, leaving a mess of pins and needles in its path.

Not that she was all into her appearance, but she looked *good* today. Thanks to Annie, she'd taken extra care with her makeup. Her sheath dress was a midnight shade of blue with a hem that hit at her knee. The color sort of reminded her of the dark sky at night when the moon was full. There was even a silver sheen to the fabric reminiscent of stars.

This was not a dress a girl who faded into the wallpaper wore. In other words, Tony would've hated it.

Ethan's gaze warmed as his eyes met hers once again, and she got more tingles. They should've been way past the tingles stage. But they still ran rampant whenever he gave her *that* look.

The one, right there, like he wanted to kiss her but wouldn't because they weren't alone in the house.

"Dad brought you a gift," Annie announced, red cheeked and running through the door with Fiona at her heels, also out of breath.

They both practically skidded to a halt.

"I did?" Ethan asked.

"Dad," Annie chided and shoved the box in Ethan's hands. The box was small, about the size of a deck of cards, and covered in yellow fabric that had been hot glued on.

Annie mouthed something to her dad and Ethan looked absolutely confused. She mouthed something else.

"Oh, right. Right." Ethan took the box and handed it to Em, their fingers brushing only the slightest.

She lifted the lid. Inside were four friendship bracelets just like the one she'd rescued from the gutter for the girls. The beads spelled out each of their names. *Ethan. Emmaline. Annie. Fiona.*

"Dad helped make these," Annie announced with pride that radiated all through her smile.

"Uh…" Ethan gave Annie a funny look. "Yes."

"This is cute." Em traced along the beads that spelled out her name. "Sweet."

The bracelets all looked the same except for the names being different—a matched set.

This was…

Huh.

"They're… bracelets." Ethan ran his teeth along his bottom lip. "Huh."

Well, with a glowing declaration like that, she would definitely *not* read too far into things.

"Yoo hoo, hello," Barbie called from downstairs. "The babysitter has arrived."

Barbie agreed to hang out with Sketch and the girls until Em and Ethan got back late.

"Hey, Barbie," Em called back, setting the box of bracelets on the dresser and trotting down the steps. "Ethan's already here with Annie."

They all followed behind her.

Barbie plastered on the smile whenever Em mentioned Ethan. Barbie wasn't dense. She knew exactly what was going on with Ethan and Emmaline's continued cookie-smashing game. Honestly, she probably figured it out a full week before it occurred.

Em just rolled her eyes.

"The girls know the rules." Emmaline was already putting on her jacket.

Ethan pulled Annie aside, and Fiona ran upstairs to get board games for the sleepover.

"You're terrified," Barbie said, getting closer so that only Emmaline could hear. "I can smell it."

"What does terrified smell like?" Em asked.

"You. Right now." Barbie wiggled her eyebrows.

"Well, you know, this is it. The end. Close the book." Em deflated at the thought. "I suppose a wedding is an excellent place for not-so-happy endings."

"Do you remember what I told you at your wedding?" Barbie asked.

Emmaline had been trying extremely hard to forget about that day, but she remembered what Barbie said before heading down the aisle.

"Weddings are not only beginnings. Sometimes, they're smack in the middle. Often, they're more at the end. The thing is, no one knows," Em repeated back to Barbie what she'd said all those years ago.

"Always be open to the unexpected, and you may find that life surprises you in the best possible way," Barbie added.

A little of the heavy lifted from Em's shoulders.

"And the last part?" Barbie made a *c'mon* motion with her hands.

"It's important that you enjoy the day, since it's a party," Em finished.

Barbie smiled hugely. "I *knew* you'd remember."

"You know." Emmaline grabbed her handbag. "Some friends might have talked about how a wedding is the beginning of the rest of your life."

"Those friends would be wrong. They never met Tony, for one." Barbie flattened her lips into a line. "Also, the wedding is only a party. The marriage is the part that you've got to worry about." Barbie reached for Em's hand and did a shimmy shake. "The point is, today you get to enjoy the party."

On that note, they did the goodbye schtick and headed to the waiting limo.

Em climbed in first. Then Ethan.

The interior running lights of the limo danced in a vibrant display of red, blue, and yellow, their LED hues interchanging as if they were en route to a pulsating night-club rather than a wedding. Meanwhile, outside, a drizzle began to form, its tiny droplets peppering the windows. This was no torrential downpour, but rather a subtle reminder that the world beyond remained beyond their control.

Ethan rolled up the divider between the back and the front so it was only the two of them.

His arm came around her shoulder and he tenderly traced the curls along her neckline, gently wrapping them around his fingertip before letting them fall back to the cascade of her spirals. The whole style would likely be wrecked if he continued with that, but it felt beyond nice, so she was not going to say a peep.

Then he kissed her, but he didn't take it further like he usually did. Instead, his eyes grew even warmer in a way she didn't know was really possible.

"I care about you a lot, Em," Ethan whispered the words, husky, and in such a way they seemed to brush against her skin.

She leaned into him and said softly, "This is how we end it, then? Caring about each other?"

He cleared his throat. "And if we didn't? End it?"

Then that would be dangerous for her heart.

"I'm falling into a whole lot of like with you," she admitted.

She swallowed because this was a gigantic step for her. Admission that he meant more than she'd been willing to acknowledge. "What I mean is—"

"I know what you mean." He pinned her with his gaze, held her in the warmth of them. "I know. Same."

Her cheeks got a little hotter at that acknowledgement because she absolutely believed him.

"What does this mean, then?" she asked.

He wasn't like the others she'd rubbed elbows with. He was really just Ethan from up the street, nothing more. Which made him everything.

His expression relaxed. His shoulders seemed to hold less tension, and his hands fell to her waist. "We keep on."

That declaration made her heart *thu-thunk* more quickly against her ribs.

She reached for his hand for reassurance because this was a big ask. Then she lifted her mouth again to his ear, and intimately asked, in a barely there, whisper, "Keep on?"

There were butterflies now in her stomach. A whole heap of them fluttering around so much it made her dizzy.

"We make a good pair," he said. "I mean, why not?"

"Why not?" She let out a long breath. "And the girls?"

"I have a feeling they've been playing a bit of match-maker of late." He pursed his lips. "With bracelets and such."

"Yeah." She pursed her lips.

"We include them in the change of plans," he said. "So they are part of this. They're kids, but they're smart and we'll all figure things out together."

"If there's an ending in the future, we have to protect them from that," she said.

"I agree. Without question. We'll protect them together. Even if we aren't together."

She scowled. "You're so not normal. But you are Ethan from up the street, and I'm kind of glad you aren't a plumber."

"I doubt the food would be as good." He touched her

jaw with his forefinger before tilting her chin up and letting that pull between them do its thing.

Then he kissed her, light on the mouth. Nothing too much, but enough to make his point that they were together, and tonight was a beginning. Not an ending.

Besides, they were headed to a wedding.

Time for a celebration of what could be.

Chapter Twenty-Five
EMMALINE

EMMALINE STILLED at the arch of flowers leading to the massive room with chairs lined on both sides of an aisle. The venue had been turned into a showstopper. The florist decorated with subtle grays and white, accented by cream gardenias, lemon leaves, and purple flowers of some kind.

The long hall with the rugged wood floor contrasted the elegant flower arrangements. The ceiling seemed to reach up, with magnificent beams holding the whole structure together.

"This is gorgeous," Em whispered, taking it all in as they moved near a table of appetizers. Little finger food bites in an array of colors and, probably, flavors.

Ethan seemed distracted. Seemed to be searching for *someone*. That someone not being her.

Her breath caught, and she went a little numb, as a memory of another time, with another man, in another life came to mind. A life where she came to events just like this and stood alone in the corner clutching a plate of food she probably wouldn't eat. No one to talk to.

She reached for Ethan's hand as a touchstone, tracing

her thumb where the sleeve tattoo smooched the cotton fabric.

"How do you know them?" Em asked, as they walked under the arch. No one was sitting yet; everyone was up talking and passing around champagne.

"Who?" he asked.

"The bride and the groom?"

"Actually, I don't." He lifted a shoulder.

"You don't know either of them?" That was super odd. Why the heck were they there, then?

Ethan had a particular look she'd seen before.

That was the look of a man with an ulterior motive.

Her mom radar pinged, and it was a good thing she wasn't on his jury because she'd definitely have predisposed ideas.

"I got invited here to do some networking," he admitted.

"That is my least favorite thing about events like this." Em grimaced. She hated the small talk part—probably why she had that tendency to fade into the background.

A man across the room waved to Ethan. Ethan waved back.

"I'm going to stay here if you want to schmooze," Em said, giving him a little nudge.

Ethan studied her for a moment. "Back in a sec then, yeah?"

She nodded, separating their hands so he could hoof it over to the guy on the other side of the flower arch.

Em was pretty sure the guy was also a Nosh celebrity, but since she didn't watch the network much, she couldn't put her finger on which show was his.

She tilted her head to the side, trying to place him but came up blank. She scanned the rest of the room, and surprise of surprises, she actually recognized some of the attendees from her previous life. They didn't seem to recognize her, though. At least there was no acknowledgement or that spark of recognition when you see someone after a long period away.

That stung quite a bit. But no one really remembered the wallpaper, did they?

"Sorry," a woman said, as Em stepped back to let her through the mass of people. Em's back hit the wall with the movement.

Staying over here was a mistake. She should've gone with Ethan. That was the more normal thing to do, anyway. She swallowed and searched the room for him, but didn't see him anywhere.

Damn.

But if there was one thing that wasn't going to happen again, it was her being pushed against the wall.

She channeled Barbie and stepped right into the fray. She searched for someone she might know or anyone who seemed kind enough to chat with.

"Emmaline?" She'd recognize that voice anywhere.

She pressed her lips together in a wide grin as she turned toward the sound. "Hey, Dr. Paul. What are you doing here?"

He laughed a hearty laugh. "I was about to ask you the same thing. Imagine finding you here."

Dr. Paul was a plastic surgeon from Beverly Hills. He may have spent his days nipping and tucking, but he himself seemed to be aging without assistance. The deep creases in his forehead and the laugh lines around his eyes were deeper since she last saw him.

"I'm not really sure what I'm doing here," she said. "My date seems to have disappeared."

"How do you know the happy couple?" he asked, slipping her a champagne flute before taking a sip of his own.

"I actually don't," she said with a shrug. "I'm here as a plus-one."

"Ah. And how does he know them?"

"Funny story," she said with a chuckle. "I have no idea."

"I love funny stories," he said. "The groom's my nephew. His dad runs the New York Nosh offices."

Ah, yes, that would be the networking portion. She white-knuckled her purse, forced herself to relax.

"I'm so pleased to run into you here. I've been trying to get Tony to connect us, but he's been a busy guy."

Oh, she'd just bet.

"Do you remember that holiday party when you sketched out those scenes for Brody?" Dr. Paul asked, looking at her like she was definitely seen.

Of course she did. "Yes."

Brody was his grandkid and totally bored at that event. He and Em drafted an entire story on the back of napkins. Brody gave the text; she drew the drawings.

"I still have those napkins you drew on," he said. "We bring them out every December. It's tradition now."

A fizzy buzz of excitement took hold. She let it, this time. "I love that."

Loved that something she'd been part of was a tradition in their family.

"I wanted to connect about possibly publishing the story through Bubbly Press someday," Dr. Paul mused. "One of the editors did the holidays with us and loved them. He mentions it every now and again."

"That's amazing." Em took a sip of champagne, happy as all heck with how this was going. "I'm on board with that. Let's do it."

"The illustrations are fabulous." Dr. Paul gave her a side hug. But her brain had gone fuzzy.

A good start…
They're just scribbles.
They're only nonsense.
They're a part of me.
They're incredible.
They matter.
They're something special.
They're a part of me.

"Sorry," Ethan came beside her. "Had to have a chat with a bloke." He held his hand out to Dr. Paul. "Ethan Greene, and you are?"

Em slid out of the conversation. Her body still present, but her mind taking a break. It didn't matter, no one seemed to notice she'd checked out.

She glanced to her purse. Then to the champagne. She tossed it back in one gulp.

A good start…

"Chat soon, Em," Dr. Paul said, pulling her from her thoughts and patting her on the arm.

"Yeah. Soon," she replied.

"Can I get you another?" Ethan asked, holding another pre-wedding champagne flute to her.

Yes. But also, "Just this one. I've got to be able to stand later so we can dance."

That got her a half smile and an eye smolder. "Yeah, 'course."

She still took the offered flute, giving a little sip to the dry Brut she never really understood why anyone liked. Her preference in sparkling wine was a nice, sweet Prosecco. Something fizzy, but not harsh.

Ethan frowned, staring off in the distance.

"You okay?" Em asked, linking her arm with his.

He held the program for the ceremony in his other hand, tapping it against his thigh.

"Good. I'm good," he said. He pursed his lips like he wanted to say more, opened his mouth, but seemed to stop himself and closed it.

"Ethan?" Emmaline whispered. "Why are we here?"

"President of Nosh is gonna be here," he said. "I need to catch him. Make a pitch, you know?"

"Make a pitch? A pitch for what?"

"New show. They're considering bringing back the meatsicle. It just needs to be signed off by the higher-ups."

Em's heart beat slower. Like it was conserving energy because it understood soon it would be broken. They hadn't talked about his career or what role it played in their tentative bid at a future together.

If he was going to be famous again, that changed things. The little bit of hope he'd given in the car started to crumble.

"They'll film at the Denver restaurant, so I won't have to upend Annie," he said, the excitement in his tone palpable. "It's perfect. Just need that final okay."

His smile was everything. He wanted this. This was good for him. But then why hadn't he mentioned it?

Then again, why would he? She hadn't exactly been a real girlfriend he should confide in.

"You're going back to cooking on TV?" she asked, toying with the stem on her champagne flute.

"Nosh is going exclusive to one of the big streaming giants. This is a big hop for me." He still tapped the paper against his thighs. "Something that's important. I was gonna wait until I know more before I said anything, but you should know since you're here. You can be stoked, too."

Stoked? Not really. Not like he'd tossed a dessert in the Crock-Pot or whipped up a batch of homemade noodles. She *would* be excited about that.

Not this.

This left a metallic flavor on her tongue.

He wouldn't be her Ethan up the street anymore. He'd be back to Ethan Greene, celebrity chef, on television weekly, and all that entailed.

She brushed a curl away from her forehead, wishing they'd styled it up so her neck wouldn't be so sweaty.

Honestly, she couldn't have been more surprised if Ethan had leaned over, told her he had great news, and then sucker punched her in the stomach. Or if he'd invited Tony to come along to the wedding with them. Or if he'd shown up in a pink sequined suit to play matchy-match with Barbie.

He turned toward her, reaching for her free hand, stroking the fleshy part between her thumb and forefinger with his thumb. What a remarkably cozy feeling, if she wasn't experiencing an odd cold finger of dread along her spine.

"Where, uh, do Fiona and I fit in in all of this?" she asked, cautiously. "After everything we talked about in the car on the way here."

The air snapped and crackled between them. "We do our best, I think. That's all we can do, yeah? We keep on."

She nodded. "Of course, yes. I mean, you do have Annie, and she has to come first."

"And I'm working this angle on my career that's going to take loads of time for a bit. There will be events like this to attend. But I'll definitely need a date." He waggled his eyebrows like she would enjoy this.

Oh, dear hell. She would not.

Why did it feel like she was, once again, being side-lined? Relegated to the bits of time he had left in his day. She'd lived this life before. She'd left it behind.

She swallowed as her heart sort of stopped beating.

Painfully so. Like she was going to pass out and the relief of being unconscious might actually be welcome.

Things weren't always bad for her with the whole sideline thing. But when life soured with Tony, instead of fixing the recipe, she tried to enjoy lemons by themselves. That hadn't worked, and when she'd realized this, it was too late to fix things. Her ex got used to Em enjoying her citrus straight, and he wasn't willing to alter his reality for her.

She'd known better than to believe celebrity Ethan was different than all the others she'd known. There was a reason she'd always disappeared before—because she wasn't good enough on her own.

"Em." He touched her waist intimately, like they were a couple for public consumption.

She'd need to invest in a new selfie stick, and just hope she didn't burn anything down this time.

"You're going back," she confirmed. "To the life before."

He nodded. "It'll ensure Annie has a good college fund, and business at the restaurants will really skyrocket with the constant advertising."

A good start…

"I had this opportunity once." She gestured between them. "In California with Fiona's dad. I…uh…stopped chasing that dream," she said, calm and totally put together. "I stopped chasing it because it's not what I want."

She stared at him, her chest heaving, and she wasn't entirely certain which dream she was referring to in that second.

The dream about being an illustrator.

Or the dream that included him.

His expression fractured a smidge with each inhale and

exhale. "You don't want it, or you don't think you deserve it?"

"Ethan, you're here to go back to a place that I'm not willing to go to."

"Don't make this something it's not," he said, stepping into her space. "We're good together. That hasn't changed. We can still be that."

"You mean friends with benefits?" she asked, keeping her tone steady, even though she felt as though she'd been tossed to the ocean waves without a life jacket.

His eyebrows fell together. "If that's what you want to call it."

She didn't know what she wanted to call this thing between them. There wasn't a word for it, really.

"Ethan!" A guy came up behind them and smacked Ethan on the back. "I have been looking all over for you."

Ethan stared too long at Em.

"You've got about a three-minute window if you come with me now," the guy said, tilting his head back toward the arch. "Use it or lose it."

Ethan didn't move.

"Go on ahead," Em said, the words a tad too mechanical. "I'll find our seats."

"Hold tight," he said, reaching for her hands and squeezing. "I'll be done quick."

This was the point, actually. Wasn't it?

They were going in different directions.

She laughed a wry laugh because, yeah, nothing good happened at a wedding.

Chapter Twenty-Six
ETHAN

HE SHOULDN'T HAVE LEFT. Not with Em all out of whack. Worst of it was, he didn't even get to talk to the bloke. He'd come back just in time for the ceremony to start and she'd been quiet ever since. Too quiet.

He wanted to fix things with her. Apologize for walking away so abruptly when she needed him.

They couldn't just *not* talk about it. Could they? Then things would fester, and things shouldn't fester. You dealt with crap before it went totally sideways. That way you didn't burn it. You merely adjusted and tweaked the recipe a little.

He did want to understand why she wasn't seeing the bright side of the whole shebang, but he didn't get it. So they should talk.

He should start the convo.

Damn, but this was why food was so much less complicated than emotions.

The ceremony finished, he and Emmaline joined the queue for the buffet along one side of the room. Honestly, he hadn't expected a buffet. But it was the new trendy thing to do among those with extra cash.

This reception space had a rustic chic look most restaurant designers would've been stoked about. Dead-set trendy. Then there were tables set for the hundred or so guests. And along the other side of the room was a huge back-lit wall of Wild West snaps.

Of course, Ethan hadn't cooked the grub for the party, but given those involved with the shindig the chicken would not be dry and the prime rib carving station would be a fave. The roasted veggies would also be far superior to the usual steamed version at catered events like this, too. But now he wasn't even hungry.

Emmaline stood beside him. She'd clenched her jaw a fair bit since the ceremony. Wringing her hands. Pursing her lips. Generally, not looking his direction.

Ethan had stuffed it up. Clarity was a pain in the ass that way.

But he'd gotten antsy. He'd wanted this for himself. Reckoned it was a good thing for everyone. With a good career he could be a good provider and a good provider made a good boyfriend, didn't it?

The last thing he wanted was to hurt Em. He'd made promises to her dad and brothers that he wouldn't do that. But he didn't use his head and now she was hurting.

She turned, must've put on a brave face, because she laughed at something the lady in front of her said. All surface bulldust, for sure. Something had dimmed, and he hated he was responsible.

"I'm really sorry," he said with his plate in his hand and hardly anything on it. "I shouldn't have walked away in the midst of our talk. And I should've told you why I asked you here. I'm nervous it might not work out, so I didn't say anything."

She nodded in reply, but said nothing.

Regret was such a dick.

"No," she finally said. Her jaw worked. "We, um…we had an agreement, and it wasn't like I was a real girlfriend. You have every right to do what you want to do with your career. I hope it makes you happy, Ethan. I really do."

"You make me happy, too, Em." He said it. He meant it.

She shook her head, still focused on the line ahead. "That's not fair."

He touched her elbow, gently, being cautious as a bloke should be when he found himself ready to hand over his ticker to a woman. "What's unfair?"

"We cannot argue while you're in a suit like that. With that accent and that hair…it's not fair," she said, this time with a huff.

He moved forward into her space, his chest brushing against her back.

"Nothing's changed for us. I still want to be with you." Ethan said it because it needed to be said.

"But I don't want this life," she countered, firmly. "I'm sorry. I can't do this life again. I knew that up front, that's why you were a safe bet. And now…"

This was a right kick in the gut.

Then her expression changed, softened, and hardened at the same time. "I can't do it again, Ethan. I just can't."

"What did you want from me, then?" he asked, already hating the answer. "When we talked in the car about making this thing between us stick?"

"All I wanted was you." She lifted her hand to gesture at him, then dropped it. "Just you. Ethan up the street. I guess I forgot who you are for a second. I'm so sorry."

That took his breath away, because when was the last

time anyone wanted just him? It'd been a while. That was for sure.

Emmaline gently chucked a roll on the side of her plate before shaking her head and heading to table ten. The one with their names on the cards.

He kept his gaze on her for as long as he could muster the strength.

Three steps, and she said nothing. Didn't look back.

Four steps, and he said nothing. Didn't move.

No one said anything, even as she sat, chucked that mask over her face—the one that said everything's hunky dory—and talked with the lady next to her like they were best friends.

Meanwhile, Ethan stood like a loser, a poser, holding on to his dinner, unsure if he was invited to go to the table with her or if he should sit in the naughty corner.

"Ethan Greene." Andrew Reynolds, head of Nosh, stepped right up to him. "Glad you could make it."

Andrew was about Ethan's age, and he was the guy who could make this happen for him. But, now Ethan was a wreck of confusion with everything.

Still, Ethan held his free hand out for a shake, even if his heart wasn't in it.

"You're a hard bloke to pin down," Ethan said.

Andrew half grinned. "I hear you want to come back to Nosh?"

"I do." Now he was conflicted, but *this* was the dream. "If you'll have me back. Things are calmer now on the homefront with Annie. I can give you my all."

When he'd left the first time, it'd been an absolute wreck.

"You are a family man now." Andrew clapped him on the back. "Always impressive."

"Indeed," Ethan said.

They went over the specifics of Ethan's pitch for his show.

"I think we can make that happen." Andrew surveyed the room, clearly searching for something or someone. "Let's *make* it happen."

Ethan should've been over the moon, but he wasn't feeling much of anything. He couldn't give up on his dream, but somewhere along the line it seemed his ticker had given itself to Em.

"Love the social media hashtag campaign," Andrew said. "Excellent attention-getter. And Em's the perfect plus-one, isn't she? Maybe she can pop into the restaurant sometime with the kids when you're filming. Give the whole family-appeal angle." Andrew was on a roll. "And when you get married, we can do a whole Nosh wedding. Really do it up. Program development likes you, Ethan. They love the blended family thing. We should roll with it."

He held his hand to Ethan, and they shook again.

"What if, uh, Em and the kids don't want to be on the telly?" he asked.

Andrew laughed as though this was the funniest joke he'd heard. Then he pointed imitation finger guns at Ethan. "Good one."

Righto, so that was part of the deal. Resigned, Ethan headed for the table with Em, unsure of anything.

"Nosh is looking like a go?" she asked, buttering her roll.

He wasn't so sure anymore. "I've been trying to get back in their good graces for years."

He should mention the terms Andrew just laid out.

"Ethan…" Em said.

"Let's eat." He tried to be charming, but he missed the mark.

She said his name softer. "Ethan…"

"Not a big deal." He forked some veggies. Then set down the fork without even trying to eat. "Will you have a dance with me?" he asked, standing and holding his hand to Em. "I mean, would you like to dance?"

She nodded. Not excitedly, mind you. And that did nothing to help his bruised pride one bit. But she gripped his palm with hers, and that touch held the hope he needed.

She stood and, secured together, they wound through the tables to the dance floor. She moved with him, off the wood grain floor, to the sealed concrete.

Glancing up, her gaze knotted with his and the string between them cinched, pulling their bodies together to slow dance. Nothing intrusive, a light brush of body against body as the band played Harry Connick Jr.'s "(I Do) Like We Do."

There was an appropriate amount of dance floor space between them, but he appreciated the way she held on. Didn't push him away. Not indecent, but not the way a woman danced with a guy she was into.

"Thank you," he said.

"For what?" she asked, taken aback.

"For being here with me."

She gripped his shoulders. "We need to call it quits when we get home—"

"They want you to be with me," he said. "The people at Nosh. It's a package deal, it seems. They want you to be the angle. You and the kiddos. I'm the family man chef. That's how they want to play it."

She tensed, stopped moving her feet, and dropped her arms from his shoulders.

"Are you asking me to do that?" She didn't stomp on his shoes, so that was definitely something.

"Tellin' you what they told me, is all." There wasn't

even an ounce of hope she'd play along. "I wouldn't let *them* push you to the side, if you're worryin' about that part."

She stiffened. Her face paled a little. "You can't promise that. I've lived in this world. I know how it works. I can't do it again."

"You haven't done it like this. Not with me." Ethan squeezed her arm. "Your bad experience isn't the only way. *We* can make this work."

"Friends with benefits, though? That's what you called us."

"Em, you said that's what you wanted." He nodded as he spoke, holding her closer. "Did I misunderstand?"

They said nothing for a beat before he had to get it out. Had to say what needed to be said. She leaned into him, hanging on as he turned them. Letting him lead and following his direction.

He wouldn't lead her off course. That's a promise he made to himself.

He moved his lips to her forehead and pressed a kiss there. It wasn't so somebody would take a pic and post it. It was authentic.

Nothing outrageous, but hopefully it did broadcast his sincerity. This was more than just the two of them.

This was more.

This was about a future.

"I'm falling into a whole lot of like with you, Em." His voice was rough as he spoke. He hadn't meant for that to happen. He'd wanted the words to be strong, firm, and everything he desired to be for her.

"I'm sorry," she murmured, but she didn't release her grip.

The words were not good.

"For what?" he asked, hoping this was something he could fix.

"That this is ending," she said, tilting her head to the right as she looked up under her eyelashes.

He nodded. This was a right bloody mess.

"I don't want to live this life anymore," she said. "I don't want to go backwards. So, I guess it's back to the original plan. It's time."

His heart genuinely hurt with her words.

Ethan cleared his throat.

She seemed to argue about something in her own head. He didn't totally dig that because it probably wouldn't bode well for him.

"I don't like this." She shook her head. "The maneuvering. That's why I got away from it. Why I came to Denver."

"Em, don't make this something it's not." He pulled her closer and held on.

But that's when she let go.

Chapter Twenty-Seven
EMMALINE

"YOU LOOK like somebody peed in your champagne, girlfriend," Barbie said from Em's sofa, Sketch cuddled right up against her. With more fabric again in his mouth… Damn, Em was going to need new socks it looked like. Annie and Fiona watched a movie in sleeping bags on the floor, surrounded by loads of pillows.

"How was the party?" Barbie asked, clicking off the television.

Well…

Emmaline blew out a breath between her lips.

"Let's head out, Annie," Ethan said, and he sounded like she felt.

"It's still early," Annie pointed out, sharing a panicked glance with Fiona.

They had left the reception early. Early enough so it was only starting to get dark outside.

This whole fiasco was a huge mistake. And they'd dragged the girls into it. No matter what their intentions were, nobody was going to feel good about it.

"Are you two breaking up?" Annie asked, and the words were a tad desperate.

"We were never together, hon," Em said, gently. "Remember? We talked about that."

Ethan knelt in closer to his daughter, so he could make direct eye contact with Annie. "Em means a lot to me. But we don't need to play pretend anymore."

His eyes met Em's and her breath caught in her chest. No one could doubt that he was a wonderful dad. A good guy, even.

Annie didn't meet his gaze, instead glancing away.

Em set her jaw because she didn't want to say something here that would confuse the situation further.

A tear threatened to fall from the corner of her eye, but she stopped it before it even made contact with her eyelid. There were no tears here. None allowed. This life she was building in Denver was not a life filled with tears.

Been there, done that. Never again.

"Have I ever told you about pearls?" Barbie asked, but she asked in such a way that even if she had told the story (which she hadn't) then she'd tell it again, anyway.

"I want to hear about pearls," Fiona said, staring up at Barbie with innocent awe.

"It's time to go home, Annie." Ethan ticked his head that direction. "We can hear about the pearls later."

"No. Not until I hear Barbie's story." Annie crossed her little arms.

"Well, to get a pearl, you have to find a clam. You with me?" Barbie asked, storytelling with her hands.

Fiona nodded.

"I thought oysters made pearls?" Annie asked.

"Aren't they the same thing?" Barbie countered. "They're both in shells, right?"

Em was pretty certain that's not how it worked.

"So you've got this clam or oyster or *whatever*. To make a pearl, something's got to get right in there and bug them. It can be an irritant like a fleck of sand, or it can be a parasite."

"What's a parasite?" Annie asked, frowning.

"Em's ex-husband," Barbie said without missing a beat.

Em made a strangled noise.

Barbie plowed right on ahead. "Or something in the ocean that just crawls in there with Mr. Clam and drives him nuts."

Ethan pressed his hands against his hips and eyed the door like it was a lifeline.

"So Mr. Clam-Oyster gets grumpy and starts covering the annoyance in snot," Barbie continued.

Em pinched her eyelids into slits and made the strangled sound again. She didn't mean to. It just kept happening and she really just wanted a bath and a do-over tomorrow.

Ethan sort of choked, but recovered.

"It's not boogers," Em confirmed.

Barbie nodded, her blonde hair bouncing. "It's clam snot. You're right. Not the same." She splayed her hands to illustrate her point. "Over time, the clam continues coating the irritation until—" She smacked her hands together.

The sound of her hands smacking together came out substantially louder than Barbie likely expected. Everyone jumped, including Sketch.

"Boom." She added the word for more dramatic effect. "You've got yourself a pearl." The last part, she said, totally normal.

Then she crossed her arms and nodded.

They all waited for the rest of the story.

Barbie, however, said nothing.

"Barbie?" Annie asked.

"Mm?" Barbie replied.

"Why does that matter?" Annie didn't seem to get the gist of the story.

Thank goodness it wasn't only Em who found herself totally lost. Barbie told a lot of stories, but usually they at least had a point.

"We have to deal with the things that bug us," Barbie said, like this was perfectly clear. "Especially when they matter. That way, we can cover them with snot and turn them into pearls." She lifted her hands like this made sense.

"I don't think I get it." Ethan seemed to reflect a lot on a story centered around clam mucus.

"When something matters, you pay attention to it. You don't just let it annoy you. You don't just let it fester. And you *don't* toss it aside. Otherwise, you won't get your pearl," Barbie said this as though the story made the gem of a point perfectly clear.

While the story did not, unfortunately, her explanation made sense. But—

"Which one of us is the parasite and which one is covering things in snot?" Em asked.

"We all are!" Barbie smiled brightly, gesturing to everyone. "You're my parasite and I'm yours. Cress is mine, and Lauren, is too. And you're theirs. And they're yours. I'm paying attention to you because you matter. And you are paying attention to me because I matter. Something happened tonight. I have no idea what, but I know that you need to rub boogers all over each other and be happy. Don't worry! In the end, we'll have a gorgeous necklace." This, she said brightly, with an abundance of fanfare.

"I still don't get it," Ethan said, seemingly lost.

"I get it." Em hated that she got it. But she did.

She might be tossing Ethan aside for the wrong reasons, even though they felt right.

Ethan looked at her as though he would like some help to understand.

"I don't want to be covered in anyone's snot," Annie said, horrified. "Can I just spit it out? The sand or Em's ex-husband?"

"You can," Ethan said, standing as though he was going to leave. "I reckon, you get to decide what relationships you're going to cultivate."

Emmaline glanced up at him.

"And which ones you're not," Ethan finished with a nod to Em. "It's always a choice."

Uh. Ouch.

Everyone stared at him, and Em realized he would walk away. The thought made her sink deeper into the carpet.

Unfortunately, that helped nothing.

"Are you going to slime her?" Fiona asked—gagged—clearly grossed out. "Like Mr. Clam-Oyster."

"I'm not sliming anyone." Ethan held up his hands as though those were words he never should've had to say. "Promise."

"That's not the point of the story," Barbie grumbled. "You're not getting it. The clams pay attention to the thing. They make it a pearl. That's the point. Don't throw aside what can be a pearl!"

"The deal was that this was only a ruse for so long." Ethan nodded, curt. "Now, it's done."

Annie's lips pressed into a thin line as Ethan took her hand and headed back to their house.

"I'm so mad," Fiona said as she tromped up the stairs.

"Baby, this was the deal all along." Emmaline shouldn't engage, but this was a genuine point.

Fiona frowned at the top of the stairs. "Annie and I want to be sisters. Girl code." With that, she flashed a peace sign.

Uh.

Emmaline started up the stairs after her so they could work through this. So Fiona would understand.

"I wanna think." Fiona crossed her arms. "Please, let me have my mind."

What could Emmaline say to that? That's exactly what she said when she also needed a minute to process.

So, she backed down the stairs. She would give her girl time to process.

"She'll come around," Em said to no one and also Barbie. She was nearly one-hundred percent certain Fiona would come around.

Fine. Maybe only seventy-ish-percent certain? But more certain than not.

Fiona said nothing, but ugh, she had that preteen flounce down as an art form. Her door clicked closed.

"So what happened?" Barbie asked, eyeing Emmaline.

"The wedding was a wedding." Emmaline moved to the kitchen, pulled out her box of wine, grabbed a glass, and pinched the spout to pour herself some red.

Barbie sauntered to the counter. "Pour me one of those while you're handing them out."

Barbie picked up her glass and took a sip. She listened while Emmaline told her all about Ethan.

Sipped her wine.

Listened some more.

When Em got to the part about Nosh and Ethan and all the things she didn't want to be, Barbie downed the whole glass like she was in college and the glass was actually a beer bong.

Emmaline continued on while Barbie poured herself

another glass, tipping the box on the edge to ensure she got even the dregs.

Lucky for them, Emmaline had a brand-new box in the pantry ready to whip out.

"I think Ethan really cares about you," Barbie said, going back to sipping versus chugging.

"Barbie."

"Hear me out, sweet cheeks," Barbie said. "You can't batch all of one profession into the asshole category. Just 'cause he's famous doesn't mean he's a prick. There are always outliers. In this case…Ethan." She waved her hand so Em wouldn't interrupt. "I don't know if you've noticed." Barbie glanced up the stairs, then leaned in. "Tony's a registered asshole. He's got the membership card and everything. But Ethan never even came up for membership." Barbie lifted the wine to her lips and somehow spoke and sipped at the same time. "That's the God's honest truth."

"The girls aren't taking this well at all. I thought we'd been careful and prepared them…"

"They've been playing you a little bit." Barbie held up her little bit fingers. "Working some preteen magic. Let's just say bracelets don't fall in gutters on their own. Grandparents don't always show up at the right time without a little nudge." Barbie made big eyes at Em. "And Ethan didn't help with all the bracelets on your curio. *And* Annie's already had her induction into the cousin troupe."

Whew. Okay.

"I should go talk to Fiona." Em looked up the stairs. But what would she say? What was left to be said?

"Give her some time. She's worried because she's confused." Barbie waved her hand. "They're like the Prawn King. They'll come around soon enough."

"What's the Prawn King?" Em asked, opening her

emergency bag of Doritos. The bag she kept for red wine nights.

Barbie's expression brightened at the Prawn King question with the same look she got when someone asked about her shoes. "Oh, let me tell you about the King of Prawns…" Then she stopped. Clicked her tongue. "I see what you're doing! Distracting me. But uh-uh, tonight is all about Ethan and Em. Prawn King will have to wait."

"Let me grab the other box." Emmaline hooked her thumb to the garage where she kept the overflow pantry. She hurried there and back, setting the box on the counter next to the empty one.

"What's your favorite part of fake-dating Ethan?" Barbie asked.

"The very real orgasms." Em dropped her head to the counter. "And when he looks at me, my insides get all fizzy." Her face warmed like she drank more prosecco instead of red. "Like champagne."

"Ooh, I love champagne." Barbie lifted her glass. "That's a good one."

"The thing about champagne is you get the lovely feeling, and then the killer headache." Em wasn't trying to be a downer. Protecting her heart made her think of all the things that could go wrong.

"Lots of people have champagne fizzy bliss," Barbie said. "With only a little headache. But that's life, not the wine."

Oh God, she was going to cry.

Dammit. No crying in this life.

A tear fell along Emmaline's cheek. Then another.

She'd survived the entire night without tears, and now they fell? It's like Barbie opened the floodgates.

"I'm sorry." Em brushed at her cheeks. "Give me a second."

"Why are you sorry?" Barbie asked.

Em shrugged between Dorito bites.

"I used to think strong women didn't cry," Barbie said, setting the rest of the uneaten chip beside her glass. "But then I realized something." Barbie drummed her fingertips along her thigh. "The strongest women I know are the ones who feel all the emotions. The ones who let the tears fall when they need to, and laugh like no one's going to judge them when something is funny. The ones who let themselves feel the emotion of the moment are the ones strong enough to withstand the force of the wind."

"I don't feel very strong." Emmaline was a lot of things, but strength was not hers right then.

"I'm so impressed that you are standing up for what you need. Telling Ethan exactly what you want. You don't want friends with bennies? Great. Don't do it. You want to be seen and not shoved in the corner? Great. You make that happen. But here's the thing, and I say this with all the love of your best friend: you haven't been this happy since Willie Redd asked you to homecoming and gave you your first kiss. Ethan's still the man up the street. He's still that guy. And going on TV won't change that."

"What about me?" Em asked.

"You're you. You're you when you're with him and you're you when you're by yourself. You're Em." Barbie waved a hand all the way down like she was on a game show and Em was the prize. "But you're happier with *him*. It's better than dating a lawyer who's never home and can't cook. I mean, look, you don't want to go on his show? Fine. Tell him to do a *My Celebrity Dad Cooks!* show and make that work. Clearly, his kid came up with a solid concept."

"You're not wrong." Em pressed at her temples.

"If you ask me, I think this whole thing is the meaning of life," Barbie said. "You're you and, I'm me, and he's him, and that's the reason we're all here on this planet, spinning around the galaxies."

"Which part, exactly?"

"All of it."

"Did you just try to unlock the secret of life?" Emmaline asked.

"That's the best part." Barbie leaned in and whispered, "Anyone who tells you it's a secret is just trying to bamboozle you into not seeing your own worth. It's about what makes us happiest. *Whatever that is!* We're told to blow out our candle because you can't shine too bright. Stay against the wall. Don't make a fuss." She waggled her finger. "But just because you blow out your candle, so the others look brighter, doesn't mean they *are* brighter. It means they're lonelier. And you're colder."

Em let out a long breath, breathing in deep, then releasing it again.

She went in for a hug. "Thank you. Thank you for being my friend and thank you for shining bright and thank you for reminding me that Ethan makes me happy."

"Now, my theory is that when you burn brightest, there's always more fuel for the flame. Thinking there won't be is what scares us into blowing out our candle. Sometimes it feels easier to stay in the dark than to embrace what we're made for."

"You're fantastic at this," Em said. "I feel like I should take notes."

Barbie went back to nibbling at her chip.

The pounding on the door brought them out of their bonding moment because it was the kind of knock that made a person's toes curl.

Emmaline hurried to the door and pulled back the curtain.

"Ethan?" She yanked open the door.

He looked confused. And wet. The rain really came down now.

"Come inside." She reached for him and shooed him inside the door. He'd changed clothes, now in jogger pants and a T-shirt, both soaked beyond belief.

"Where's Annie?" Em asked, glancing behind him.

No one waited there.

He held a sopping note in his hand out to Emmaline. "I don't know."

Chapter Twenty-Eight
ETHAN

ANNIE WAS SET on getting herself a mum. Ethan was ready to tear his hair out.

Her note was brief and said basically that she'd run away. If she actually hadn't left, that note would've been a ripper to show her when she was older.

As it was? Not cute at all. She'd taken things too far.

In the last few days, he'd sort of started to question if the girls were pushing him and Em together. But it was all innocent, so he hadn't minded. Ignored it, even.

"Fiona's not in her room." Em rushed down the stairs. "She's gone, too."

Ethan's headache pounded and his chest felt like someone had dropped a boulder on it.

Fiona's note was the same as Annie's: they'd decided to run off and be sisters together.

"We can't just wait them out," Ethan said, fussing with the note. "Hoping they'll be back." They'd get hungry and tired and eventually come home, sure. But they couldn't wait for it to happen.

He gulped. It was a big world out there and two little

girls could be genuinely hurt before they made their way back where they were loved.

"Ethan," Em said, shaking her head. "I think we need to look for them. I don't think Fiona's bluffing."

The urgency of Em's worry broke him out of his own head.

They called for help. While Ethan and Em figured out what the girls were wearing, and all the things a parent never wanted to have to think about, Barbie had reached out to all of Em's firefighter brothers. Then her dad. Even her odd Uncle Jerry, who also worked on the force. Then Lauren and Cress. Jack and April. Everyone.

Because there was absolutely no evidence the girls had been taken, this was definitely a relief. Though there had been some hard questions about it from Em's dad, given Ethan's celebrity status. Everyone in the neighborhood combed through Ethan's backyard and home. Em's too.

With Ethan's help, and James's talent for strategizing, they created a neighborhood grid to comb through. As they were all heading out to search, Ethan was not about to be left behind. But it was pointed out that he needed to stay put for when they came back. Also, he couldn't leave Em. Not like this.

He stayed behind.

"I never believed I was a witch. Not since I was five and James convinced me I was part paranormal," Em said, crossing her arms around herself. "But I'm melting a little more every moment that goes by."

"They're gonna be fine." Ethan said this to himself, also to Em.

She still wore her flimsy dress from the wedding.

"Kids do this all the time. They're just confused," Em agreed.

Ethan had a headache brewing at full force. "It's my fault. The whole charade was my idea. This is my fault."

Em shook her head. "No, I agreed. I kissed your cheek. I played along. I get the blame."

Lauren handed a bottle of water to him, but he didn't take it. Em took one, though.

"Kids make mistakes, too," Lauren said. "It's not always anyone's fault. Sometimes, it's just about being a little human person and learning from mistakes."

"They're just confused," Em said, again.

He hated that he'd had quite a bit to do with that confusion.

Ethan didn't reply other than to nod, but he continued gripping Em's hand like it was all he had left. She gripped his right back. If there was one good thing about this situation, it was that they were a team. In this together.

She'd already phoned a friend—her family—and there was no audience to ask about a solution. In the game of *Who's Going to Find the Girls?*, they were stuck with only hope and determination.

"Ethan," Em said. Her throat worked against emotion.

"It's gonna be fine." He wrapped his arm around her shoulder.

"Em"—her father jogged to where she stood with Ethan under the porch light—"you're gonna freeze. Go put on some clothes."

"It's not like I'm standing out here naked." She crossed her arms, clearly ready to dig in and not move an inch.

But her dad was right, she should put on something that wasn't so flimsy. Maybe something flannel. So he pushed her along.

"I'm not leaving." She squeezed Ethan's hand and it felt like they were together again, and not fake. But for real.

"Go get warmed up," he said, and he kissed her forehead. "I'll wait here."

He had nowhere else to go. He stood, staring into the darkness, hoping the answers would come.

"Fiona?!" Em called from right near her house.

He glanced that way.

Then she was shouting, "Over here. Fiona's here!"

Ethan's heart worked overtime as he bolted up the sidewalk. Em had pulled Fiona from a bush, and he searched the area for his Annie.

"Where is she?" he asked, and his voice cracked. He started searching through the bush, but there was no Annie.

Fiona started to cry. "We were just gonna stay away 'til you guys said you'd be boyfriend and girlfriend. But then it got super cold and it rained, and Annie didn't wanna come back!"

Em was holding her daughter and Ethan's arms had never felt so empty.

Chapter Twenty-Nine
EMMALINE

THEY'D GONE HOME to get Fiona warmed up.

"Mom?" Fiona asked. She frowned. "Umm, I think I maybe know where Annie might be."

"Why didn't you tell Uncle Lance and Grandpa when he asked?" Emmaline would dissect that later with her daughter. "Never mind. Where do you think she is?"

"I kinda think she might be, like, in the playhouse." Fiona glanced to her window. "If I was really sad, that's where I'd go. And, like, everyone's already looked back there so it's safe."

Emmaline glanced out the window to the backyard. She'd already turned on the porch light, but there was no movement in the playhouse.

Whatever, she needed to check. The guys could do another sweep of the backyard when they got there, but she'd do hers now.

"Call Uncle Lance and tell him what you told me. Tell him I'm going to look." She grabbed a flashlight, didn't even put on a coat, and headed outside.

If Fiona's hunch was correct, then Emmaline did not

want Annie to bolt. She didn't say anything as she searched around roses, behind the tree, and the playhouse. Nothing.

But then…a little niggle of something had her peering into the tube.

Right into the eyes of Annie.

There had been a lot in her life that she'd found relief over, but nothing was as sweet as finding Annie cuddled up in a plastic play tube.

Annie seemed to deflate at Emmaline's presence. But since she was the one who was there, and she was a grown-up, she'd be the one to coax her out.

"Hi." Em military crawled into the tube. Ack, it was tight in there. She really should've changed into something other than her dress when she first got home. For real.

"I don't wanna talk," Annie said, her French braid a mess, laying on her side, her hands under her cheek.

Emmaline spent a lot of her life relating to that. "I don't really want to talk to anyone else, either. But since I'm a grown-up, I have to." She rolled her eyes. "I think I'll just stay here with you, if that's okay?"

Annie didn't respond, so Emmaline took that as an affirmative that she could stick around. They sat awhile while the rain fell, patting the top of the tube with droplets. The sound was actually soothing, like one of those meditation apps Em had on her phone.

If Emmaline was correct—and she figured she was—Fiona had alerted the uncles, and the guys would all descend on her backyard shortly.

Which meant she needed to convince Annie to evacuate her hidey hole and connect with her dad before things got more serious and official.

"You're not gonna marry my dad," Annie said this as though it were already fact. "You won't be my mom."

"But, you know what? Your dad and I are still friends.

And I'll always be your friend, too." Emmaline didn't intend to squirm uncomfortably.

"He's the best," Annie said, wistfully. "Why wouldn't you want him?"

Oh, the innocence of a girl who adored her father.

"I'm still learning to be me," Emmaline said. "Your dad is really nice, and I like him a lot. But I need to be me before I can be something more than just friends with your dad. Besides you don't have to be married or related to be a family. You don't even need a mom to be a family, or a dad. You just have to have a whole lot of love. That's enough. Barbie's my family. And Lauren and Cress. Jack is your dad's family as much as your gramma and grampa. As much as you. Because everybody cares for each other."

"That's easy for you to say. You're just you."

Annie wasn't wrong. Sometimes, simplicity made the most sense.

One would think so, right?

"I lost sight of who I was before I came to this house. This neighborhood. My life was so different, and I didn't really like it all that much." Emmaline scooted closer because her feet were seriously getting cold. "I love Fiona. But she was like the only good thing there."

"I didn't like before, either," Annie whispered. "Before Dad."

"Do you want to talk about it?" Emmaline asked, her stomach sort of rumbling because she'd pretty much skipped dinner, had a few Doritos, and a half a glass of wine.

"No." Annie pinched her lips together.

Emmaline could respect that. "No matter what happens with your dad," Emmaline said, "you and Fiona will stay friends. You and I will stay close, too. And that's more family than anything else. I promise you."

"I wish you weren't nice to me," Annie said, turning her face up toward Emmaline. "'Cause then I wouldn't want you to stay."

"I know what it's like to run away," Emmaline said, pushing the toe of her shoe into the planks of the playhouse. "But you think about what you're running away from versus what you're running away to." Hey, that sounded like something Barbie would say. "You've got a good gig with your dad. Have you tasted his eggs?"

The rain was moving into more of a drizzle than a downpour. That was hopeful.

Annie gave Emmaline a look like she had her number, but she wasn't dialing it.

"Why'd *you* run away?" Annie asked.

That was a hard question with a simple answer. "Because I wasn't happy. I knew I couldn't be happy there." Emmaline kept going. "No one noticed I left for a very long time." The rain thumped against the top of the tube, where it flowed off the roof of the playhouse into a stream of heavy water. "Your dad noticed right away that you're missing. He's been really worried right from the beginning."

Still nothing. The rain only *thump, thump, thumped.*

Emmaline military crawled a little farther in, about as far as she figured her hips would allow. "Everyone wants you to be okay. Me, especially."

"Why?" Annie asked, looking at her little hands.

Well, that was another simple answer. "Because we all love you very much."

"I wish I had a mum."

Emmaline's throat clogged. That was not easy at all.

Emmaline's heart hurt for her. "You are an awesome kid. And I think you are pretty special to have Ethan as your dad. No one else gets to call him their dad."

A tear fell down Annie's cheek. Emmaline felt that trail of wet right in the smack dab center of her heart. But like Barbie had said, only the strongest women were willing to cry.

"You will *always* be first for him. And he's super worried," Emmaline said.

Annie wiped at the tears with her wrist. "He's going to be so mad at me."

"Maybe." Emmaline figured the truth was going to always be the best with Annie. "But I think you should tell him what you told me, so he'll know. And he can help you see how much you mean to him."

"You're really nice." Annie stared at Em like she was her everything.

Emmaline had no problem reciprocating. "You're really nice, too."

"I'm getting cold," Annie said.

"Me. Too." And uncomfortable to boot.

Emmaline moved closer in toward Annie, even though she was not dressed for the playhouse or the tube. "Sometimes hugs help. Can I give you a hug?"

Annie nodded.

Emmaline did more of the military crawl, but…uh. There was no forward movement happening for Emmaline. She was half in, part out of the tube, and there was likely not enough butter or WD-40 in the world to get her moving.

Oh no. She tried to move back, but her hips were sort of turned and there was not room to turn over and slide out.

This children's tube clearly wasn't built for adults who enjoyed any amount of Rice Krispies treats.

"Annie." Emmaline looked at her. "I'm stuck. Give me a pull?"

Emmaline gave Annie her hands. Annie did not have a problem maneuvering in the tube. She pulled and huffed and pulled, but Emmaline was really stuck.

"You're not moving," Annie said, dropping Emmaline's hands.

Nope, she wasn't. "I think we are going to need some help."

Damn. Damn. Dammit. Damn.

"Emmaline?" Mom called from the porch. "Where are you?"

"I'm in here," Emmaline yelled. "I've got Annie."

"She's stuck," Annie hollered. Then she got right up to Emmaline's face. "I'll get help."

Emmaline nodded, because it's really the only thing she could do. "Go find your dad first. He needs to know you're okay."

"Okay," Annie said.

"Pinky swear?" Emmaline moved her pinky toward Annie.

Annie looped her pinky with Emmaline's. "Swear."

Then she crawled backward out of the tube, leaving Emmaline alone, in a cocktail dress, in her backyard, sorta freezing.

Funny thing about being wedged in a tube like this—it gave a girl some time to think.

Time to process. Time to ponder.

Time to plan.

Chapter Thirty
EMMALINE

FAMILY WAS what they made it, and Em was on her way to figuring things out about who she was and who she wanted to be. Emmaline, Ethan, Annie, and Fiona could have a makeshift family and it wouldn't be perfect, but that's what would make it wonderful. She wouldn't settle for scraps, but she wouldn't expect Ethan to, either. Or Annie or Fiona, for that matter.

She wasn't ready to marry the guy, but maybe she was ready to think about for-real dating, and not run as fast as she could away from a potential forever with him. Ethan deserved the benefit of the doubt that he really was different than the other famous people in her life.

"Em?" Ethan called.

"In here," she called back, still from the inside of the tube. Time was a funny thing when a girl was stuck in playground equipment. She had no idea how long she'd been there, but it felt like forever. She'd tried a few more times to remove herself from the plastic cocoon, but it was a no go. "You're with Annie?"

"Annie's okay. She's with Cress," he said from the vicinity of the playhouse. "Annie says you're stuck."

"How stuck are you?" Mom yelled, louder than entirely necessary. Emmaline could hear them just fine. *Thankyouverymuch.*

"Pretty stuck." Emmaline didn't attempt to extract herself again, seeing as it only wedged her deeper into the tube.

Someone climbed up the ladder into the playhouse, the *thunk* of their footfalls coming her direction. She hoped it was Ethan, or her mom, because her dress had hiked itself up around her thighs during the didn't-help maneuvers.

"My hips don't fit in here." This was obvious but still required saying.

"Ethan here," he said, as a hand trailed up the inside of her calf. "I'm gonna pull you out."

"Maybe put my dress down first?" She let her head fall to the inside of the tube because she seriously couldn't believe she got stuck. She lifted her head and hit it again.

Stuck a-freaking-gain.

And this time she was wearing a cocktail dress!

A rough, male-sized hand she hoped was Ethan's gently tugged the fabric back over her legs.

"Still me," he said.

He gripped one ankle. Then he gripped the other, and he pulled.

She made a groaning sound that was not very attractive. At all.

Also, okay. Ouch.

There was something happening as he pulled that involved science and physics, but it wasn't enough. She didn't budge.

"James?" Ethan said, footfalls moving away. "You want to help me, mate?"

James tried as well, but still Emmaline did not budge.

"She's really stuck," Mom said, and a smaller hand patted Emmaline's ankle.

"I don't do anything halfway," Emmaline called back, a little muffled because she'd given up on lifting her head every time she needed to say something. Her neck was seriously getting a crick in it.

"We're gonna have to cut it," James announced. "Only way to get her out."

Well, fabulous.

"Where's Jim? Or Sam?" Mom said, her voice already trailing away. "Tell them we need the saw. Sam's the best with it."

Emmaline resigned herself to waiting when Ethan's head came into view from the opposite side of the tube, illuminated by a flashlight.

"Hi," Emmaline said, her cheek resting against the plastic.

"Hi." He did that thing where he sort of grinned, but not really. She'd really grown to like that expression.

She studied his gaze and the way he stared at her like the rest of the world didn't matter when they were sharing the same space.

"I found Annie." She smiled brightly.

Ethan didn't come all the way in. Probably because he'd get even more stuck than her. But she could see his eyes and understood the depth of what he meant when he said, "Thank you."

"Um. Do you want to pull this way?" she asked.

Because maybe that might work better? It seemed like that would be a good idea right about now.

"I thought, actually, maybe we could talk for a sec," Ethan said, reaching in to trace her jaw with his fingertip. "While I've got your attention, and you've got mine."

"You're soaked," she said, but at least the rain had stopped so he wasn't getting more soaked.

"I don't care."

She wriggled and made some forward movement. "You're crammed in a tube with me."

An uncomfortable tube.

"I don't care," he said, again.

Well, that made one of them.

"I'm hungry," she said, appealing to his inner chef.

"Lucky for you, I have a ripper set of skills that'll help with that when you're off the playground equipment." With that, he full-on smiled.

"Hah."

"Unless you want me to yank you by the head, it's not going to work from this direction either," he said.

Unfortunately, he was correct.

"I was wrong to put you after everything else on my list. It wasn't fair. I need you to know how grateful I am that you were my partner tonight." He lifted a hand to the side of her cheek. "Thank you for finding Annie."

She would've nodded, but space was tight. "You need to talk to her. She's got a lot more going on in her head than I think she ever told you."

He nodded. "Yeah. I got that. Her mum hasn't been involved in ages, and I guess I thought that meant the wounds were healing. But I think it's only making them deeper. I'll be making some calls tomorrow. Getting her some help."

Speaking of help…

"Ethan." Emmaline wished she could scrub her hands over her face. "I'm figuring out who I am and what I want to be. That's the journey I've been on."

"That makes me happier than you can know."

"But I'm tired of doing it alone." So, so tired of doing it by herself.

That seemed to get his attention. He stilled.

"I want to keep giving us a try. I was ready to give up, but I don't want to," she said with absolute certainty.

"Em, that's…" His expression broke. "The only thing that's made me more scared than the girls runnin' off was thinking I'd lost you for good."

"I'm not going to do your new show, though. I've had time to think on it, and I just don't want that. Part of figuring out who I am, and what I want to be, means I can't do your show. I want you to do it. Do it with Annie. But…. I… I have my own dreams now." She breathed a massive sigh of relief from speaking the words out loud.

"I'm proud of you for sayin' what you want and what you don't want. Good on you for makin' your stand and holding that ground." He nodded, holding her gaze with his.

"It's just that's yours. The show is about *you*. The things you love and who you want to be. It's not mine. It's not me."

"I'll always support you, Em. Just tell me what you need and it's yours."

She nodded. "Okay."

"So what happens next?" he asked. "With us?"

Another deep breath. "I've been thinking about that a lot since I've been in here."

"What'd you come up with?"

That was the thing, right? "I was hoping we'd feel that out together."

"That's what you want?"

"I figure that if we both do what we love to do, give each other space and room to grow, then as long as we meet back together at the end of the day, the rest of it won't matter." She paused, took a breath.

"I'd like to kiss you right now," he said with that low bedroom note in his voice. "You know that?"

Emotion clogged her throat because she had this with him, and it wasn't a ruse.

"I'm all in this with you," he said, his fingertip against her lips.

She liked that. Really liked that.

"Me, too." *Yes. All the yeses.*

Visions of a future with the two of them came to her mind's eye. Visions that didn't freak her the hell out.

"Em?" he asked.

"Uh-huh?" she asked, breathy.

He touched the tip of her nose. Who knew that a touch like that could turn her on like that while stuck in a playground tube?

"Make me the happiest bloke and be my girlfriend," he said with more seriousness than she expected. "For real."

"For real." She agreed with a short laugh. "Okay."

He reached for her hand and wrapped a friendship bracelet there, tying it on in a knot and for the first time in a long time, she wasn't afraid because whatever came next, it would be filled with color and flavor and all the brushstrokes anyone could dream up.

"I guess we gotta get you out of this tube. I'll make us all some dinner. Then we curl up on a couch with the girls and watch a movie. Then we do it again tomorrow. And again the next day."

"And again," she agreed.

Honestly? It didn't matter if they were in the bedroom or holding hands walking around the cul-de-sac. All that mattered was that they were together.

Chapter Thirty-One
EMMALINE

EMMALINE SKETCHED for days after they removed her from the tube.

Cut the tube from around her, whatever. Same difference, right?

Ethan worked out the details of his new Nosh contract for his Cook with My Celebrity Dad show where he'd teach other celebrities how to cook along with him and Annie. The spark of the concept was her genius after all.

Em illustrated an entire story about an excited little girl who made drawings that no one thought were any good, except her and a handsome chef who only happened to look a touch like Ethan Greene. Those drawings came to life, and the little girl's world became pretty spectacular.

Emmaline could relate to the story because, while life was still hard, it was also beautiful. Most of the time, it was fun.

There were moments, because she was a mom, where she wished she could crawl into the tube again and get stuck there for a while. Long enough for a solid time-out.

Those moments were not the usual. Not her *normal*, for lack of a better word.

Annie was doing better. So was Fiona.

They'd all started spending more time together, and the girls adjusted to their respective parents' official relationship status. No overnight sleepovers, yet. They wanted the girls to be more confident in their relationship before they introduced that kind of change.

They were going fast. And yet, they were also going slowly.

Time was a funny thing like that.

So, while they sorted their stuff, she drew, and she still designed billboards, too. Still created business cards. Still made up the direct mailers that would fill mailboxes for insurance agents all over the globe. Hey, sometimes a job was a job. And that was enough when everything else was so great.

Then she sent off her book and hoped it might catch the eye of an agent or an editor, or someone who believed in her project as much as she did.

She stared at her face in the mirror. "I can do this."

Maybe if she said it enough, it might come true.

Today she sat at her desk, drawing a kitten that looked a lot like Pepper and a dog that looked a bunch like Sketch. The two of them were unlikely crime-fighting pets. The house was quiet since Fiona was at day camp, but soon enough it would fill up. Family and friends would all find reasons to pop in.

Drawing a final whisker on her kitten, she chewed at the end of her felt-tip pen. Perhaps a little more shading around the paws?

The dryer buzzed, announcing it'd finished the cycle and needed to be swapped.

And the microwave dinged, reminding her she'd put her mug of coffee in there before she logged in.

She'd realized a few things in the last weeks.

Life wasn't about finding normal.

Life was about finding the extraordinary in normal.

There would be arguments, and there would be anger. But there would be happiness, and there would be laughter.

The entire array. They'd have it all.

She deserved it all. And so did they.

Epilogue
ETHAN

Three years later…

"LITTLE MUCH, DAD." Annie eyed the tray of s'mores ingredients he'd put together for their night. "Don't you think?"

"I think Emmaline is going to take some convincing." He broke up another bar of Valrhona French chocolate to set beside the charcuterie of marshmallows, gluten-free graham crackers, and the Belgian chocolate Fiona preferred. "Did you and Fiona finish up over by the pit?"

Annie gave a teenage grunt of affirmative as a response.

Given he was nervous as all hell, he didn't push it.

"You wore your bracelet?" She had the bracelet with her name on her wrist.

The girls used to wear their friendship/family bracelets always, but time passed, and now they only pulled them out on special occasions.

She made an *uh-duh* sound.

Do not push.

He didn't push, but he went in for a hug. "Thanks, love."

"Don't make it a thing," she said this, but she still squeezed him.

Annie had grown quite a bit in the last few years, both physically from a girl into the start of a woman, and emotionally, too. She'd spent a lot of time working through everything with her past. There was a whole airport full of baggage there, but she'd done the work to unpack it. Honestly, he had baggage, too, and she helped him learn to unpack it, as well.

Annie adored Emmaline and, in return, Em adored her right back.

He loved Fiona like she was his own daughter, too. Happy to be the one who got to show her how a bloke should treat her mum.

He shook out his hands and did a little boxer bounce. He had this.

He had to remember that tonight, no matter what happened, they were a family. That wouldn't change.

"You can stop freaking out now, Dad." Annie rolled her eyes in the way she'd gotten so good at recently.

"I'll stop when it's over." After she'd given her answer. A woman who let a bloke redesign her entire kitchen for his own personal playground would not say no.

Even if she hated weddings. Right?

It didn't even have to be a big thing. They could pop over to the courthouse and leave with the same last name. Figuratively. She didn't have to take his name. In fact, he wouldn't expect or even ask her to take his last name. Not when Emmaline Eaton's name was about to be on the cover of so many children's books it made his head spin.

She'd become something of a celeb in her own right within the children's book publishing world. It helped he talked about her and her books all the bloody time whenever he was on the telly.

They'd had a lot of adjusting to do, but they'd done it as a team.

"Are we going to eat first? Or go right for the s'mores?" Fiona took the stairs two at a time on her way down.

Her mum hated when she did that. Always worried she'd end up in the Emergency Room with a broken arm.

That only seemed to encourage Fiona to do it more often.

Like Annie, Fiona had also grown into a top-notch human. She also wore her bracelet.

Fiona inherited her mother's creative side and took as many art classes as she could. He'd met Tony, her dad, and quickly realized she'd inherited his height. Because the girl already towered over her mom and Annie.

She had more to go to top him.

"I vote food." Fiona raised her hand and headed to the oven. "I'm starving."

"We have to wait to see if Emmaline ate at the airport." He forced himself to stop fiddling with the tray.

"She ate in Phoenix." Annie held up the screen of her mobile.

Ethan scowled at his little girl. "You asked her?"

He'd wanted everything to be a surprise.

"I'm hungry now." Annie shrugged in the teenage way he'd become used to. "Figured I'd find out… What's wrong with that?"

This was okay. He and the girls would eat while Barbie, Lauren, and Cress all tag-teamed to pick up Emmaline at Denver International Airport.

Emmaline thought he had a restaurant thing tonight.

That's what he'd told her so her friends could pick her up and he could get things ready here.

"You know if she flips out, it doesn't mean anything?" Fiona asked. Not helping his anxiety levels in the slightest. "That's just Mom."

"I know." And yet, his palms began to sweat more and more the closer the time came to her return.

"Should we wait in here or go outside?" Annie asked.

The answer to that was simple. "What would we normally do? We keep things normal."

"Normally you'd snog her until she turned blue, and then you'd help her"—

Annie made air quotes—"unpack. But you're at a restaurant thing, so…"

Fiona snorted.

His cheeks burned. Clearly, they had not been very sly in their attempts at alone time after she returned from her trips to visit authors, her publisher, and bookstores all over the country.

"Outside." He picked up the tray and strode to the backyard.

Much of it was the same—the same playhouse, same Adirondack chairs, same patio. But they hadn't replaced the tube after they cut it up to remove Emmaline. She figured the girls would be too old for it soon, anyway. Also, no one wanted anyone else to get stuck inside.

The thing was a hazard.

Instead, they converted that area into a family zone with a fire pit for summer s'mores nights.

Emmaline had done that.

She'd asked his opinion, and he'd helped with the install. But back then, this had only been her house.

Back before Ethan and Annie had moved in. Before they'd remodeled together so the girls could have separate bedrooms, even though they were best mates who preferred to camp out in the other's space.

Before they'd decided—with an abundance of encouragement from the girls—to be a family who lived under one roof, shared one grocery bill, and operated as a unit.

Sketch barked at the front door as it opened.

"Hey," Emmaline called. "I'm home."

He got light-headed. Dear God, he was going to stroke out.

Aborting the mission seemed like a good idea. He should do that. Should call it off. Eat a s'more and snog his girl.

Annie flanked him on one side. Fiona, on the other.

"What're you doing?" he whispered.

"Making it so you don't lose your nerve," Fiona muttered. "Don't worry, we've got a plan for her, too."

Nope. He didn't like that. These two…they were hell on parents when they worked together.

But he didn't have a second to say it before Emmaline breezed through the back door. Her traveling clothes were nothing outrageous—just jeans and a T-shirt with one of her characters on the front. A beagle named Sketch.

"Ethan, you're home." Her eyes lit right the hell up.

Yeah, when she walked outside, and her gaze caught his, she may as well have been all decked out in a fancy frock because she knocked him for six with emotion that settled in near his heart.

"Hey, girls." She strutted toward the three of them, handing out a round of hugs, ending with him.

"Hi." She held on as she leaned back. "You're here."

"Hi," he replied. "I am."

He loved this woman.

She got a funny look on her face before she tossed her

arms around his neck and, well, kissed him until he probably turned a little blue.

"This is so ridiculous," Fiona said under her breath.

"Will they ever grow up?" Annie asked.

Emmaline smiled against his mouth. "Hi."

"Hi," he said again, grinning against her lips.

Fiona and Annie made in-tandem gagging noises, but now seemed like a good time to get down to it.

He'd been planning this for months. Waiting for just this moment.

"Didn't you have a thing tonight?" Emmaline asked, squashing her eyebrows together and letting go of his neck to pull her sunglasses from her head and stick them in her purse.

He didn't move. Couldn't form a sentence.

"Why are you acting like this?" she probed.

"I'm not acting like anything." Was he?

"You're acting weird, Dad," Annie confirmed.

Fiona nodded. "You are."

"Are we having s'mores night?" Emmaline glanced around them at the fire pit burning away, the tray of fixings he'd set on the table there, and the chairs all set up with their marshmallow skewers. "Fancy."

"Dad." Annie raised her eyebrows. "Just do it now. Get it over with."

"Do what now?" Emmaline's smile kinda faltered into frown territory.

"Well." Ethan rubbed her arms, elbow to shoulder. "I had a plan tonight."

"Uh-huh?" she sort of asked.

He waved a hand toward the barbie. "We were going to come out here and eat s'mores with the girls."

Emmaline laughed uncomfortably. "Okay."

He was making this way more uncomfortable than he

needed to. He took a deep breath and said, "And then I was going to ask you to marry me."

She blinked. Super hard.

Went white.

"Like right now?" she asked.

He nodded.

"Give her the ring, Dad." Annie nudged him with her elbow.

Righto. The ring.

The girls helped him pick out the ring since he knew nothing about rings. His girls had fancy tastes, turned out. Emmaline would probably like it. He hoped. Especially since it was a whole group effort.

He couldn't help but notice that Fiona had moved to behind her mom and stood conspicuously there. Apparently, she was to stop Emmaline if she fled.

Not a good omen.

He took a breath. Reached into his pocket, and dammit, he was going to do this right.

Ring box in his hand, he flipped it open and knelt on one knee.

Emmaline's eyes got wider.

Annie moved quickly beside Fiona, apparently prepared to offer defense, and not let Emmaline through should she decide to flee.

His throat was super dry. His fingers numb. His tongue not really working.

"I love you," he said. "Nothing changes, except some paperwork. And we get to have a party."

"Dad!" Annie gasped. "That's your proposal?"

"That's what he's been working on?" Fiona said out of the side of her mouth.

Emmaline scrunched her face with what looked like an abundance of questions.

He took another crack at it. "I love you. When I think I can't love you more, you surprise me, and it just keeps growing. I love how you adore my daughter, like she's your own. I love how you love me back. I love your daughter like she's my own. And… I don't want to go through life without you. Will you marry me, Em?"

A tear fell down her cheek. Then she let out a chuckle from deep in her belly.

"Okay." He nodded, about to stand up. They'd still get s'mores. "It's okay. I knew it was a long shot."

"Yes, of course, I'll marry you, Ethan," Em said, grabbing his arm before he could turn away. "But—"

"But?" he asked.

"It's not just a party. It's important that you know that," she said urgently, as she reached out to touch the diamond in the center of the ring. "Before we get to the vows. Because they matter. It's not just a party."

Righto.

"Okay," he said again.

"He's seriously got to up his game," Annie whispered to Fiona.

He pulled the ring from the silk and slipped it on her finger. He stood. Kissed her. Disregarded the girls and their gagging noises.

"Glad that's settled. What's next?" Emmaline asked.

He lifted a shoulder. "I mean we could do the cliché thing and get married."

He touched the tip of his nose to hers, and she melted into his arms. Totally melted. "I could be down with that."

So could he.

"Something simple? Nothing over the top," she went on.

He nodded. "Good call."

"Ethan," she said.

"What's up?"

"I love you, too." She grinned at him.

He opened his arms then and waved for the girls to join them in a family hug.

And, yeah, he noticed there were smiles all around.

"Here's to the future," he said. "Let's light it up."

There's more Em and Ethan!

A special bonus scene Christina created especially for newsletter subscribers!

Claim your copy of the bonus scene at:
christinahovland.com/emmaline-bonus

Acknowledgments

Emily Sylvan Kim, thank you for believing in Emmaline and helping me to bring her story to print. You are more than an agent and friend. I love that you believe in the characters and the story as much as me. I am so happy you are on my team.

Kristi Yanta, I'm so glad we finally had another project to work on together. Thank you for being the ear and the voice of reason I needed during the editorial process. I am so grateful for you.

Thanks, as always, to my family: Steve and all four of our children. Mom, thanks for giving me a writing cave to escape into. Sereneti, thank you for always enjoying my stories and telling me so.

Thanks to those writer friends who keep me grounded: Dylann Crush, Serena Bell, Jody Holford, Brenda St. John Brown, Claire Marti, CR Grissom, AY Chao, Patricia Dane, Molly O'Hare, Gail Chianese, and so many others.

Thank you to Autumn Gantz my publicist and manager. She's the one who keeps things moving with Team Christina.

Thanks to Amanda Wallace who is always so upbeat and helps me manage my social media.

Karie you make me so happy. Thank you for being my bestie. The Thelma to my Louise… or vice versa. Whatever we decided.

Gretchen… what can I say? You're the bomb-dot-com. I'm so blessed you are in my life.

Gina, thanks for being my movie buddy and always having a listening ear.

Denise Allen—my friend and supporter—thank you for loving my books and always being there for me.

Thank you to Tara Wine-Queen for alpha reading the first chapters.

Erica Russikoff, thank you for the awesome line edits!

Shasta Schafer thanks for being my proofreader.

Beth Carbutt, as always, thanks for being my editorial goddess—even on the fly this time.

Suzie Waggoner, thank you for being my Typo Terminator. Make no mistake, if you've found a typo in the book it's because I made a change after Suzie's thumbs up.

Amy Andrews and Sam Eeles, thank you for being early readers and checking in on my Australian hero.

Declan at Writerful did a sensitivity read for Ethan, and I want to thank him for being so flexible and kind with his comments and suggestions.

Thanks, also, to the team at Blue Nose Audio for the fantastic narration and audiobook production.

And thank *you*, yes YOU, for making my dream of being an author a reality. This is a pretty great job I've got!

About the Author

Christina Hovland lives her own version of a fairy tale—a retired artisan chocolatier turned romance writer. Born in Colorado, Christina received a degree in journalism from Colorado State University. Before opening her chocolate company, Christina's career spanned from the television newsroom to managing an award-winning public relations firm. She's a recovering overachiever and perfectionist with a love of cupcakes and dinner she doesn't have to cook herself. A 2017 Golden Heart® finalist, she lives in Colorado with her first-boyfriend-turned-husband, four children, the sweetest dogs around, and Mayonnaise the wonder cat.

Chapter One

Becca

NEON BEER SIGNS totally signaled a new beginning. Sure, a girl might not think it possible, but Rebecca—Becca—Forrester was out to prove they could. The scent of hops and bourbon paired with the blast of music through the speakers and constant hum of life in the background at Brek's Bar in Denver, Colorado. Outside, the snow had turned to a slushy mess. Inside, the bar warmed her like she'd taken a shot of top-shelf whiskey.

Oh yes, this joint was the perfect place for a fresh start that did not involve anyone else or the baggage they dragged along with them.

"Why do you want to wait tables here?" Brek asked, giving a dose of emphasis on *here*. "I'd have thought you'd prefer some place with tablecloths."

Becca laughed. Brek was as biker as biker got—long hair, leather, and an abundance of tattoos. His wife was... not. She was a financial planner, and Becca's friend.

Becca shook her head. She definitely didn't want to

wait tables anywhere else. "I'm looking for the diviest dive I can find."

The idea to wait tables was a complete one-eighty from her recent past as a certified behavioral counselor, but she wouldn't go back. Not yet. Especially not when she was having a perfectly lovely time at the local go-to spot for great music in Denver, hanging with her friends, and harassing Brek into hiring her as a part-time waitress while she took a life break.

"Diviest dive? Well, I guess this is your place." Brek flashed her a smile.

"Exactly." Becca tucked a lock of her thick, brown hair behind her ear, where it belonged but never stayed. "Until I figure out what comes next for me."

"You can live the dream right here with me." Brek patted the bar top like it was a living, breathing thing. Something he adored.

Sigh. Someday she wanted someone to look at her like Brek looked at his wife and his bar top.

Not now. She was on a break from all of that—the relationships, the responsibility, everything—but, someday, the adoration thing would be fun to have, too.

He'd created the perfect dive bar atmosphere—neon lights on the dark wood over the bar with his name lit up in blue. The wood paneling covering the walls was new enough to make the place look well-kept but beat up enough that it didn't look like he had tried too hard. Aesthetically, nothing matched. Yet everything still worked together. The place was definitely Instagram-worthy.

The darkened room hopped in preparation for the band to take the stage. A vibe she loved pulsed through the air. That feeling right before music blasts and the lights come to life. Yep. This was exactly what she wanted for her present life: loud music and the familiar faces of the bar's regulars, with no further obligation for the mental or physical well-being for those around her.

Also, the best bands played at Brek's Bar. Sometimes, because he had the connections, Brek brought in huge names. Like *huuuge*. Waiting tables here was perfect for a recovering groupie on hiatus from life.

"You can start next weekend?" Brek asked.

"Next weekend would be perfection." Becca glanced at her friends, mingling across the room.

Then *Linx* entered Brek's Bar. Becca choked on nothing but air.

Linx. Walked. Through. The. Door.

Bassist for Dimefront. Hot as all hell. Heartbreak in leather pants when he took the stage.

She, on the other hand, was only hot when she wore a sweater. Definitely not heartbreak in any kind of clothing. Unless… Could a woman be heartbreak in yoga pants? She was sure that wasn't possible. She shook the thought from her head as he moved her direction.

Her mouth didn't just go dry; her entire body froze in time.

Tonight, he'd ditched the leather and wore shredded blue jeans instead. Lanky, with ridiculously long dark hair, stubble that was a half day away from being a full beard, and all the charisma of a man who could get tens of thousands of screaming fans on their feet with one chord on his guitar. He scanned the room like he owned the joint.

Brek may have owned the bar, but Linx owned the room.

"Looks like my current assignment is here," Brek said, offhand with a touch of growl.

"Linx is your assignment?" Okay, she tried to resist sliding her gaze back to Linx, but she failed. Every woman in the house got the Linx grin as he continued his slow saunter through the room.

"I'm his babysitter…" Brek said, glowering in Linx's general direction.

Crumpet crap-ola. Her blood seemed a whole lot thicker and her skin a whole lot thinner when he sauntered toward Brek… and her. The blue neon halo was a nice touch. Well done, universe. Well done, indeed.

She sighed because…. Linx.

All eyes were on him. Every woman in the room got a solid eye canoodle as he strutted right up to where she stood across from Brek. His eye canoodle could likely get a girl pregnant. She sucked in a breath and braced for her turn.

Linx moved less than an arms-length away, and her heart stuttered like he'd asked her to remove her panties. Surely, he wouldn't recognize her. It'd been years since they partied in the same circles.

She held her breath because she couldn't take the risk of his scent. Not because she had any special superpowers that involved scented rock stars—that she was aware of— but she knew he smelled amazing. Rock star heaven and concerts and something musky, like oak trees in the rain.

"Do you want me to wait for the drinks, or do you want to send them over when they're done?" Becca asked Brek, ignoring the fact that Linx was right-freaking-there doing some kind of intense handshake thing with him.

"You should definitely wait," Linx said, blasting her out of her knickers with that smile of his.

Yes, she often thought in British slang that she'd picked up one summer on a European Dimefront tour. She really took to their language choices. Refined, but still rather raunchy.

Like her. Rather, who she wanted to be.

She slid her gaze up the length of Linx—long and lithe. Not beefcake, but definitely built. He had more of a runner's build. Muscle and sinew, but not overdone.

He leaned against the bar top, a look of pure happiness on his face. This wasn't a cat's-got-his-cream smile. This was a cat's-about-to-play-with-his-dinner-before-devouring grin.

"Becca, this is Cedric," Brek said, slinging drinks like a pro.

Cedric?

Right. Sure, yes, she knew that was his given name. Cedric Sebastian, wasn't it? Last name was Lincoln, and all the original members of the band took a nickname that had an x at the end. Together, they made a triple-x, which they found hysterical, as pointed out in multiple Rolling Stone articles.

"Becca," Linx—er, *Cedric*—stretched her name across his tongue and played it like an instrument.

He held his hand out to her. *What to do? What to do?*

She could touch him. She should touch him. He was expecting her to touch him.

Do something already, Becca.

She was overthinking this way too much. So she gave him a solid handshake.

The way he squeezed her palm was nearly erotic. For no good reason, either. It was just a handshake. He didn't make any lewd gestures or anything.

Still, the bar seemed to zip to a pinprick and focus on Linx.

"Becca is a friend of Velma's." Brek tossed Linx a look like her dad used to give her when he thought she was going to use very poor decision-making skills.

Becca extracted her hand from Linx's grasp. She noted how he kept the touch for as long as she'd allow.

"I like Velma." Linx grabbed a pretzel from the bowl on the bar and flipped it into his mouth.

"I do, too." Brek continued working. "That's why I'm making it clear to you that *Becca* is a friend of *Velma's*. Which means stop looking at her like that."

"Like what?" Linx held up his hands.

"Like you want to make her Denver," Brek said with a growl.

What the heck did that mean?

Linx popped another pretzel into his mouth. Somehow, he chewed, smirked, and smoldered, all at the same time.

"She's not Denver. Denver is Denver. Becca is Becca."

Brek crossed his arms. "You and I need to discuss what you're allowed to do and not do while you're visiting."

Linx held his palm to his heart and wobbled dramatically. "I am offended."

For the record, he didn't sound offended.

"It's not visiting if I bought a house. That makes it my home," Linx said to Brek.

He bought a house in Denver? Huh.

Perhaps Becca wasn't the only one in the midst of reconsidering life choices.

"You *bought* a house in Denver?" Brek asked. "I thought it was a vacation rental."

"It was," Linx said with a shrug.

"The landlord was being a total dick about Gibson, so I made him an offer." Linx did the pretzel thing again.

"Who's Gibson?" Becca asked.

Not that she had any real reason to be part of the conversation, but Linx hadn't asked her to leave.

"His cat," Brek said, arms still crossed.

"He's more than a cat." Now Linx crossed his arms. "So what if I bought one little house so he has a place to live?"

Brek shook his head. "Whatever, man. You do you."

"That's my plan." Linx slid his gaze to Becca. "Unless Becca wants to sit here and have a drink with me? Then we can see what happens."

Linx gave her a charisma-soaked smile.

Ah. There it was, her eye canoodle. She felt that stare deep down in her soul.

Yeah. Total player.

A player who went through sex partners like they were potato chips. This was according to his bandmate, Bax, and general female knowledge when meeting a player of his magnitude.

Back when she'd followed Dimefront concerts she'd had her eye on Linx. Something about him was like a magnet, pulling her in his direction. She had wanted him. Full. Stop.

But Linx was bad news for her. He rocked a total love them and leave them vibe. The kind that made a girl like Becca—someone who tended to see only the good in people and, therefore, fall for the wrong men—step away. He had just the right amount of baggage for her to want to unpack. And he was exactly the type of guy to pick up those suitcases and leave town right after she committed to the unpacking.

So she kept far away from his wandering gaze, preferring to observe him in his natural rock star habitat, and not let her heart, or body, get involved.

Brek handed a bottle of Coors to Linx.

"I've actually..." Becca jerked her head toward her group of friends. "Got to get back."

"That's a drag." Linx shrugged and gave Becca an extra-long, excessively thorough glance.

She shouldn't have done it. But she did. Yes, she totally canoodled him back.

"Becca?" Brek's voice cut through whatever the heck was going on between the two of them.

Brek had, of course, known Becca during her groupie days. Back then, he'd managed Dimefront and she'd been a Ten, the pet name they called their groupies. The Grateful Dead had Deadheads, Justin Bieber had his Beliebers, and Dimefront had their Tens. She'd spent a summer being Queen of the Tens.

This was not something she shared regularly. With anyone. No one else in her real life knew. Not even her best friends. That summer had been her first attempt at a life vacation. And it'd worked. Lucky for her, Brek didn't, and she was quoting here, "Broadcast shit that wasn't his to tell."

She let out a long breath and turned to Brek. He glanced pointedly to the order he'd prepared.

"Thanks." She snatched the remaining drinks and—and this was the hard part—she walked away without looking back at Linx and his neon halo.

Enjoyed the sample?
Played by the Rockstar is Available Now!